D1170253

REVIEWS

"A claustrophobic chamber piece set inside a modern apartment tower, C.M. Forest's Infested has the gritty feel of early Cronenberg and Romero. The wild, fast-moving plot and gruesome set pieces will delight readers with a taste for the strong stuff."

—Nick Cutter author of *The Troop* and *The Deep*

"Swiftly moving between grisly encounters, action set pieces and peeled away reveals, C.M. Forest's Infested holds nothing back. This is pacy, gory, relentless fun graduated from the old school with honors."

—Andrew Pyper, author of *The Residence* and *The Demonologist*

"From the outset, this breakneck horror tale never lets up. Fans of 70s James Herbert and David Cronenberg are going to love this well written, skin crawling splatterfest!"

—Dave Jeffery, author of the *A Quiet Apocalypse* series

"Forest's 'Infested' is a claustrophobic nightmare! This book had me racing to see just what will happen, while squirming the entire time. Loved it!"

—Steve Stred, author of *Sacrament* and *Mastodon*

"INFESTED is the best debut horror novel I've read this year. Can't wait to see what crawls out of CM Forest's skull next."

—Drew Starling, author of *Sentinel* and *Nothus*

"C.M. Forest has created an image-induced nightmare of skittering little legs and creepy crawly carnage resulting in one heck of a traumatizing good time... Infested is a full-tilt 10 out of 10 on the heebie-jeebies scale, and a 5 out of 5 stars on the Horror Bookworm Recommendation scale"

—Mike from Horror Bookworm

INFESTED

Copyright © 2022 by C.M. Forest

All Rights Reserved

No part of this book may be reproduced in any manner, or transmitted in any form or by any means, electronic, mechanical, photocopying, recording or otherwise, without express written permission by the author(s) and or publisher, except for the use of a brief quotation in a book review.

This book is a work of fiction. Names, characters, places, events, organizations and incidents are either part of the author's imagination or are used fictitiously. Any resemblance to actual persons, living or dead, or actual events is purely coincidental.

Hardcover ISBN: 978-1-990245-59-6
Paperback ISBN: 978-1-990245-58-9
Digital ISBN: 978-1-990245-57-2

Edited by Lyndsey Smith & Michelle River
Cover Art by François Vaillancourt

Eerie River Publishing
www.EerieRiverPublishing.com
Hamilton, Ontario Canada

INFESTED

C.M. FOREST

ALSO BY C.M. FOREST

NOVELLAS:

We All Fall Before The Harvest (2022)

EERIE ANTHOLOGIES:

It Calls From the Veil (2022)

INFESTED

C.M. FOREST

FOR MY MOM

CHAPTER 1

THE 25ᵀᴴ FLOOR

A deep, rumbling crash caused Olivia to open her eyes.

Confusion rolled through the landscape of her mind, even as a second clap of earth-shaking thunder filled her ears. She couldn't tell if she had been sleeping or not.

"What?" The question fell from her lips malformed, a mix between a word and a moan.

No remnants of a dream hung throughout her consciousness. Only a void. Her bewilderment deepened when she realized she was lying on the floor. The plush carpet of her bedroom flattened against her stomach and chest.

Why am I on the ground?

No reasonable explanation presented itself.

Olivia took a deep breath and willed herself to remember, at the same time doing her best to keep the panic nipping her consciousness at bay. The memories were reluctant to appear, while anxiety grew wild like a weed.

Finally, she was able to piece together a jigsaw puzzle of recollections.

She had a drink with her husband, Liam, who had returned home from work in unusually high spirits, a plastic bag full of Chinese food in hand. Once the combination dinners were finished, they had broken out the vodka from the freezer. *Then a movie?* It was at this time her memories lost coherence, became a foggy mess of snapshots.

Liam carrying her to bed.

The sound of his phone ringing.

And then...nothing.

The void.

Whatever had happened, one thing was undeniable—her head hurt like all hell. She usually took it easy when drinking, having discovered in her youth she was a cheap drunk. It didn't take much to produce a hangover, and she'd suffered through quite a few in college. But those days were over, and this time was different. She'd never woken in such torment before. Besides the splitting sensation sliding across her cranium, her mouth was completely dry. When she did manage to swallow the minuscule bit of saliva she could produce, her stomach protested painfully with a severe contraction. The acidic taste of bile rose in the back of her throat, coating the inside of her mouth.

Lightning illuminated the world outside. The white light blared in through the bedroom windows like the prying beam of a searchlight. A second later, a booming explosion of thunder literally shook the room around her. Both effects, especially the noise, reverberated through her head, turning her skull into a gong.

Biting down on her bottom lip to distract the agony in her head, she got her hands underneath herself and pushed off the floor. As soon as her face was free from the carpet, she could feel wetness on her cheek, but Olivia couldn't fathom what she had been lying in. Her fingers groped around in the dark and found a smooth, thin object her brain instantly catalogued as her phone. She turned on the screen and let out a pained moan at the sudden brightness, directing the device toward the floor.

A large, mostly soaked-in puddle of vomit spread like a lily pad where her head had been lying. It turned the already dark carpet black. Olivia squinted past the searing migraine, sure she could see bits of rice in the mess—not the leftovers she was hoping for.

The smell of booze, mixed with her purged dinner, made her gag.

"Liam?" She meant to yell, but her voice was a dry rasp. It also brought an unwelcome sensation—a sharp, angry cramp snapping closed on her stomach like a bear trap. "Ow, fuck." She dropped to her rear and pressed her back against their bed, wrapping her hands across her stomach.

Only after the agonizing contraction finished did she notice how hot her bedroom was. A line of sweat had already started to collect at her hairline, as well as under her neck, armpits, and breasts.

Is the air conditioning off? If so, she couldn't imagine why. They were in the middle of a heatwave.

"Liam, I need help." The words came out a little stronger this time, enough, at any rate, to reach over the edge of her bed and wake her husband. She expected to feel the sheets pull, the mattress shift, as Liam rolled over to see what was going on. But the bed remained still.

Olivia turned around slowly and peeked over the side of the queen-sized mattress with her phone in hand. Although the bedding was rumpled, the bed itself was empty.

"Liam?" she called again. Still, her throat was so dry, raw, she doubted her voice would be able to make the trek through their apartment, especially with the storm assaulting the building.

She sighed and gripped the edge of the bed, hoisting herself to standing. Even as she changed elevations, she knew it had been a mistake. The sudden bodily shift caused the sharp pain in her stomach to return, and with it came a retching wave of nausea. Olivia could again feel the bile rising in her throat like a foul rodent emerging from its hole.

The sensation was enough to propel her forward, around her bed, and toward the en suite. The bathroom was small, just a toilet and sink. She ignored the light switch, slapped her phone down on the edge of the vanity, and made for the bowl.

Olivia dropped to her knees and leaned over the porcelain rim. The scent of piss greeted her. Liam rarely flushed after peeing—he said it was a waste of money. She heaved several times, but all she could produce was a small bit of phlegm and stomach acid. It did the trick though, and the vicious assault on her belly eased.

Dragging the back of her hand across her mouth, she reached out and flushed the toilet but remained hunched over the bowl—the porcelain cool and comforting against her sweating skin. Olivia took in large mouthfuls of oxygen and felt her stomach settle even further. Each breath added another brick to the foundation of stability she knew she would need to go vertical.

Feeling physically sound enough to stand, she pressed all her weight onto the rim of the toilet bowl and carefully rose. An uncomfortable cascade of sensations went through her, all which seemed to originate from her gut. Her stomach had become a poisoned well, feeding death to the rest of her body.

A trembling quake of muscle and tendon rippled through her limbs, and she felt completely drained. Once sure she wasn't going to have a repeat fit of nausea, Olivia turned around slowly and gripped the edges of the sink.

With a sigh, she decided to get a better look at herself and reached across to the light switch just inside the door. When she toggled the switch, nothing happened. The power was out.

No wonder it's so hot in here.

She grabbed for her phone, activated the screen, and held it up next to her head.

"Jesus Christ," Olivia muttered, staring at her reflection in the mirror above the sink.

Pale to begin with, her fair complexion looked downright wraith-like in the gloom of the bathroom. Dark circles hung under her eyes. Her black hair, already prone to knotting, was a mess of tangles. Dried puke had twisted several clumps of strands into grotesque dreadlocks.

Unable to recall the last time she had felt so wretched, she couldn't imagine drinking so much that this was the result. It just didn't make sense.

Olivia returned her phone to the edge of the sink and twisted the faucet with the engraved C on it, holding her hands under the cold stream before splashing it onto her face. She repeated this action three times until the collar of her top—a Nine Inch Nails T-shirt she wore to bed—was soaking wet. The coldness of the water not only pushed back the oppressive heat, but it also worked at clearing her head. It took a bit longer to rub the vomit out of her hair, but eventually, she managed to scour the remains of her stomach contents from her locks.

Feeling as close to human as she was likely going to without a shower and a full night's sleep, Olivia dried her hands and face on a towel hanging from a brass loop next to the sink and returned to her bedroom.

She rounded her bed at a glacial pace and stared down at the mess she had left on the carpet. It looked like a crime scene under the light from her phone and was going to be a bitch to clean up.

"Liam?" A bit more gusto this time. Enough, she reasoned, to cover the distance to the living room at least, but again, her husband failed to respond.

Olivia attempted to form a narrative of the evening's events. Obviously, as embarrassing as it might be, she had imbibed more vodka than she should have and had paid the price. When exactly she ended up on the floor, or why Liam wasn't in bed, she couldn't say.

Rain lashed the glass of her bedroom window, even as another burst of lightning turned the night sky into day. In that moment, Olivia could see how dark, how menacing, the low-hanging clouds looked.

It seemed the storm was just beginning.

CHAPTER 2

She was struck by the stillness which greeted her upon exiting the room. Thick darkness obscured the small hallway connecting the bedrooms—the master and the guest—to the living room. The faint, corpse-grey light from her phone did not do much to penetrate the distance before her. Olivia flipped the device around and attempted to activate the flashlight, only to be denied. Her battery was at less than ten percent.

"Fantastic." For a moment, she actually started to turn back toward her bedroom and the phone charger next to her bed before shaking her head.

The power's out, stupid.

Olivia had walked through her home many times in the dead of night, but this time, it felt different. Even as she rounded the bend, she felt as if she had wandered into an alien landscape. The shadows cast by the low light coming from her phone screen created holes in the floorplan, and previously lit corners became pockets of unimaginable depth, like some colossal hand had reached down and twisted her home like a Rubik's Cube. It still held the same shape, but everything else was wrong.

An assault of lightning followed by a protest of thunder pulled her gaze to the large, floor-to-ceiling windows at the back of the dining room.

"Liam? Where are you?"

She realized she was afraid. A perk of residing in a brand-new high-rise building was a sense of security—the fears one faces while living in a house or smaller abode mostly vacant—but as she continued treading the dark waters of her apartment, she did not feel safe at all.

Alongside the dining room was the kitchen, but her feeble light did not reach the full extent of the room. The stainless steel appliances were completely lost to the null, but it did reveal enough of the countertop to make visible three items. A bottle of vodka—the sight of which made Olivia's guts squirm like a heap of nightcrawlers. The note pad from the fridge—meant for grocery lists, with a cartoon dog on the top corner of each page saying into a word balloon, *I dog-gone forgot*. And the last item, an object she hadn't seen in their home before—a prescription pill bottle.

Regular strength Tylenol gave Liam's stomach fits. The man would be tormented by cramps if he ingested the kind of pharmaceutical alchemy prescribed by doctors. Olivia had no such problems with drugs—prescribed or recreational—but given her husband's physical constitution in regard to the former, and outright disapproval of the latter, their home was narcotics free.

"That's weird."

With the delicacy and precision of an archeologist resurrecting an ancient artifact, Olivia carefully lifted the pill bottle and held it before her face. She squinted at the label stuck to the side. Most of it had been scratched off, but she could just make out *30 tablets Temazepam*. She shook the container. It was empty.

"Temazepam?"

Another cramp caused her to lean forward, and the pill bottle fell from her fingers, bouncing hollowly along the marble countertop before rolling to a stop next to the vodka. Olivia bent over the island and rested her face in her palms, taking in a few deep breaths. She glared at the liquor bottle and pulled it toward her with shaking fingers. The movement sent a small eighty-proof tsunami splashing along the inside of the glass. It was still three-quarters full.

"Jesus, I *have* become a lightweight."

The missing booze, which had been split between her and her husband, did not seem like enough to give her the mother of all hangovers.

Once the cramping passed, she turned her attention to the note pad. A page had been torn off, leaving a jagged swatch of paper still clinging to the strip of glue on the top.

Olivia knew the pad had been blank. She had bought it at the dollar store shortly after moving in, and in the preceding six months, neither her nor her husband had written a single item on the list. Why Liam had ripped a page free was beyond her.

On the fresh page, though, she saw he had scrawled something.

0725

Olivia scrunched her eyebrows together. *What's that mean?* She instinctively thought of every four-digit code she knew—numbers for banking, or passwords—but nothing matched.

She continued to stare at the digits until her phone vibrated in her hand. The sudden movement caused her to jerk and flip the device around. Less than five percent battery. To punctuate this statement, the screen dimmed considerably, making the device all but useless as a source of light.

"Damn it." She sighed, placing her cell amidst the other articles on the countertop. Another item lost to the darkness around her.

Outside, the wind whistled and howled. Olivia let the mystery of the pill bottle and the number on the pad rest for a moment and pushed herself away from the island, carefully starting across the dining room toward the balcony door. If she pulled back all the curtains, she might be able to add a bit of light to her surroundings. Plus, she was curious how bad it had gotten—or was getting—outside. She needed something to take her spinning mind off the mysteries filling her home.

The view from the balcony was both impressive and completely uninspiring at the same time. Being on the twenty-fifth floor presented an amazing look at the world around the high-rise, the problem being, at present time, the view only presented unbroken horizon. The New Leaf

Building was just the first in a planned group of structures which would be the start of a burgeoning neighborhood. At least, that was what she had been told upon moving in. But, after six months, not a single bit of construction had begun on any other project.

Olivia pressed her fingers against the glass of the sliding door—the panes had retained some of the chill the air conditioning offered before the hydro went out—and stared off into the night. The New Leaf was surrounded on all sides by trees, with a thin, black road cutting through the flora, leading away from the tower all the way to the highway. Rain, riding chaotically on currents of frenzied wind, lashed against the balcony. Olivia could also feel this, small vibrations through the window, entering her fingertips. She suddenly needed to go out, to experience the storm.

A humid gust greeted her when she pulled the door open. Freckles of rain spattered against her cheeks. It wasn't the level of refreshment she had hoped for. The rain itself was warm and stank like pennies, but still, the air was moving and went a ways toward further clearing her head.

She sighed. Somewhere in the distance was their previous home, a three-story slum buried in the heart of the city. No matter how late at night, the sounds of humanity would come through their windows while living within that old building. Olivia loved it. Liam hated it.

The day he came home all a bluster, excited news brimming from his lips, she knew things were going to change. His employer had started a partnership with a construction conglomerate, and as a perk of the deal, he—and any other staff who wanted to take advantage of the offer—would be given a full year, rent-free, in a new high-rise apartment building in the countryside. How far in the countryside, he hadn't known at the time—it turned out to be nearly an hour—but said the commute would be worth the free rent. When she noted they only had one car, and it would mean both having to quit her job and being stuck at home, Liam was quick to point out a year's rent was greater than the pay afforded by her part-time employment at a used bookstore. He also reminded her of her desire to get back into writing, promising to turn the spare bedroom into an office.

So, she agreed to the move, and within a week, they were packing boxes.

Olivia had to admit, the relocation had been exciting at first. The New Leaf Building was a vast improvement over their previous home. The apartment was easily twice the size of the one they had left behind. The exhilaration was short lived though, as the realities of their new dwelling began to weigh in.

Liam was almost always irritable. Already prone to working late, the commute only added to his frustrations. He even occasionally stayed with a friend in the city on the nights it was just too late to make the trek home. Olivia herself couldn't find the motivation to do much of anything, certainly not rekindle her love of writing—though she tried. Instead, she would sit on the balcony and pine for their old home, a place which felt increasingly farther away, like the ground between the two locations was growing, stretching.

All these problems seemed secondary to the one facing her now—finding her husband. Olivia scurried back into her apartment and slid the door closed, leaving the storm behind. She tried to recall if they had any candles or a flashlight stashed somewhere, possibly tucked into a drawer or in one of the boxes in the spare room, but was brought to a mental halt when she glanced across the span of her home.

A glowing red light was coming from the front door of their apartment.

Between the confusing state of her awakening and the unsettling absence of her husband, Olivia had missed something while moving through her home. She stepped forward. The glare was emanating from the hallway outside, a crimson haze invading through the partially open front door.

Olivia felt her heart begin to thud.

The sensation was so strong that, for the first time since waking up on the bedroom floor, the general turmoil in her stomach and the dull ache in her brain was completely forgotten.

Because, even as she squinted, she was sure someone had been standing out there.

CHAPTER 3

Olivia took a quick step back, keeping the door in her sights and knocking into the glass of the balcony.

"Hello?" Her voice cracked as she spoke, the single word sounding more like the croak of a frog than English.

Fumbling through various scenarios in an attempt to explain what she was seeing, Olivia settled on the most worrisome.

Somebody was about to enter her home.

She almost called for her husband again but kept her mouth shut. Unless he was playing a particularly mean joke, Liam wasn't there.

Eyes wide, she stared at the sliver of red light peeking around the edges of the door. Had it been open the entire time? Had she walked right past it upon leaving her bedroom and not even noticed? Or had somebody, the shadow in the hall, opened it?

Her breath came fast and hard, and it made her lightheaded. The distance between her current location and the apartment door felt insurmountable. She could never overcome the space between the two before whatever was in the hall could push its way in.

Olivia sucked in a lungful of air and forced her legs to move. She scurried through her dining room, past the kitchen, skirted the living room, and with her hands out, pushed the front door closed. Only with the snap of the deadbolt locking into place did the air exhale from her body.

"What the fuck is going on?" she whispered. She turned around and propped her back against the door. Even supported by the sturdy wood behind her, she felt weak, like she would collapse to the floor.

A quick, frantic patter vibrated through the door. Olivia yelped and skittered away from her position.

Somebody is definitely out there!

She rushed forward once again, yelling, "Who's there?" Olivia pressed her face to the surface and peered through the peephole.

The red light of the emergency lamps cast a bloody haze on the section of hallway opposite her door. The patterned wallpaper—an elegant floral print—was reduced to a crimson collection of red shapes. Off to the extreme left and right of her fish-eyed view, the corridor fell into a shadowy pool. From what she could see, the hallway was vacant.

"If somebody is out there, you better stop it now! I'm going to call the cops if you don't!" She actually hoped for someone to appear, to stand up from a crouched position and stare back. As awful as it would be, she would at least be able to confront it.

But nothing stirred beyond the door.

"Fuck this," she said, leaving the door behind.

She wasn't going to call the police, not yet, but she would call Liam. Why her husband was not home was a mystery she couldn't wrap her head around, but it was a mystery which was easily solved. He would not have gone anywhere without his phone.

Olivia collected her own cell from the kitchen island, swiped away the returned warning of imminent battery failure, and brought up Liam's number. Strangely enough, she hesitated. Her thumb, poised over the call button like a guillotine, remained still. A deep sensation of foreboding, like she really did not want to know where Liam had gone or what he was doing, filled her, a swirling paradox of curiosity and utter dread, the idea that to learn the truth would forever change her life. Dismissing the unwanted feelings with a frustrated sigh and a headshake, she dialed.

A part of her expected to hear his phone's ringtone jingle through the stillness of their home. Like she had somehow managed to miss him completely, thanks to the darkness, and had moved right past him without noticing. Whatever she was expecting, it wasn't what she got. Instead of the call going through at all, the line simply went dead. She tried a second time and then a third before pulling her phone away from her ear and inspecting it. She had no signal.

"What? That's not possible," she muttered to herself.

She wondered if a drained battery could cause a poor connection. As far as she could recall, it had never been an issue before.

"That's great!" Olivia blurted, dropping the device back onto the countertop.

She began to pace, not really sure what was the best course of action to take. The New Leaf was a wireless building. Something which had never been an issue before, thanks to the nearby cell tower, but if for some reason the cell signal was compromised, then she was completely cut off from the outside world. Olivia rubbed her eyes—her head still sang a chorus of torment—and took a handful of steadying breaths.

"Think. Think. Think. Where would Liam go? Why?"

The answer to both things came to her at once.

The phone call.

A vague, ill-shaped piece of the evening's events started to materialize in her mind's eye. Once she was in bed, the world fading fast around her, she had heard Liam's phone ring. Whoever had called him must have required his attention. She glanced toward the front door and, more specifically, the small set of hooks stuck to the wall next to it. Even in the dark, she could see the glint of his car keys.

"So, whoever called you was in the building?"

That seemed unlikely. Liam had told her only a few of his co-workers had taken the rent-free offer, and of those who had, he was not friends with any of them. As for the other tenants, Liam worked so much he wouldn't know half their neighbors even if he ran into them.

Yet the evidence was there. Somebody had called him, causing him to go out. But he knew he wouldn't be gone long so left the front door unlocked—something he was prone to do when running down to his car in the garage.

Her deductions did not explain the note pad with its seemingly random number, nor the odd pill bottle, empty of its contents, left behind in the kitchen, but those questions were secondary in her mind behind finding her husband.

Olivia returned to the peephole and looked out. The red haze was almost surreal, like she was not viewing the space just steps away through a warped piece of glass, but rather was peeking through a tear into another reality altogether. Whoever had tapped her door was apparently gone. She wondered briefly if it could have been a burglar but then rejected the idea as being too outlandish. The New Leaf was a safe, secure building, and as far as she had seen, no weirdos or psychopaths lived within its walls. Whoever had made the noise was probably just a confused neighbor.

"It's nothing." This verbal reassurance did little to quell the dread which had started gnawing at her guts like a rat.

Olivia slipped on her sandals and reached for the lock. The sound—a deep clunk—made by the deadbolt retracting into its base made her regret the action almost immediately. She let her hand hover over the knob for several seconds before giving it a twist and pushing the door slightly ajar. Even though the peephole had promised empty hallway on the other side, she had still expected, in that moment, for an arm to reach in and grab her, or a face to suddenly appear in the curtain of red light spilling between the door and the frame, but neither thing happened.

She pulled the door open farther and leaned forward, sticking her head out through the gap. As soon as she did, she could hear something. It wasn't a knock or thump or bang, but rather a low, warbling sound. A sound which couldn't be mistaken for anything else.

Somebody was moaning in pain.

CHAPTER 4

As the door opened, the pained wailing became more pronounced. It sounded like a woman but was hard to tell, due to the guttural nature of the noise.

Olivia peeked through the gap and peered up at the twin lights stationed above her door. The red bulbs looked like two bloody eyes bulging from the wall. She had been vaguely aware of their presence, but like with most utilitarian things, she had become conditioned to not notice the emergency lighting. Her forehead wrinkled in confusion.

Why in the world would the light be red? Why not use white bulbs?

She couldn't fathom the lighting being at all useful in a real emergency. The crimson glare, coupled with the tight confines of the hallway, gave everything a claustrophobic feel, like she had wandered from her twenty-fifth-floor apartment into the cramped space of a submarine suspended in the ocean depths.

Any more thought to the back-up lighting situation was brushed aside when the wailing intensified for a moment. The sound, which crept along the walls like a wave of spiders, invaded Olivia's thoughts, and she couldn't imagine what could cause a person to make such a noise.

She glanced down both sides of the hallway. Her apartment was located on the left side of the building—only a few units from the stairwell. She could barely make out the metal door, the glowing exit sign above it lost in the sea of red produced by the emergency lights. Off to the right, the corridor was reduced to a series of crimson spotlights, each one highlighting another door—some housing neighbors, others unoccupied.

The New Leaf Building had a unique shape. It resembled a capital D. The front of the building followed the arch of the D, while the backside, where Olivia lived, was flat across. Because the hallway itself was curved to match the front exterior, she could not see farther than the very top of the arch. For a moment, while her eyes adjusted to the poor conditions, she feared she would have to walk to the far side of the hall to find out who was making all the noise.

But then she saw them.

About four or five doors down, on the same side of the hall as Olivia, was a figure hunched partially inside one of the shaded areas between lights. The sight of this person—a writhing mass of near-shapelessness—caused Olivia's heart rate to gallop.

"Liam?" Her husband's name leapt from her almost of its own accord.

She slapped a hand across her mouth and watched the person on the floor, expecting them to rise, to turn toward her, to rush her. But the crying person did not stand, or really even move much at all. They just continued to moan.

Olivia stepped out from her apartment, checked to make sure the lock would not re-engage when the door closed, then gently eased the door shut behind her. The brass numbers fronting her home, 2506, caught the red light and sent it back out in a series of bloody, twinkling stars. She started moving away from her home, her legs trembling under her weight. After only managing a few steps, something snatched her attention, pausing her forward momentum.

A series of sounds worked their way through the wall next to her. Small crashes, like items being pushed off a table or shelf, cut through the plaster and drywall to reach her. She looked at the door to the apartment where the noises had originated—2507. The place belonged to a young couple,

Nico and Chloe Pantazis. The wife worked for a large pharmaceutical company and was constantly out of the country for some reason or another. Olivia had chatted with the husband, Nico, on a few occasions, but most of the conversations revolved around his home country of Greece, or his young son, Rian. The boy was on the spectrum for autism, and even though he could name the capital of every country in the world and knew the scientific name for most species of lizard, he needed constant care.

She was going to knock on the door but came up short. Whatever was happening inside probably had to do with Chloe and Nico's son and was none of Olivia's business. Besides, banging on the neighbor's door at one in the morning, wearing a T-shirt and sleep pants, reeking of vomit and looking like a reanimated corpse, was not the best option.

Nope, she would continue to the sobbing woman, make sure she was okay, then return to her apartment, hopefully finding Liam along the way.

Olivia started again toward the slouched figure and could feel rivers of sweat begin to run down her back. She would never have imagined the building could get so hot. It felt like she was navigating through a giant, curved oven, the emergency lights acting like the elements, cooking everything caught under the glare.

The gloomy shroud began to pull back, like the layers of an onion, and the identity of the person became clear. It was Mrs. Elliot. Olivia was sure of it.

The Elliots, a retired couple, lived four apartments over from Olivia—the last unit before the elevators. She and Liam had been introduced to them when the building first opened. The old lady was something of an elitist, which was expected, Olivia guessed, considering the woman's husband had owned a chain of grocery stores in the city. What really struck Olivia as funny, though, was the old man, Willum Elliot, was not that way at all. If anything, he was the textbook definition of grandfatherly.

With the realization it was Mrs. Elliot she was looking at, slumped like a vagrant against the wall, Olivia quickened her pace.

"Mrs. Elliot?" Olivia was almost afraid to speak, to disturb the woman. The scene before her was horribly amiss.

The question did not reach beyond the woman's sorrow, however, and she continued to bellow and moan, unaware of her audience.

A wave of foreboding seemed to radiate off Mrs. Elliot like a flashing danger sign. It was obvious something was wrong, that Mrs. Elliot was in distress, but it went deeper than that. A vein of profound disquiet ran through Olivia, and the hairs on her neck stood on end. She wanted to turn her back on the old lady and return to her apartment, wanted to change her clothes and climb into bed, wanted to wake up in the morning and find Liam lying next to her and all the unwanted mysteries of the night to be a thing of the past. Olivia wanted all these things but knew running away would not change the fact this woman was obviously in serious distress.

She looked down at the woman for a moment, hoping Mrs. Elliot would notice her, would see she was being observed and would compose herself, maybe even be embarrassed for making a scene in the first place. It would save Olivia from having to do anything at all. But that did not happen. Instead, the old lady continued to weep and quiver, oblivious to her surroundings.

Olivia cleared her throat and tentatively reached out, placing her hand on the woman's shoulder. It felt bony under her touch, like Mrs. Elliot was a collection of twigs draped in a thin layer of cloth instead of a human being.

As soon as her fingers fell on her, the old lady twisted her head up toward Olivia—her face a mask of gore. Several gashes leaked blood down the winding crevasses of her wrinkled cheeks.

Under the red light, the blood shone like liquid ruby.

CHAPTER 5

Olivia jumped back, her left side colliding painfully against the frame of a nearby apartment door.

What the fuck happened to her? her brain screamed.

The old woman, her head bobbing in the air like a cork on the water, leaned forward and peered at Olivia. Her mouth hung partially open, her lips drooping significantly at the corners. In the hellish light engulfing them, Olivia could see just the tiniest reveal of tongue when Mrs. Elliot licked along her bottom teeth, which resembled river-smoothed pebbles in her mouth.

Olivia pushed herself away from the doorframe and took a stuttering step toward the downed woman. Her first attempt at speaking produced nothing more than a wheeze of air. Clearing her throat, she tried again.

"Are you okay?"

Mrs. Elliot did not respond. Instead, she continued to stare off into the distance, like she couldn't see Olivia at all.

Squatting down—careful not to touch the woman again—Olivia cleared her throat a second time and said, "Can you tell me what happened, Mrs. Elliot?"

Somewhere along the length of the hallway, a door slammed closed.

The bang yanked Olivia's attention from the old lady. She looked around for the source of the noise, but it was almost impossible to pinpoint its origin.

"What's going on here tonight?" she muttered.

When the old woman answered her question, it surprised her nearly as much as the shutting door.

"Willum." The name slipped between Mrs. Elliot's quivering lips with a slight hiss.

"Your husband?" Olivia quickly looked around, like the old woman speaking his name aloud would produce the man. "Is he here? Is he okay?" She had not meant to overwhelm the poor thing with a barrage of questions, but was so thirsty for answers she couldn't help it.

The elderly lady stared blankly, and for a moment, Olivia wondered if maybe she had been mistaken. Maybe she had heard a name woven in a painful exhale where there wasn't one. And then Mrs. Elliot said it again.

"Willum."

Olivia nodded. "Yes, your husband, Willum. Where is he? Is he hurt too?" Her tone grew evenly with her unease. Fear sharpened her tongue.

Finally, the bloodied Mrs. Elliot appeared to focus on Olivia. She lifted one hand from the floor—a bloody palmprint left behind on the low-pile carpet—and cupped the side of Olivia's face.

She hadn't been expecting the contact and, once the hand was there, did not want to upset the traumatized woman further by removing it. Olivia could feel the sticky-wet blood coating the inside of Mrs. Elliot's palm cling to her cheek.

"Mrs. Elliot, what happened? Is Liam here?" She wasn't entirely sure why she asked about Liam, but her state was bordering on frantic.

Mrs. Elliot's tongue snaked out several times, leaving a glistening film on her lower lip. "He hurt me."

Olivia pulled away, returning to her feet and taking a step back. The woman's hand, free from Olivia's face, fell dead to the floor.

"Liam did this?" Her mind recoiled at such a thought. The idea itself was somehow corrosive to her mental being.

Slowly—almost mechanically—Mrs. Elliot turned her gaze away

from Olivia, letting her sight settle on a nearby open door. Apartment 2510. Although she had never been inside the apartment, Olivia knew it belonged to the Elliots.

"Willum hurt me. He took the girl," Mrs. Elliot whispered.

"Oh...I thought...," Olivia stuttered. She wasn't sure *what* she actually thought. Liam was capable of anger, but she couldn't imagine him getting physical with anyone, especially an old lady. Leaning closer to the injured woman, she asked, "Wait, what girl?"

Mrs. Elliot shook her head and began sobbing again, the tears cleaving trenches in the blood.

Could Mr. Elliot have done this? That didn't jive with her memory of the old man. It wasn't just that he had seemed so kind and gentle. No, the real reason she couldn't imagine Mr. Elliot beating his wife was because he was in poor health. He needed a cane to get around, and even then, it was obvious each step was a struggle for him. In comparison, Mrs. Elliot was a fairly sturdy woman, still healthy for her advanced age. But what else could the answer be? The proof was sitting in a bloody heap before her. Whether she could picture it or not, it seemed Willum Elliot had laid a beating into his wife.

Olivia felt suddenly dizzy. The hallway twisted around her like a living thing—the humid air its hot breath. Fighting through the vertigo, she reached forward and plucked a few strands of silver hair—which had become stuck in the tacky blood—out of Mrs. Elliot's face.

"I can't believe he did this to you."

She imagined Mr. Elliot, his withered frame hunched slightly, smacking his wife around, his liver-spotted fist sinking into this poor woman's cheek and spittle flying from his clenched, coffee-stained teeth. Old and sickly he might be, but he was still a monster, it seemed.

Staring at the cuts along the woman's forehead—little gaping mouths decorating her wrinkled flesh—almost made Olivia sick. A ripple of nausea, much like she felt upon rising from the floor in her bedroom, sent a wave of agony through her guts.

"Did you call...someone? Like, for help? The police?" She thought of her non-functioning phone and wondered if the problem spread further than her own device. Not that it mattered, Olivia knew. Mrs. Elliot could have called the cops, but given the location of the New Leaf Building, it would take some time before they would arrive.

The question went unanswered, and the old woman looked away from Olivia, her eyes glazing and distant. She started to moan again. The conversation, if one could even call it that, was apparently over.

Olivia turned away from the beaten woman, directing her attention to the darkness of the elderly couple's apartment. She rose to her feet and took a hesitant step toward the open door. It was utterly black past the threshold. A vertical pool of ink.

A long, growling rumble of thunder caused the New Leaf to vibrate.

The sound of nature's fury achieved what Olivia couldn't and pulled Mrs. Elliot back to reality. The woman's body jerked, and she brought her wide eyes to bear on Olivia. "She was looking for somebody. A boyfriend, I think. She seemed distressed. I talked to her, but then Willum...I thought he was sleeping. He grabbed her. He pulled her inside. I tried to stop him, but he hurt me."

"Your husband..." Olivia scratched her head as she spoke, trying desperately to make sense of the limited information she had been given, a task made all the more difficult given the foggy state of her own brain. "Willum brought a woman from the building into your apartment? And they're in there right now?"

The old woman nodded once.

Anxiety—of the prickly sort—made Olivia's body itch, and she approached the open door. She did not want to go inside. Olivia felt frayed, gutted, a filleted version of herself, and every action felt like the wrong one. The only sure things were, Mrs. Elliot was a mess, and the man who had apparently done it was inside. And to make things worse, he might or might not have a girl from the building in there with him.

Before she could come up with another solution, Olivia found herself pushing into the murky passageway leading into the Elliot's apartment. Behind her, Mrs. Elliot—with blood dribbling down her face—began to sob once again.

CHAPTER 6

Olivia strained her eyes, willing them to pierce the sheet of darkness which had engulfed her.

"I know what you're doing!"

It was a lie of course. She had no idea what the old man was up to, but she felt the need to say something. There was no reply. The only sound filling the air around her was the sorrowful cadence leaking from Mrs. Elliot.

The blackness of the Elliot apartment was overwhelming. She wished she had taken the time to search for a flashlight before venturing from her place. But how could she have known what she was going to be walking into? The walls of her reality had peeled away while she lay on the bedroom floor, revealing a strange, unfamiliar world underneath.

"Mr. Elliot." She licked her lips. "I know you're in here. Come out now, or...or I'm calling the cops!" A small quiver scurried through her words, revealing how paper-thin the conviction behind them was.

Olivia turned back to look at the old lady in the hall, now framed in black by the open doorway.

What if Mrs. Elliot is wrong? The woman had clearly been beaten up—there was no doubt about that—but what if the assault had caused something to break loose in her aged brain. For all Olivia knew, whoever had assailed the old lady had fled. There might be nobody in the Elliot apartment at all.

Still, she figured it was better to check.

Just inside the doorway, sitting in a large wooden pot decorated with tribal designs, was Mr. Elliot's cane, beside two upside-down umbrellas. The head, which peeked up over the lip of the pot like a gopher, was that of a silver mallard. It was polished to such a shine it fully reflected the red light seeping in like a mirror.

Olivia couldn't imagine the man getting very far without his walking aid.

She stared at it for a moment before pulling it free from the confines of the wooden pot. The metal handle was oddly cool given the rising heat. The cane was sturdy. She realized it would make a nice weapon, if need be. Which, she supposed, was why she was compelled to reach for it in the first place.

Holding it before her, she moved forward. Slowly, dimly, objects and shapes began to materialize around her. These things, which felt as much like alien creatures hiding in the dark as they did furniture, gave Olivia the impression of being watched. They seemed to move and sway, ready to attack. Paranoia filled her thoughts. She became sure somebody was standing just beyond her extremely limited vision, watching, waiting.

Straight ahead, she could make out narrow, vertical slivers of nighttime light peeking through the blinds covering the dining room windows. Hurrying forward, left hand groping the air before her, Olivia reached the window and pushed the blinds aside. Still holding them, she twisted to look at the room behind her. In the low light, the shapes and forms had become a clutter of antique furniture. It seemed she had been in danger of being attacked by a Chesterfield. The only thing watching her was a cabinet jammed full of trinkets. She wanted to laugh and knew she probably would do just that, but not until later, not until she was back in her own home and all the craziness was behind her.

Using the cord at the edge of the window, Olivia drew the blinds completely open and took in the ferocity of the storm outside. The trees surrounding the New Leaf rocked and swayed violently. Sheets of rainwater ran down the glass.

With the darkness repelled, even just a little, Olivia felt her confidence grow, and she looked over the main living area of the Elliot's apartment. The layout was a near match to her own. She had only ever been in one other apartment in the building, Chloe and Nico's, and since theirs was on the front of the building—along the bow of the D—it had a slightly different floor plan.

One thing which caught her attention, though, was the vent cover along the dining room wall. Enough dim light made its way through the large windows to reveal something had apparently jarred it loose, causing it to hang open. The rectangle beyond was completely black. Somewhere buried deep inside the sheet-metal intestine, a wild tapping echoed forth.

Olivia told herself it was the sound of the metal heating up under the oppressive pall of warmth filling the New Leaf. But the explanation felt as hollow as the shaft exposed before her.

She stepped away and spoke into the empty room. "Mr. Elliot? Are you here?" For a moment, she thought she heard something—a deep coughing—but the noise was gobbled-up wholesale by the rage of the storm.

Olivia peeked into the darkness of the guest bathroom and the kitchen. Both appeared empty, although she wasn't about to wade in any further to investigate.

After moving back to the front door, Olivia looked out on Mrs. Elliot again. The woman had sunk to the floor even more so than before. It looked like her body had crumbled under the weight of her sorrow, leaving her a sack of powdered bone and cartilage. She convulsed in time with her sobs.

Where the hell is everyone?

The New Leaf was sparsely populated, but there were still people living there. *How is it possible that no one can hear this poor woman lying in the hallway?*

Olivia pushed the door open as wide as it would go in an attempt to allow as much of the red light into the home as possible. She turned her attention toward the hallway, which led deeper into the apartment. Dark spots could be seen on the carpet, a wild pattern of circles, like tiny black holes in the floor itself. It was impossible to be sure, but the reality of the situation made Olivia fairly certain it was blood. She wondered how much of the stuff the elderly woman had lost before finding herself slumped in the corridor outside.

She stepped around the stains, frightened at the prospect of checking the rest of the rooms. Her mind tried to fill in the blanks as to what she would find there. All the scenarios were horrifying. She knew, no matter what sight awaited her, emergency services would be needed. She wondered again at the state of the cell signal. What if there was no way to reach 911?

Olivia took a deep breath.

The emergency light did not reach very far into the hall, but with the cane held ahead of her like a lance, Olivia faced down the darkness and continued forward. As she did so, the wail of Mrs. Elliot's crying was replaced by a new sound, a deep *shunk*. The noise repeated. And then again.

Again.

It was a horrible sound, one which reminded Olivia of herself, trying to pull a booted foot free from the mud as a child—a wet, sucking sound. A sound which had no place in a high-rise apartment building.

Wanting the noise to stop, Olivia slapped the cane against a nearby wall and shouted, "I've called the police, Mr. Elliot!"

Shunk!

Ahead of her was the first of the two bedrooms. A faint glow of soft orange light came from underneath the door. It took a moment for Olivia's eyes to adjust enough to even be aware of it, but once they had, it glared like a thin, horizontal beacon.

Shunk!

She thought about knocking, but that seemed absurd under the circumstances. Instead, she planned to grab the knob, throw the door open, and confront the old man. Before she could though, something slammed into the door on the other side. The light along the bottom was smothered.

She couldn't see the knob twist, thanks to the dusk of the small hallway, but she could hear it. A slow, persistent squeal followed by a click. The door fell open a few inches. Through the gap, Olivia saw two things.

The first—and what appeared to be the source of the light—was an e-reader. The device leaned against the bottom of a highly polished wooden chest next to a bed with a ruffled comforter hanging limply off the side. A red smear of something on the e-reader's screen had turned the normally white display a sickly orange.

The second sight to greet her increased in gruesome detail as the door widened, like a picture coming into focus. Lying on the floor, her body bathed in the e-reader's light, was a woman. She wore grey exercise tights—with a large, pink heart across the ass—and a purple sports bra. The woman was positioned awkwardly on the ground. Her head and face had been reduced to a chunky pulp, making any identification on Olivia's part impossible. Resting against the ruin of her head was an oval hunk of glass. Flecks of skull and brain, along with a healthy wash of blood, nearly covered the entirety of the object. In the dim light, the words, *Willum Elliot – Businessman of the Year – 1996*, could be seen. Olivia realized the *shunk* had been the sound of the award being driven repeatedly into the corpse's head.

She raised her free hand to her mouth, her palm effectively trapping the scream threatening to erupt.

Blood-stained fingers appeared around the edge of the open door and heaved it the rest of the way. Standing before her—backlit by the e-reader—was Willum Elliot. He was not a big man, but in that moment, he seemed to completely fill the frame. His boney arms and legs looked stick-like contrasted with his sagging, paunch of a belly. He was wearing boxer shorts and a white undershirt, both articles of clothing spattered with blood.

All these details, like individual drops of rain, were lost in the storm that was Mr. Elliot's face. His mouth hung open at an impossible angle. Several of his teeth were missing, and the corners of his lips were torn and bleeding. Multiple lines of blood and saliva hung in ropes off his chin.

"Mr. Elliot?" she whispered.

As soon as the name left her mouth, something physical left his.

It appeared quickly, a shiny black head preceding a segmented body. A large insect, about the size of a small cat, emerged from Willum Elliot's damaged maw amid a series of retching coughs and burps. The creature climbed up the elderly man's face, horrid little legs finding purchase in the folds of his skin. It stopped once it reached his forehead. Clinging there, half-free from the old man's mouth, the bug began to hiss.

Olivia could not stop her scream this time.

CHAPTER 7

Terror, cold and dark, howled through Olivia. Her throat burned as the scream blasted from her lips. A river of urine slid in hot winding paths down the inside of both her thighs, soaking into the cotton of her pajama pants. The apartment around her seemed to constrict, and her brain tried—and ultimately failed—to come to terms with what exactly her eyes were seeing.

The insect twisted and shimmied from its position on the old man's face. In the little bit of light provided from the e-reader, it looked more like a living blob of oil than a solid thing. Mr. Elliot himself was frozen—the withered muscles of his arms and legs taut, sacks of loose skin and aged fat hanging from the undersides. He made no move at all to pull the nightmare free from his mouth.

As the bug continued to climb the landscape of his face, it shifted enough to the side—almost reaching Mr. Elliot's left ear—for Olivia to get a clearer look at it. The shape, although blown-up to horrifying proportions, was vaguely familiar.

When Olivia was eleven, she had spent a week at her aunt and uncle's cottage in Northern Ontario. It was the last real vacation she had taken with her mom and was one of her fondest memories. Seven days of swimming, hiking, and her uncle's cooking. Plus, she got to play with her cousins—twin girls a year her senior—every day. It was while out with her cousins, exploring the woods, the lone dark spot of the whole trip occurred.

The three girls had come across a dilapidated structure a half-hour's walk from the cottage. It looked like it might have been a cabin at one point, but time, weather, and neglect had broken the back of the place, leaving it sunken in the middle. Weeds, plants, and trees grew in tangles from the windows, the glass long gone. Olivia wandered around the side of the wreck and saw a smaller structure out back, recessed from the main building.

It was an outhouse.

Unlike the cabin, the outhouse had managed to remain mostly erect. Even the door, with a halfmoon carved near the top, appeared sound.

Neither of her cousins wanted to go near the wooden box, insisting there could be nothing good inside. But Olivia, being younger, wanted to prove to the older girls she was fearless so sauntered over and opened the door. What she had not told them was she had to pee quite badly and was afraid she wouldn't be able to hold it until they got back to the cottage.

The inside smelled damp, like soggy newspapers. A deep green fungus lined the nooks and crannies. It looked soft and cool. One step in led to a raised bench with a hole cut through it. The wood of the bench was frayed and peeling, the hole itself a black circle with no immediate bottom.

Deciding to get it over with as fast as possible, Olivia closed the door—there was no latch—dropped her shorts, and sat with a thump over the opening. As soon as her ass hit the wood, she felt the entire structure shake. A wet crack, like the sound of a broken bone, issued from the bench beneath her. The seat collapsed.

Olivia screamed. Folded in half, she fell through the hole, her butt smacking the soft ground, her feet sticking up through the opening.

Her cousins called from the outside, asking if she was okay. But when she opened her mouth to respond—embarrassment already setting in—something fell on her face. She snatched it free from her cheek and held it up. Pinched between her fingers, illuminated in a spotlight shaped like the moon, was an earwig. Revulsion stiffened her limbs, and she flicked the hideous insect away.

She struggled to free herself, and her foot slammed against the side of the outhouse. The tiny structure rocked, and somewhere in the darkness along the ceiling, a piece of wood broke loose. It tumbled down onto her head with a small *thwack*. Olivia rubbed the spot and peered up into the black above her, just as it began to rain earwigs.

They skittered across her face, burrowed into her hair, and slid down her top. Blind panic electrified her body, lifting her from the hole. Bursting through the outhouse door, shorts around her ankles, she began to scream and dance, causing bugs to fly from her body. Her cousins, both with matching expressions of horror on their faces, watched in stunned silence.

She had occasionally relived that moment over the years since, always in the middle of the night, when a stray itch materialized seemingly out of nowhere. Her mind would picture those awful things, bodies the color of black coffee, oversized pincers gnashing, scurrying through the folds of her pajamas. Only after turning on the lights and inspecting her bed would she return to sleep.

That day in the woods came back full force as she watched the thing begin to navigate Willum Elliot's face.

It's a goddamn huge earwig, her mind screamed. But that wasn't quite accurate. It just looked like the bug which had terrorized her youth. This was something different, something she had never seen before.

A thin pair of antennae swayed in the air above the old man's mostly bald pate. They were hard to see, looking more like wisps of string caught in a breeze than anything else, but they were there.

"Mr. Elliot?" Olivia's voice had been reduced to nothing more than a breath of air, a whisper, but it was enough for the thing before her to react.

The insect quickly retreated into the old man's mouth, its carapace scraping against the few remaining teeth hanging in his destroyed maw as it did so.

There was a second, a brief moment, after the creature disappeared into the black hole of Mr. Elliot's smashed orifice when nothing happened. It was as if time had simply stopped—Olivia standing frozen to the floor, while the blood-spattered man before her was as still as a storefront mannequin.

Silence descended through the apartment.

And then, in a sudden fit of tightening muscles, Willum Elliot burst back to life and launched himself at her.

CHAPTER 8

Olivia took a step back, raising the cane—the thin, black, lacquered wood of the walking aid acting as a barrier between them. It did nothing to stop Mr. Elliot's momentum. His full weight collided with her, pushing her back, slamming them both against the far wall of the hallway. A storm of framed photos poured down around her from the impact.

She screamed and pushed against the man, but he was rabid in his assault and quickly threw her to the floor.

The deep pile of the carpet under her felt like an insult, a soft cushion to lay upon as the grim reaper descended. The old man followed her down, collapsing like a bag of sticks and wet clothes on top of her. Olivia opened her mouth to protest, to question, to scream, but all those things were silenced when he brought his fist crashing down onto her face.

She had been hit once before in a field hockey melee, and later by a boyfriend with a drinking problem. In both instances, she had given better than she had received, but neither time had the blow been so devastating as the one Willum Elliot delivered. It rocked her head, squishing the back of her skull into the lush carpet. No sooner had his knuckles left her face when another clenched fist slammed down.

Through the assault—which had taken on a strange, surreal quality, like the first punch had knocked her loose from her body—Olivia could see his slack mouth waving, ropes of saliva catching the light from the e-reader. Only when she felt one of her molars crack in half, the piece of tooth disappearing down her throat, did she return to her body, fully understanding this man intended to kill her.

In a snap, her fear and confusion broke. A new, deeper instinct took root...survival. Hot currents of adrenaline arced through her limbs. She swung her arms violently into the man on top of her, while kicking and bucking her legs. Her hands, flailing through the air, slapped against his face, his lower jaw swaying with each hit like a punching bag.

One of the old man's fingers snaked into Olivia's mouth. She could taste the dead woman's blood coating his hand and retched when her gag reflex kicked in. Olivia bit down with everything she had, her teeth easily penetrating the aged skin of Mr. Elliot's fingers, coming to a crunching halt on the bones. She was rewarded with a fountain of fresh blood. It filled her mouth before spilling down her throat. Her body arched painfully as she heaved. The bite, which must have hurt like all hell, did not faze the monster straddling her. In fact, all her fighting did little good to dislodge the elderly man.

In the weak light, Mr. Elliot's tight fists—his knuckles, a series of four boney knobs, stood out like rocks glued to a baseball—arched back through the air before slamming down on the side of her head. The blow, which oddly did not hurt that much at all, caused the world around her to shimmer and darken.

Olivia had only ever been knocked out once in her life. Another field hockey mishap had done the trick then. Still, she could remember the sensation clearly enough to realize another impact like the last would send her off into the black, and then she would be at the mercy of the man...the thing...on top of her.

Her fingers raked across the thick carpet, plowing grooves in the pile like a till through the soil. Every muscle, every bone in her body, screamed to fight back, but the weight of the man was too much to overcome. Her arms thrashed around wildly in search of something to force Mr. Elliot off her.

When her hand slapped against the body of the cane, she did not at first even feel it. Only when her groping digits curled around the smooth shaft did a portal of coherent thought open in her mind. Olivia swung the walking stick up from the floor and brought it across Willum Elliot's face. A vicious snap rocked his limp, lower jaw, sending a spray of spit down on her. The man reeled back, his movement portraying insult more than injury.

In a quick, frightening motion, the bug crawled free again. It pulled itself out, and strands of saliva slipped free from its grotesque body, falling in a slick curl along Olivia's chest. She brought the cane up again. The silver mallard, reflecting the e-reader light, looked like a miniature shooting star arcing across the blackness of night. The head of the stick connected firmly with the insect. A wet cracking sound proceeded a frenzied hiss from the thing, before the man—and bug—fell completely off of her.

Olivia sucked in a mouthful of air, not realizing until the moment the weight atop her was gone that she had been close to suffocating, thanks to its presence, and rolled to her hands and knees. Off to her right, she watched as the bug—a fury of spastic vibrations—sucked back into the old man's mouth. Mr. Elliot started to climb to his feet.

She stood up, her body quaking with fear, and made a break for the hallway door. The distance was practically insignificant while running, but still, she was overcome with the sensation the nightmare behind her would catch her before she could exit. That his fingers—nails black with congealed blood—would bury themselves in her hair, yanking her back into hell. She had lost one of her sandals in the fray, which caused her to hobble slightly.

Each step closer to the patch of red light leaking in through the main door gave her hope she was leaving her attacker well behind, Olivia screaming the entire time she ran.

Just as she reached the threshold between apartment and hallway, she was pushed from behind. She briefly wondered how a man well north of seventy could catch her, but this thought, like the world around her, was turned upside down. Her feet smacked together, and she tumbled forward into the hall, her remaining sandal spinning through the air like a frisbee.

Confusion momentarily took over as Olivia was suddenly looking at the tortured face of Mrs. Elliot. The old lady's eyes stared ahead, dim, unfocused. She opened her mouth to speak, but whatever Mrs. Elliot was going to say was instantly silenced when her husband roared free from their home and began stomping his foot into her face.

Crab-walking away from the scene, Olivia couldn't take her eyes off what she was seeing. The retired grocery store owner, his knobby knees looking swollen in the red glow of the emergency lights, brought his bare foot down repeatedly onto his wife's head. Olivia let out a strangled, horrified yelp. Turning away in a drunken shock—not before witnessing the big toe on his left foot fold completely back on the old woman's forehead, a position it could not achieve without breaking the bone—she scrambled to her feet and began sprinting for her apartment.

Her legs felt weighted, like her bones had been laced with lead, each step down the blood-red hallway a colossal achievement. As she ran, new details began to emerge from her surroundings. A dark smear on a doorknob, a tear in the wallpaper, a neighbor's door slightly ajar. All signs her environment had changed while she had slept. She had been so consumed with her own situation, she had completely missed these things.

Thunder, the sort which sent children scurrying into their parents' beds, covered the sound of Mr. Elliot's foot obliterating what was left of his wife. Olivia was thankful for that, for even as she ran, even with her heart pounding in her ears like a marching band drum, she could still hear that awful sound.

She stumbled past Chloe and Nico's place, the door wide open. Somewhere in the back of her mind, she recalled having heard noises from within, but the memory felt ancient, like it had happened to her in another life. Desperate for help, she turned to enter her neighbor's home but came up short when she saw her own door, farther down, also open.

Had Liam returned?

"Liam!" His name came out warped and distorted, buried under sorrow and fear. She was crying so hard she almost choked.

Olivia stumbled into her apartment, once again closing and locking the door.

CHAPTER 9

"**L**iam!" Olivia shuffled forward, her body sagging under the weight of the trauma she had suffered.

She could see across the distance of her living and dining rooms, all the way to the open blinds of her front windows. The tumultuous sky, a sea of low-hanging clouds which slid across the dark horizon, dumped copious amounts of rain on the land. The furniture felt odd and out of place in the gloom, like she were mentally trying to meld the décor from the Elliots' and her own home together.

"Liam, where are you!"

Her body was shaking, a reaction completely at odds with the sweltering temperature filling her home. The tremors radiated out of her muscles in near-violent waves. It made her want to collapse, to fall to the floor where she could scream and cry, but even then, she doubted such actions would quell the quaking. More than anything, she prayed her husband would come out from the blackness of her home. He would know what to do.

But he didn't. Her apartment was as silent as it had been when she left, a mausoleum of domestic living.

Olivia ran to the kitchen, liberated her cell phone from the island, and dialed 911 while returning to the living room. Even though her earlier attempt to call out had ended in failure, she was still hopeful. A brief clicking sound emitted from the device before the call was dropped. Still no signal.

"Fuck!"

She threw the phone onto her couch. It bounced off the cushions and clattered on the hardwood next to the piece of furniture. Olivia felt faint. Her head throbbed, and sweat trickled from her hairline, sliding down the sides of her nose, stinging her eyes.

What's going on? Why is this happening? She attempted to work through the events as they had been presented to her, and no matter how hard she tried, they just didn't make sense. There was literally no way she could explain any aspect of it.

Her body demanded movement, so she began to pace through her living room. Each step was frail, unsound, but her legs—shaking as they were—held. She wanted to break down and cry, but she knew from experience crying wasn't going to make anything better. It never did. Tears weren't going to erase the nightmare she'd wandered into. If she wanted answers, she was going to have to find them.

She scooped up her phone, activated the screen, and held it before her. The depleted battery left it weak and dim, but she would get whatever light she could out of the device before it died. Olivia moved away from the couch and shuffled into the dining room.

Something in the corner of the room caught her attention.

The murky light coming through the windows, coupled with the faint glow from her cell, cast a thin haze of pallid illumination, just enough to define the outline of the air vent stationed in the wall. Much like the one she had seen in Mr. and Mrs. Elliot's apartment, it hung open. She had completely missed this detail while passing through the room earlier.

A series of clanks resonated from within, causing her to jump back. She had heard similar noises in the Elliot's home, but these were much more pronounced. The sensation of closeness was near overwhelming. Olivia froze in place and looked up. It was a metallic sound, mixed with a soft scuffling noise, like an impatient child tapping their fork on their dinner plate.

Something was in there.

Images of the creature which had apparently nested in old man Elliot's face sprung immediately to mind. She stumbled backward, almost tripping in the process. If one of those bugs was in there, about to burst from the black square of the vent shaft, she didn't want to face it without a weapon.

With a final, plaintive beep, her phone died.

Feeling suddenly exposed, Olivia groped her way to the kitchen and began fumbling with the cutlery drawer. The handle was all but lost to the gloom of her home, but after a few attempts, her fingers wrapped around the brass knob, and she yanked the drawer open—the silverware inside rattling and clinking like windchimes. It was almost impossible to differentiate between the various utensils, but she knew where in the drawer they kept the butcher knife, so it only took a couple attempts to pull it free from the sea of cutlery.

Olivia, brandishing the knife, hesitantly returned to the dining room, her gaze locked on the darkened vent now mostly obscured from sight, so focused on that single spot. When a sound suddenly erupted from deep in her apartment, in the short hall leading to the bedrooms, she yelped and dropped the butcher knife. The tip of the blade stuck in the floorboards next to her feet with a twang, an inch shy from severing her baby toe.

"Liam?" Her voice had taken on a wild, crazed jitter. When there was no response, she pulled the knife free from the floor beneath her and moved over to the hallway.

Dark grey light filtered through the open door to her bedroom like brackish water. It cast a ghoulish pall over the section of hall immediately outside it. Olivia squinted to draw more detail from the environment around her.

"Please, Liam. Please tell me you're here," she begged.

In the low light before her, something small cut through the hallway. It moved fast, a tiny blur racing across her path. It was gone as quickly as it had appeared.

Fear spiked through Olivia's body, and she twisted in an attempt to train her gaze on what was before her. A diminutive form, barely visible, moved from behind a small bookshelf resting against the hallway wall.

It was a boy. A thin arm stuck out from the side of the shelf, and tufts of brown hair brushed against a skinny neck.

There was only one child she knew of on her floor—Chloe and Nico's son, Rian.

"It's...It's okay." Olivia couldn't imagine what the boy must have seen to drive him into her apartment. She could barely understand the sights she had already witnessed herself.

Rian jerked once at the sound of her voice and, in a spastic motion, scurried out from the side of the bookshelf to stand before her.

The kid was naked, except for a pair of underwear—Iron Man flying across the front. Blood covered the smooth skin around his hands and feet. His lower jaw, badly broken judging by the way it hung slack, almost reached his chest. Strands of drool dripped from split lips. An insect, glistening with mucus, pulled itself free from the boy's mouth and twisted to look at Olivia.

She screamed at the sight.

The bug sunk back into Rian's throat. A moment later, the boy charged at her. He ran in a slightly hunched manner, like a skinny Quasimodo. Oddly, in that moment between seconds, she found herself wondering if his crooked posture was a result of the creature, or some other medical condition she had been unaware of.

When he fell upon her, it was with a vicious ferocity, his hands a storm of fury. Olivia felt his nails rake the sides of her neck. Although he clearly meant to kill her, the boy was much lighter than Willum Elliot, so instead of being driven to the ground, she was able to lift the child and throw him free of her.

"Rian! Rian, stop!" she pleaded as the boy flipped over the side of a chair. "Please, it's me, Olivia! Remember? I bought you that toy lizard, the one with all the colors. It made a sound when you pressed its head. Please!"

Olivia had seen the garish, plastic reptile in a gift shop. It sat in a bin full of other toy lizards and snakes, the kind of things mass produced in China and sold in discount and dollar stores across the country. Cheap. Disposable. But something about that specific toy had caught her attention. Maybe it was the colors, which were brighter than the rest, or possibly the spiked fin riding the lizards back like a lethal spine, but whatever it was, she knew Rian would love it. The fact it let out a sad, digitized roar when you pressed its head was the cherry on top.

Liam had rolled his eyed, but it was worth it when Olivia had later presented the gift to the child. Rian was not overly affectionate, as far as she had ever seen, but he wrapped his arms around her in a tight hug that day. It was one of the highpoints of her life since moving.

If he heard her now, talking about the gift, he gave no indication. Instead, as soon as he landed, he rushed her. This time, he alternated between running and scurrying on all fours, much like a lizard himself.

The knife cut through the air without much thought. Olivia had forgotten she had been holding it. She simply swung her hands to keep the boy at bay.

The stainless steel slid across his narrow, sunken chest. A curtain of blood began flowing immediately from the wound, but the injury did nothing to deter the child, who simply resumed his mad dash toward her.

Olivia watched stunned as the boy leapt through the air, his delicate fingers transformed into angry claws. Just before he reached her, she closed her eyes and jabbed the butcher knife out. She would not have believed a blade, even a sharp one, would be able to penetrate a body so easily, but with her forward thrust, added with the boy's momentum, nearly the entire blade disappeared into his belly.

Blood dribbled down the handle of the knife, finding access between Olivia's clenched fingers. It was hot and slick.

"Oh god, I didn't—"

She was cut off as the child continued to fight toward her, his actions pushing the blade in even farther, only stopping when the handle abutted the soft skin of his stomach.

He's not going to stop! The realization flashed in her mind like a neon sign. She had stabbed him, most likely a mortal injury, and yet he did not react to the wound at all. His entire being appeared to be focused on attacking her. His broken mouth swayed and drooled, and a thing so horrible Olivia couldn't imagine conjuring it in her worst nightmare burrowed somewhere down his gullet.

She thought again of the hug he had given her that day, his arms small but strong. The joy in his eyes.

Olivia released the knife and kicked forward, launching the little boy across the living room. She did not wait to see him land. Instead, she twisted around and made for the door. Pulling it closed behind her, she fell into the hallway.

Movement dragged her gaze farther down the corridor.

Crawling from the dark void of her own apartment was Chloe. The woman was a mess of blood and injuries. A gaping wound on the side of her neck pumped blood in spurts.

Behind Olivia, Chloe's son, the small boy who had just attacked Olivia, the child she had just stabbed, began scratching at the door.

The two women locked eyes. Olivia was brutally aware of the blood soaking the front of her shirt. She had likely just murdered this woman's son. Horror and fear burned on Chloe's face. Olivia felt like she should help her but was on the verge of shutting down, so she just watched as her neighbor pulled herself along the carpet toward her.

Chloe only made it a few feet before collapsing in a heap, a trail of blood, black and shiny under the red emergency lights, revealing her tortured trek. Olivia was sure an insect was going to burst free from Chloe's mouth.

Instead, the dying woman spoke. "Eosphoros."

With the word out, Chloe appeared to deflate, like the word itself had been keeping her going, and now that it was gone, she had nothing left.

Olivia rose to her feet and began stumbling toward the stairwell. Before she could make it there, the door across the hall from her opened up, and a thin man emerged. The ruby light caught his glasses, turning his eyes into twin glowing crimson circles. She tried to react, but there was nothing left.

In an instant, his arms wrapped around her in a tight bear hug. She could feel herself leave the ground, bodily lifted from her position, and dragged into his apartment.

She couldn't even muster a scream.

He kicked the door closed behind them, the snap of the lock sounding like a gunshot.

CHAPTER 10

EARLIER

"**I**'m not sleepy."

Liam was pretty sure that was what Olivia was trying to say, even as he laid her in their bed, the thick, downy comforter embracing her.

He enjoyed keeping the apartment cold but, in that moment, regretted it. He wanted to take his hands off his wife as fast as possible, but he felt she needed to be under the bedding to sell the illusion.

It had been a tremendous effort, marshaling the woman from the living room to the bedroom. He was nearly a foot taller than Olivia and had almost eighty pounds on her, but with her limbs having fallen into near uselessness, she kept stumbling. After tripping over her clumsy feet for a third time, he swore between gritted teeth and scooped her into his arms. The term *dead weight* came to him several times during the trek, especially when passing from the hallway into their bedroom, an action which transported him back six years to their wedding day.

After the small ceremony—mostly close family and a few friends—he and his new bride returned to their dump of an apartment. They had been living together for almost a year at that point, but still, upon exiting the elevator—a narrow cube which shuddered like all hell while in use—Liam hefted Olivia up and completed the time-honored tradition of carrying the bride over the threshold.

Olivia had protested, but it was half-hearted at best and even became a burst of merry laughter as the act was completed. He could so clearly remember the look of joy in her eyes. Twin pools of love and longing which made him want to drop her and run. When he looked down at Olivia's face this time, her eyes were mostly closed—just a hairline sliver of pupil peeking out. Her mouth hung partially open, a dab of saliva already gathering at the corner of her lips. She looked pale, waxen.

Liam pulled her cell phone out of her pocket and placed it on the bed next to her. He had checked the device, and although the battery was low, there was still enough juice for his purposes.

Satisfied, he spared one last look at the woman he used to love and then returned to the living room.

Liam pulled his phone from his pocket and checked the time. It was getting late. He didn't want to dally any longer than absolutely necessary. A few last-minute preparations were needed, and then he would grab his keys and be out the door. In the morning, he would return home and finish the charade.

He snatched the remote from the coffee table and shut off the television before returning his attention to the table for the two glasses sitting on its surface. His drink—mostly Sprite with a dash of vodka—was still half full. He knew he would be driving and did not want a random roadside stop to nab him with booze in his system. Olivia's glass, one which had housed much more than just vodka and Sprite, was empty. A fine, almost invisible ring of white sediment circled the bottom.

He hurried to the kitchen and placed both glasses in the sink, rinsing them thoroughly but leaving them there. Liam had walked through the construction of the scene he was creating in his mind so many times it felt almost automatic. The glasses were important, but not as much as the other items.

After moving over to one of the cupboards, Liam pulled the pill bottle—now empty—from the back. He had purchased the pills from some random drug peddler downtown. The dealer, a thin, haggard fellow who was probably ten years younger than he looked, was leaning in the doorway of an empty butcher's shop.

Liam had passed the guy several times—always crossing the street before doing so—but a week ago, he had seen the man in his usual haunt so had remained on course to walk by him. Once next to the drug dealer, Liam stopped and, as casually as he could, inquired about the medication. He had been prepared to abandon the question altogether if anything but a yes or "Sure" came out of the dealer's mouth.

As it was, the man smiled—a grin a few Chiclets shy of a full count—and told Liam to come back tomorrow at the same time. No price was mentioned, but Liam knew he would pay whatever the pusher asked.

Sure enough, the next day, the grim man held out the small orange bottle. He even gave it a musical shake to celebrate the deal. Cash was given, the pills were taken, and Liam vowed never to walk that block of the city for as long as he lived.

Liam placed the pill bottle on the kitchen island next to the bottle of vodka—still in its place from earlier—and went to the fridge, pulling the grocery list free.

"Okay." He blew out a long, steadying gust of breath. This was going to be the hardest part, and he knew it.

He had been practicing his wife's handwriting for weeks and thought, if he kept it short, not even an expert would be able to tell the difference. Not that he thought it would come to that, but still, better safe than sorry. After another breath, he leaned over the pad and began to write. It flowed so fast, so easily, he let himself begin to relax. This slip in attention ultimately cost him though. Halfway down the page, he reverted to his own penmanship and produced a looping bow on one of the letters. Olivia's handwriting was a reflection of herself—quiet, restrained, boring. There were no flourishes at all. Cursing, he tore the page free and prepared to make another attempt.

The sudden ringing of his phone halted his progress.

Liam scrunched his forehead in confusion. It was late, too late. The only person who would call him at such an hour would never do so when he was at home, certainly not on this night.

For a moment, he thought the ringing might rouse Olivia but then rolled his eyes at the thought and brought his phone up.

"Who the fuck is this?" he muttered upon seeing a series of digits he did not recognize.

Accepting the call, he sidled the phone up to his ear and asked, "Hello?"

The voice on the other end began speaking almost immediately. Liam opened his mouth to interrupt them, to demand just who the hell they thought they were, but the words being uttered through the earpiece reached him, and all he could do was stand in silence.

He listened, nodding his head occasionally, like the disembodied voice on the other side of the connection could see him. At one point, just before the call ended, he rushed over to the kitchen island, grabbed the pen, and jotted down a series of numbers as they were told to him. With the one-sided conversation over, Liam put the phone down.

At some point during the brief call, a line of sweat had broken out on his neck. The collar of his shirt was cold and damp. He stared at the number.

0725

"Fuck."

Everything he had done, all his planning, was being unraveled before his eyes.

"Fuck!"

This time, the word propelled him into movement. Phone still in hand, he rushed to the front door. Even as he put his shoes on, he was dialing a number.

As the call attempted to connect, Liam entered the hallway of the 25th floor. He pulled the door behind him but did not engage the lock. He didn't plan on being gone long. Maybe he could still salvage the evening.

He turned around and nearly collided with one of his neighbors—a tall, gangly man with glasses. Liam had never seen the guy before.

"I'm sorry," the man said with a stutter.

Liam forced a smile and gave a dismissive wave. He didn't have time for pleasantries.

When the voice on the other end answered, Liam felt a moment of relief. "Hey, babe, it's me. Wait," he quickly added to get his words in. "I did it. I really did it. But...there's something else. I just got a fucking crazy phone call."

Aware the stranger was still staring at him, Liam pulled the phone closer to his ear and lowered his voice as he hurried down the hall.

CHAPTER 11

The apartment, awash in the flickering light of several candles, was a frenzied commotion of dancing shadows. It gave the scene a strobe-light effect, like everything was moving slower than normal.

Olivia's abductor, arms wrapped around her tight enough to impede her breathing, pulled her deeper into the place like a fish hauled from the lake. Playing the part, she began to thrash but had such little energy that any resistance was minimal.

"Please! Calm down!" The man's voice was high, flighty. His breath, a brief gale of humid air, brushed across the side of her face. "We're safe in here."

The word "safe" acted like an anchor, pulling her down. A series of mental breakers began to flip inside Olivia, causing the fight to leave her body.

"I'm going to let you go, but you have to be quiet. Do you understand?" he asked.

"Yes," she whimpered.

"Okay. Okay." Slowly, the tangle of arms encompassing her loosened and then slithered away like twin snakes, retreating on either side of her body, allowing her captor to shift around and stand before her.

The man came into focus. He was young, thin to the point of being outright skinny, and at least a head taller than her, but his narrow frame seemed to negate that height instead of accentuating it. He was dressed in beige cargo shorts and a navy-blue T-shirt—the words *University of Toronto* written across the front in faded white letters.

"What is going on?" The question barely managed to crawl from her lips. She felt like she was going to be sick, that she could very possibly puke up all her organs in a wet pile at the stranger's feet.

The man stared at her for moment before shaking his head. The movement was clipped, almost bird-like. "I...I don't know."

"It's a nightmare," she cried. "We're stuck in a fucking nightmare."

He reached out and wrapped her once again in his arms. This time, the gesture was soft, comforting, telling her to let go. She pressed her face into his chest and began to sob, held in the stranger's tight embrace for several seconds.

"It's okay. It's okay." He spoke in a soothing tone, but it was not quite enough to camouflage the fear buried beneath.

Olivia wanted to believe him—she really did—but she knew it was a lie. It wasn't okay. It was a very long way from being okay at all.

With her tears abating, she started to feel foolish. She literally had no idea who this guy was, and yet she was bawling her eyes out—into his shirt no less! It took great effort to pull back her sorrow, but after a moment, she managed.

She wiped the moisture from her cheeks before using the back of her hand to collect the running snot—a shiny mark on the front of his top revealed she left some on the fabric.

"Thank you. I don't know what the fuck is happening here, but I had to get away, get away from..." She couldn't say the boy's name, not yet. It was too new, too horrible to let it leave her lips.

He brushed off her thanks with a brisk flick of his hand, followed by a quick stab at his glasses to push them back up the bridge of his nose. "Well, I couldn't leave you out there with those things."

"I didn't even know anybody was living in this apartment." She shook her head. "I thought it was empty. Christ, am I glad I was wrong."

His eyes shifted about for a moment before he chuckled—a self-conscious sound. "I just moved in today. This is not how I thought I would meet my new neighbors, but I guess we take what we can get. I'm Alex."

No hand was offered. Instead, as he spoke, he returned to the front door and dragged a stout waist-high shelf in front of it. Olivia doubted the piece of furniture would be much use as a barricade, but any added reinforcement was welcome.

"My name's Olivia. I live across the hall."

A strange, awkward silence followed in the wake of her words. Alex smiled, but it was an uncomfortable expression which looked out of place stretched across his face. She was hit with the impression the man did not smile often.

With her eyes accustomed to much dimmer conditions, the candles in Alex's apartment pushed away the darkness surrounding them. She looked over her neighbor. A smattering of acne scars stood out like craters on the lunar landscape of his forehead and cheeks. His hair was choppy, uneven, almost as if he cut it himself. But even with these defects—or maybe in spite of them—he was a surprisingly handsome guy. She was never good at pegging a person's age but figured Alex was in his early-to-mid-twenties.

His apartment reflected his recent residence. There was almost no furniture—only a small couch, coffee table, and a round dinner table which looked like it was found on the side of the road and would be lucky to seat two. His balcony door was fully open, which caused the candles nearest the door to sputter in fits.

A manic flash of lightning bloomed beyond, followed by a damning crash of thunder.

Alex followed her gaze and nodded. "I should probably close that," he said quickly, his finger again attempting to force up his glasses, even though they were firmly set on his nose. "The rain is coming in, but it's just so hot."

He started toward the open door, or at least that's where Olivia thought he was going—maybe to close it—until he turned right, beyond the couch, and headed for the kitchen. When he reached the island, he hastily closed the lid on a laptop she had failed to notice earlier. Excitement filled her at seeing the device.

Without thinking, she blurted, "Is your internet working? We have to get help!"

"I wish it was, but the building's wireless. No power, no Wi-Fi. Trust me, I tried. Besides"—he scooped the computer up and slid it into a black bag sitting on the floor nearby—"the damn thing died on me."

She kept forgetting that nothing worked. It was as if her brain could only handle so many problems, and the power being out didn't make the list.

"I was doing some work when all this"—he waved his arms through the air around him and walked back to her, dropping the bag on the couch as he did so—"happened."

"What's your work?"

"Oh, um." Alex looked around the room, his hands finding his pockets. "I'm a reporter."

Even buried up to her neck in chaos, she found the reply an interesting one. "Really? Do you write for a paper, or online?"

"No. I mean, not yet." He refused to meet her eyes as he spoke. "I'm sort of freelance at the moment."

"Well." She forced a smile. "I guess you just found a hell of a story."

"I guess I did. I was actually working on a story when the power went out." His gaze shifted briefly to the ceiling. "And then there was the bang."

"What bang?"

"Huh?" His face twisted in confusion. "The *huge* fucking bang! The one that shook the building. It sounded like something exploded." His thin eyebrows momentarily bunched together. "You didn't hear it? I thought we were having an earthquake or something." He removed his glasses and used the bottom of his shirt to clean the lenses. "It sounded like a tank rolled into the side of the building. It damn near knocked me out of my chair."

Olivia realized whatever cataclysmic event he was referring to obviously happened while she was unconscious on her bedroom floor. "I didn't hear anything. I don't know what's going on. I...I wasn't feeling good, I think. It's kind of a blur. I guess I slept through it. When I got up, the power was out and Liam—my husband—was gone. I went looking for him, but found..."

A replay of Mr. Elliot stomping on his poor wife's head flashed across her thoughts, sending a stab of nausea through her gut.

"I found all this."

"You must be a *heavy* sleeper. I literally thought the building was going to fall down, it was *that* loud."

How drunk was I? she wondered. Was it possible to sleep through such a din, even drunk?

Seemingly unaware of her internal pondering, Alex continued. "Not long after, I heard people in the hallway. They were in a panic. I went to see if I could help, and—*Jesus*—I saw one of those bugs crawl right down a guy's throat. It happened so fast! Nobody knew what to do. We thought he was dead. We just stood there, stunned, and then..." He wiped a hand across his mouth, as if trying to block the story from continuing. "Then he gets up and starts going crazy!"

"You're lucky you didn't get hurt." Pain still radiated from her jaw, thanks to Mr. Elliot. "What happened after that?"

Alex ran his fingers through his hair and sighed. "I ran back here and locked the door. I've been hiding ever since."

A thought came to Olivia. "How long ago did all this happen?"

He appeared to think about it for a moment. "I mean, I wasn't really looking at the time, but it has to have been at least a couple hours."

"A couple hours!"

Somehow, this revelation was almost as shocking as the insects burrowing down peoples' throats. Although she hadn't stopped to actually think about it, somewhere in her mind, she had decided the madness had erupted just before she had returned to the land of consciousness.

"How is that possible? Where's the fucking police?"

Alex apparently had no answer.

CHAPTER 12

Olivia sat on Alex's couch, a bottle of water gripped in her hands. The air coming through the open balcony, a continuous howl of wind, did nothing to sap the heat from the apartment. If anything, it made it worse. The currents carried the sticky weight of humidity, slathering it across everything.

"Thanks for the water." She spoke numbly, the words barely having enough heft to escape her mouth. "Do you think the police *are* coming at least?"

Alex, standing off to the side near the kitchen island, shrugged. "I hope so but kind of doubt it. If they were called, they'd be here by now."

It was exactly what she had been thinking, but hearing the man verbalize it set a horde of pins prickling across the back of her neck.

She took a small pull from the bottle. The water inside was cool, refreshing. The liquid tried to push the heat away, but it was a losing battle. "I wish I'd never left my apartment." She spoke into the lip of her plastic container.

Alex sighed and walked over to the couch, sitting down heavily next to her, the cushion beneath her slouching to one side at his added weight. "How do you think I feel? I wasn't planning on moving in until next week."

She looked at his grim face and let out a sad chuckle. "Okay, you win."

"Did you find him?" He asked, his tone dropping to a whisper.

"Who?"

"You said you were looking for your husband. Did you find him?" His eyes shifted as he spoke, giving Olivia the impression he was afraid of her answer.

"No, I didn't."

Alex appeared to ponder this for a moment. "I think I saw him."

Olivia stiffened, and a bit of water sloshed from the bottle. "You did? When? Was he okay?"

"Whoa," Alex quickly said, apparently realizing he could have broached the subject with a bit more care. "It was earlier, before all this. I was just coming home and was nearly tackled by him leaving your place."

"Was he okay? What was he doing?"

"He was...he was just walking. It was only a second or two."

Olivia slumped back into the couch. "Dammit, I wish I knew where he was. I just want to know that he's okay."

"Well, maybe he went for help. Who knows, he could be coming back with an army of cops."

"Maybe."

It was a nice thought, but somehow, she doubted it. Liam was born of inaction. He wasn't lazy, but rather hated dealing with things.

Just recently, on a rare trip to the city, they had stopped for lunch at an Italian place. When their order came, Liam sighed and shook his head. Instead of chicken in his pasta, there was shrimp. In all the years Olivia knew the man, she had never once seen him eat seafood. Knowing her husband well enough to realize such an inconvenience could likely spoil the entire day, she volunteered to notify the waiter of the mistake.

"No, it's fine," he snapped. "We just won't come back here." He then proceeded to meticulously eat around the tiny, pink crustaceans, all the while complaining about it.

That is, until the waiter popped back around, and then he was all smiles.

Olivia tipped the bottle for another swig and wiped the excess water from her tender lip. She suddenly did not want to talk to this stranger about her husband. Clearing her throat, she asked, "So, what brings you to the luxurious New Leaf Building, Alex from apartment twenty-five-o-five?"

He rubbed his hands on his knees and pursed his lips in thought. "Well, um, I have some family nearby, and they were able to pull some strings and get me into the building. Not just anybody can live in the New Leaf."

Olivia tilted her head at this. "They can't? Why?"

He cleared his throat. "Well, that's the question, really. After I got accepted to live here, I, ah, started to look into the owners, Conrad and Vera Anderson."

"Conrad and Vera Anderson? Never heard of them," Olivia admitted.

Now that she thought about it though, she realized she was completely ignorant regarding who actually owned the building. She assumed it was run by a faceless corporation, not a husband-and-wife team.

Alex nodded, as if he expected just such an answer. "I'm not surprised. The Andersons are...elusive, to the say the least. But they are quite powerful. Their net-worth is well into the tens of billions."

Olivia whistled. "Shit, I wish I was a part of that family."

Her words elicited a series of uncomfortable coughs from the young man. He tried to turn the reaction into a laugh but failed utterly. "Yeah, well anyway, I got a tip that the couple would be living on site, in the penthouse, until the entire New Leaf venture is complete."

"You mean when the other buildings are finished?"

He nodded.

"What was the story?" Olivia gulped another mouthful of water, each splash of liquid further soothing her tumultuous stomach.

Alex adjusted his glasses and frowned at her. "Was?"

"Well, yeah, *was*. Whatever you were writing about has obviously changed, right?" Olivia tilted her chin toward the front door and what lay beyond.

"Oh, right! Yes, of course. Well, I was writing about the breadth of their empire, a vast conglomeration comprised of hundreds of companies. But I suppose you're correct. That hardly matters anymore."

"What do you think they are?"

"Who? The Andersons?"

"No, the bugs!"

"I don't know. It's like they're drawn to people, and then they...infest them."

The thought of an insect sliding down her throat, its body a wriggling mass of legs and shell, almost made her gag. "The people, the Infested, why are they acting like that? Why are they trying to kill everyone?"

He opened his mouth to reply but then closed it and sadly shrugged his shoulders.

Outside, the storm continued to buffet the building. It came in waves, like the crashing surf, periods of cataclysm dancing to the sound of a horrible cacophony of roaring thunder and howling wind.

Olivia was sure Alex would close the balcony door, but he surprised her by leaving it wide open. She could see the rain in the orange glow of candlelight, puddling along the hardwood around the opening. Her first thought was of the damage allowing the water to remain might cause the building, but then she figured it didn't matter. Tomorrow, when the sun rose, the New Leaf would be swarming with police and investigators. It had to be. A little bit of water damage would be the least of anyone's concern.

She had recounted the attacks from the old man down the hall and the boy next door. Alex listened intently, his face a rictus, like her words had flavor and the taste of said flavor was extremely sour.

"And you couldn't get through on your phone?" he asked when she mentioned the device.

"No, nothing. Although, like your computer, it was all but dead, so maybe it was just my cell and not the service. How about you? Any luck on your phone?"

"No. Or rather, I don't know because I don't have one."

It was Olivia's turn to look sour. "You don't have a cell phone? I thought only grandparents and weirdos looking to get off the grid didn't have a cell phone."

"I communicate online, or not at all." He gestured toward the laptop bag, still resting on the floor. "And although I wouldn't mind getting off the grid from time to time, I'm not quite there yet. And given that I still get carded whenever I go into a bar, I think it's safe to say, I'm not a grandpa either."

Olivia smiled, which in turn caused her lip—swollen at the hands of Willum Elliot—to split like a grape, a wasp-sting of pain as the tearing of such delicate tissue caused her to flinch.

"You're bleeding," Alex said, coming forward to look at her.

She reached up and touched the abused skin around her mouth, her fingertip coming back with a shiny red cap.

"Um, if you want, you can use the bathroom. Maybe clean up a bit?" His voice was soft, sympathetic. He pointed toward the small hall leading to the bedrooms. "You'll have to use the master bath though. Something's wrong with the plumbing in the guest one."

She followed his gesture, letting her gaze fall down the hall. The last time she had made her way to a stranger's bedroom, an old man with a serious bug problem had beaten the shit out of her. But then again, she could really use some freshening up. Her pants, damp with piss, stuck uncomfortably to her legs and rear, and the drying blood at her hairline itched like all hell.

"Okay. Yeah, that would be nice actually." Thinking for a moment as she stood up, she added, "I'm so sorry. I can't even begin to imagine how bad I must smell."

Alex shook his head, a shy smile across his face. "No, no, you don't. You really don't."

Olivia stared at him for a moment, and his smile widened.

"Okay, yes, you do smell, but it is totally understandable."

She couldn't help but to laugh. It felt nice, the worry momentarily sloughing off, but it only lasted for a second, and then the fear rushed back in, filling the void, leaving the two of them standing quietly together.

"Do you mind if I take one of the candles...and a knife?"

CHAPTER 13

Holding a candle in one hand and a fillet knife in the other, Olivia made her way down the short hall to Alex's bedroom.

Alex's apartment was pretty much the antithesis of the Elliots' place. There were no exotic trinkets from world-spanning vacations sitting atop antique end tables, no photographs in elaborately carved frames hanging from the walls. Even the carpet felt somehow reduced, a lesser version of what covered the floor down the hall, which was impossible since all the units had the same carpet. He had just moved in, but for some reason, Olivia thought it did not matter when he took up residence. One day or one year, either way, the hallway she traversed would be bare.

The candle, a thick jar of scented wax with three wicks sparking from the top, produced a penumbra of orange light revealing the dimensions of the space. The spare bedroom door appeared before her, like a ghost materializing from the dark. It was closed. She imagined the room would be full of boxes, a temporary storage unit for the detritus of Alex's life. A holding pen for the things which did not rank high enough on the value chart to be unpacked immediately.

The master bedroom was open. She was thankful for this, wasn't sure she would have been able to muster the courage to open the door. The determined light from the candle attempted to reach past the frame as she approached. A deep fear something was in the room, waiting for her, began to pick at her insides. She raised the blade. Alex had offered to come with her, but she had said it wasn't necessary.

Now she was starting to regret that decision.

"Stop it," she whispered to herself. But the words were shallow.

Olivia took a deep breath and pushed past the threshold, entering Alex's sleeping chambers. He had mercifully left the bedroom blinds open, allowing a dim blanket of nighttime light to seep across the floor. A series of boxes sat along the window, appearing like the silhouette of a cityscape against the backdrop of the stormy night. In the middle of the room was his bed, a simple, double mattress on a frame. And that was it. No dresser. No end tables. Just a bed and some boxes.

Before making her way to the bathroom, Olivia walked up to the windows. A secret hope she would spy an envoy of approaching red and blue lights, flashing beacons of safety pulsing through the storm-tormented foliage. But there was nothing. A horizon of swaying trees, which became lost to the dark beyond that.

As she was about to turn, something sitting on the nearest box caught her eye. She held the candle before her and saw it was a letter. The paper, which was partially folded, was addressed to somebody named Meredith.

Olivia was about to turn away from the missive—clearly it was none of her business—when the light from her candle lit upon the letterhead. It read: *From the desk of Conrad Anderson.*

The owner of the building?

It somehow fit, she guessed, that Alex would have a letter from the man—he *was* writing an article about him—but still, why was it addressed to Meredith?

Olivia looked over her shoulder to make sure Alex had not snuck up on her while she had dallied. She placed the candle and knife down on the box and picked up the letter.

Meredith,

I know that we have not spoken for quite some time, but understand that I still care for you. I wish that we could go back, all of us, to the past. I would like to think if we could, I would be able to change things. Force a different outcome. For it is now, that I am getting older, I realize how important you are to me...to us.

Please, if you have any forgiveness in your heart, I am ready to fix what has been broken. I should never have let my own prejudices cause such a rift. Family is the most important thing. It is stronger than the hardest mountain and deeper than the darkest depth. I hope you consider my offer. If you do, I can be found overlooking our newest endeavor, The New Leaf Project.

I miss your light, Meredith. Please return home,
Conrad.

Below the man's name was the address for the building. Olivia read the short letter through a second time and still couldn't figure what any of it had to do with Alex. Had he stolen it? It clearly wasn't meant for him, yet here it was, sitting casually in his bedroom.

She was about to read it a third time when she heard a small cough from the hallway behind her.

Heart stuttering, she quickly placed the letter back how she had found it, scooped up the candle and fillet knife, and rushed across to the bathroom. Just as she was reaching the bathroom door, her forward foot making the transition from carpet to tile, she heard Alex enter the room.

"Everything okay?" he asked, coming around the corner, the flame of the candle in his own hand trailing an orange line through the air like a phantom.

"Sorry," she sputtered, her mind trying to come up with an excuse which was probably not even needed.

Thankfully, Alex provided one for her.

"You must be a wreck—no offence," he quickly added.

"Yeah, this hasn't been the best night."

Alex continued forward until he was standing right in front of the boxes. He looked down at the letter, his gaze lingering on it for a beat longer than anything else, before looking back at her. "I just remembered,

I might actually have some clothes for you to change into. You probably want to get out of those ones. I'll take a look while you're freshening up."

Contemplating his tall frame, Olivia doubted it. The man was certainly thin enough, but what she really needed were pants, and anything he had would definitely be too long. Still, she thanked him anyway.

After placing the candle and her weapon on the edge of the sink, Olivia turned to close the door behind her. As the gap between the door and the frame shrunk, she caught a glimpse of Alex's face. He began to look through the various boxes, and his smile quickly fell away, revealing a scowl which had been hiding underneath. Just before the door clicked closed, she saw him lean back, grab the letter, and crumple it up.

CHAPTER 14

Olivia felt her body relax as soon as the lock was thrown on the bathroom door. For the first time since leaving the confines of her home, she felt safe. No strangers, no Infested, just her, alone in the bathroom.

The mirror, an exact duplicate of her own, revealed her current state. The person peering back was near unrecognizable. Several bruises discolored the surface of her face, darkening her complexion enough she felt she could pass for a different person altogether. She leaned forward, turning her head to the left and right, cataloguing all the damage.

Considering the violence of his attack, Mr. Elliot had not inflicted as much trauma as she would have suspected, although she could see four crooked lines wrapping the side of her neck from Rian. The most startling aspect of her appearance was her swollen lip, which had split along the middle, a slice of angry red against pink. A small pool of blood had collected between her bottom lip and chin.

Olivia flipped on the cold water and cupped her palms under the stream for a minute, the liquid spilling across her hands and falling between her fingers in tiny waterfalls. She spied a washcloth folded on the back of the sink and grabbed it. After soaking the fabric, she began cleaning herself as best she could, starting with her mouth.

A brief knock issued from the bathroom door. The sound was soft, muted, like Alex was going through great pains to keep it from being as harsh as possible.

"Olivia?"

She turned off the tap and took a half-step toward the door. "Yes?"

"I, uh"—he cleared his throat—"I found some clothes for you."

She hesitated at the door, her hand hovering over the lock. Alex might have saved her life, but the man was still a stranger to her. He might be dangerous. This line of thinking was ridiculous, she quickly reasoned. If he had ill intentions toward her, there had been many opportunities to act on them already. Still, as she twisted the lock, she couldn't quite shake the feeling Alex was not what he seemed.

"I found this." He pushed some clothes forward as soon as the door was open. "Most of my stuff probably won't fit you, but these might."

"Thanks. Anything is better than what I have on."

He hovered for a moment in the opening, an odd expression pulling at his face. She thanked him again and closed the door.

Olivia examined what he had given her. She wasn't sure what she expected, but a simple grey dress and black leggings had not been it. Did Alex have a girlfriend? There had been no sign of anybody else living in his apartment, and he certainly didn't mention anything about having a wife or girlfriend, but that didn't mean much.

Oliva stripped out of her shirt and pants, the latter of which was damp and reeked of urine, and threw both into the bathtub. Going back to the washcloth, she re-wet it and began cleaning her legs and thighs. She rinsed the cloth several times afterward, then, declaring it a lost cause, tossed it into the tub on top of her soiled sleepwear. She vowed to buy Alex a new one if she made it through the night.

The clothes he provided were still too large for her. What probably was a short dress on the owner went past Olivia's knees. If Alex did have a girlfriend, she was as tall as he was. Thankfully, the leggings were snug enough, and once Olivia rolled up the bottoms a few times, they fit comfortably.

Fully dressed, Olivia looked over at the door handle. She was loath to leave the bathroom behind. The sense of dread she felt at the idea of entering a wider space, a space with dark corners and hidden places, made her stomach hurt.

She knew she was being childish. Liam would have been quick to call her out on such behavior. Besides, she figured if the Infested got into Alex's apartment, it would only be a matter of time before they came for her. Imagining Mr. Elliot, or even Rian, sharing the small confines of the bathroom with her made her want to cry.

Straightening the unfamiliar dress, she took a breath and grabbed for the handle.

"Oh good, they fit," Alex said, springing from the side of his bed as soon as she stepped out of the bathroom.

She smiled at him, her hands awkwardly pulling at the sides of the dress. "Yes, thank you. Are they your girlfriend's?"

Alex turned away and quickly began straightening his bedding, an unnecessary action since the sheets were only slightly rumpled from him sitting on them. Over his shoulder, he said, "Oh, yeah. Yeah. We broke up, but I guess I still have some of her stuff."

Before they left the bedroom, Alex in the lead, Olivia glanced back toward the box which had held the letter. She opened her mouth to inquire about it but then thought better of it. She had already intruded by reading the thing. To pry further would be downright rude.

Instead, she remained silent, collected the knife and candle, and followed her host out of his bedroom. The letter and its implications were left somewhere in the darkness filling the space behind them.

CHAPTER 15

Olivia's thoughts bounced through her head like a pinball. She wasn't sure how—or even if—she was digesting everything. Too many elements buggering all reason had befallen her. Somewhere in the primal regions of her grey matter, an ancient voice whispered she was losing her mind. And maybe she was. If there was one thing she knew, it was that humans weren't built to deal with freakshow nightmare-fuel like the Infested.

Once back in the living room, Alex pulled a pack of cigarettes out of his pocket. He said something about trying to quit, apologized, and then offered one to Olivia. She waved away the offer but still accompanied him to the open patio door. Even though Olivia was exhausted, she felt an overwhelming urge to keep moving, that to fall into complacency was to invite death.

"The storm is getting really bad," Alex said, the words sneaking past the cigarette already stuck in his mouth.

Olivia found his comment to be an understatement. The world outside appeared every bit as volatile as the one within the building. Angry tridents of lightning blasted the earth, and barking claps of thunder raged across the landscape. It reminded Olivia of a bad storm she had witnessed with her mother at the age of eleven.

They had gone shopping for new clothes. Summer was almost over, and the first day of school was quickly approaching. When they exited the store, the sky had been transformed into a wide sheet of black clouds resembling an inverted mountain range. The clouds looked so low Olivia was sure, had she been able to reach just a little higher, her fingers would push right through the underside. She imagined it would feel similar to poking into the skin of a rotten peach.

Her fascination had quickly turned to worry when she saw the expression on her mom's face. The woman was the embodiment of fun and carefree, yet when she had peered up at the bloated clouds scraping by, she looked afraid.

The ride home had been hectic. Branches—unwilling rockets powered by the violent winds—assaulted their car. The next day, Olivia heard the storm had spawned a tornado.

Even though it was too dark to clearly see the clouds outside now, she knew that, had they been visible, they would look exactly the same as those she had witnessed as a child, the kind which could birth such a disaster.

It took Alex several attempts to light his cigarette, but when he finally did, the pleasure he felt with the first inhale of toxic smoke was unmistakable.

"I really have been meaning to quit," he said. "But after tonight, I may put it off for another six months. It's going to take a *lot* of cigarettes and some hefty therapy to get past all this shit."

"I just wish it wasn't so hot." Olivia pulled at the collar of the dress she wore. Sweat had already glued the fabric to her body.

Alex looked down at his own attire. Two dark circles hung from the armpits of his T-shirt, a third from the collar. "This night would be so much more manageable if the damned air was still working."

As soon as he mentioned the air conditioning, Olivia turned to look at the vent she knew sat in the wall off the dining room. She recalled the open grates in both her home and that of the Elliots. And worse still, she remembered with perfect clarity the awful sounds issuing from within. Alex's was neatly secured though, a rectangle of metal slats with slivers of darkness beyond.

"What is it?" he asked after taking a drag from his cigarette, the end erupting into an angry red eye of fire and ash.

She wasn't sure exactly, but a picture was starting to form in her mind. Walking closer to the vent, she recounted her discovery of the opened shafts.

"You think..." He flicked his cigarette out through the balcony door. The wind snatched the slender stick and carried it away. "You think that's how they're getting in?" As he spoke, his voice rose in concern.

Now that it was out in the open, a concept she could view, approach, that was exactly what she thought. Taking a step back, she looked over at Alex and said, "You have any packing tape?"

She stepped back, and Alex climbed down from the chair he had used to reach the vent. Shiny, clear tape—a crazed cross-hatch of adhesive— covered the entirety of the vent. During the process of applying the tape, Olivia had been sure one of the bugs would rush forward and slam itself against the metal grate, its chitinous exoskeleton clanking against the tines like some horrific bell. But none did.

"I don't think a bull could get through that." He slapped the roll of packing tape into the palm of his free hand as he spoke. "Should we do the rest?"

She started to nod but then stopped. There was no need to secure the others. Olivia could picture all the vents in her own home. A strange truth presented itself to her. The dining room grate was unique, a one-of-a-kind feature in each unit. All the other vents were wide and thin, too thin for one of the bugs to push through. No, just that single opening was large enough.

He bit his bottom lip and adjusted his glasses while she revealed her revelation. When she was finished, he said, "That's really strange," before hurrying off to the living room.

Olivia was about to follow but stopped when she saw a trio of faces peering at her from behind the modest dinner table.

What is that? she almost blurted out but maintained her composure enough to keep the question internal.

Keeping an eye on Alex, who appeared lost amongst his own meager assortment of furniture, she approached the unexpected sight. It turned out to be a painting, a family portrait, and it was quite large. The sort of thing she imagined she would find in a stately manor, not the new apartment of a rookie reporter.

She moved around the table for a closer look. The artistry was impressive, even under the less-than-optimal lighting conditions. The portrait featured an older man and woman standing behind a chair. The painter had captured a remarkable sense of wealth and poise in the couple, who looked to be in their fifties but in good health. Sitting before them was a little girl of about nine or ten. Her white dress, which seemed to spread before her like a blossoming flower, gave the child an air of timelessness.

This is so weird. Why would Alex have this?

"My grandparents." Alex's voice floated in from over her shoulder, causing her to jump.

Olivia spun around. "Sorry," she blurted. "I wasn't trying to be nosey."

He held his computer bag but placed it on one of the chairs so he could take the painting from her and rest it atop the table, the circumference of which was barely enough to contain it. His focus on the folks portrayed on the canvas was near absolute.

Olivia cleared her throat, suddenly feeling like an intruder, like she was coming between an argument. "Did you paint it?"

Her question pried a chirping laugh from his lips and managed to pull him away from his apparent revere.

"I can barely draw stick-people. Seriously, I almost failed grade three art. Do you know how hard that is? No, my grandparents had it commissioned a long time ago."

Returning to the faces, delicately recreated in oil on canvas, Olivia could see the resemblance between them and Alex. "So, these are your grandparents. They look awfully important."

Another laugh, this one much sadder. "Yeah, you could say that. I lived with them for quite a while."

She waited for him to elaborate, but he never did.

"And the little girl? Is that your mom?"

Alex scrunched his eyebrows, like her question was of an outright bizarre nature. "What?" After a second, his expression relaxed and he continued. "No, not my mom. It's my sister. She died, along with my parents, when I was a kid."

Olivia slid her fingers across the face of the child, the dry paint creating stiff ridges and valleys. "Oh my God, I'm so sorry. She looks like you."

Alex cleared his throat and then returned the painting to its place behind the table. As he did so, Olivia caught a glimpse of a small, brass plaque along the bottom of the frame. The name Meredith jumped out at her before the entire thing was hidden away once again.

"How come you're not in the picture?"

With the portrait safely tucked away, Alex seemed to relax a bit. "I was away at school when it was commissioned. Truth be told, I'm not upset about that."

"If you don't mind me asking, how did your sister and parents pass?"

Alex fidgeted with his glasses for a moment, clearly uncomfortable with the subject. Before Olivia could retract the question though, he said, "They died in a plane crash."

His words bored through her core like a diamond-tipped drill, exposing the heart of her buried sorrow. "My mom died in a crash as well."

"Oh..." Alex shuffled awkwardly. "Was it a plane crash?"

Olivia sighed, already regretting saying anything. "No, not a plane. A car. It was my seventeenth birthday, and it was cold out, way colder than it should have been for early November. She, my mom, wanted to spend the night together, go out for dinner, see a movie, the same thing we had done every year for each of our birthdays since Dad left. But..." Olivia felt the tears begin to come. They fell freely from her eyes, and she didn't attempt to stop them. "But I had wanted to go out with my friends. She was hurt, I could tell, but she wanted me to be happy, so agreed."

Alex stood unmoving as she spoke, clearly uncomfortable with her account, but she was too far in. Nothing would stop the rest of the story from coming.

"The funny thing is, I didn't even want to hang out with my friends that night. I wanted to spend the evening with my mom. But it's lame for seventeen-year-olds to hang out with their moms, so I ditched her for them.

"It had just started to snow as we left our house. The kind of snow that looks fake, fat bits of fluff instead of frozen rain. We didn't really speak as we drove. I could tell her feelings were hurt. We had just turned a corner when she said she wanted to give me some money to spend with my friends. She undid her seatbelt and reached into the backseat for her purse. Neither of us saw the ice. It was crazy. One second I was wondering how much cash my mom was going to give me, the next we were sliding. Our car jumped the curb, and we slammed into a telephone pole."

Olivia reached up and caressed a thin scar behind her ear, a memento bought and paid for by tragedy on that chilly night.

"I was hurt but not too bad. When I finally became aware of what happened, I looked over at the driver's seat, and all I saw was snow. Giant, picture-fucking-perfect flakes drifting down onto her empty seat, and all I could do was stare in confusion.

"Then I remembered. Mom had taken off her seat belt. When we hit the pole, she had flown through the front window.

"I found her on the road, ahead of the car, snow collecting on her clothes and hair. Her chest was rising and falling so fast, like she had just run a marathon. I called to her, but she didn't answer. The closer I got, the more I realized she was not okay. A red halo was staining the snow around her head. Bits of glass from the windshield had become lodged in her face. I can still remember the way it twinkled in the streetlight as she shuddered on the road."

"Jesus, I'm so sorry." Alex stepped forward with a stutter, his arms hitching up, filling the space between them. He hesitated only for a moment, before wrapping her in a hug.

Olivia tried to smile, hoping it would show how strong she was, but the effort refused to reach her lips. "No, I'm sorry. That was too much. I don't usually talk about that night." She rubbed her eyes. "Anyway, she was in a coma for a year, but that was just a formality. She had died that night on the road. What was left was just an echo of her. She was taken off life support just before I turned eighteen. And every single day since that cold night, I wish I could go back, slap, punch, bite, or even kill myself, anything to stop my mom from getting into that car and driving me somewhere I didn't even want to go."

Pulling free from the embrace, she snatched the tears from her cheeks.

"Anyway, I met Liam a couple years later. I thought I was dead inside, you know? Incapable of love. But then this man comes into my life, and we connect and something in here"—she patted her chest—"fired back up. I was whole again. I had a reason for being. He is my everything."

CHAPTER 16

The elevator, a metal-lined cube with three columns of buttons shining like fireflies, dinged triumphantly just before the doors slid open.

Olivia stepped out into a long, dim hallway. She looked to her left, then her right. Both directions presented the same sight—an endless corridor of rot and ruin. Warped doors made of wilting wood jutted from sagging frames like crooked teeth.

When she turned back around, she found the decay had already seeped into the elevator itself. The reflective metal had run brown with filth. Red freckles of rust spread like mold. The buttons—glowing plastic circles moments before—flickered madly, many having fallen to darkness. There was no going back.

The hallway filled Olivia with a deep apprehension, like it could only lead to some awful, ruinous destination. She did not want to venture its length, but nor could she stay within the elevator forever, so with a trembling pulse, she stepped free and began walking. Her shoes crunched over fragile bits of dirty plaster and yellowed paper. The smell of wet fabric, like clothes forgotten in a locker, permeated the air. Above her, the cicada buzz of the fluorescent tubes—of which only every third one worked—appeared to fold in on itself, creating a multi-layered symphony of static.

The first door she came upon looked into a room. Two beds on wheels with retractable railings sat unoccupied, both heavily soiled. The stained bedding on the first was pulled tight, the corners tucked, the pillow sitting like a plump, yellowed sack at the head. The second bed, however, bore signs of having recently been disturbed. Brown sheets with spots of wear straight through the fabric lay crumbled and discarded along the far side. The pillow, which had a black fungus sprouting along its top, was cratered where it appeared a head had rested not that long ago. Olivia brought a hand to her mouth, sure she would be sick, but nothing came up.

Beyond the beds, a single window stood in the middle of a decrepit wall. Small armies of paint chips had collected along the bottom of the window frame. The glass was dirty to the point of being opaque.

Olivia knew, if she were to walk up to that glass and scratch away the grime and grit, she would see a parking lot three stories down.

The room was not her destination though, and so she continued on. Just as she moved away, a shadow fell across the glass from the outside. It was fleeting, but in that moment, through the layer of neglect built-up along the pane, she had seen multiple limbs.

Each room she passed presented the same image. Two decaying beds. One made, the other not. The greyed-out window. And the shadow.

Somewhere in front of her, a slow warble of music, the audible equivalent of a Dali painting, stretched like molten plastic through the air. Olivia recognized the song at once, and it broke her heart. She had heard it many times as a child, drifting through the speakers of the radio sitting in the kitchen, filling their house with melody. It was her mom's favorite song.

The words *Intensive Care Ward*, accompanied by a blue arrow, stood like a faded ghost under the dirt of the wall next to her. Olivia felt her knees threaten to buckle under the weight of the letters. Those three words, Intensive Care Ward, had become synonymous with pain and torment for Olivia.

She wanted to stop her forward march, but her feet continued to crunch over the debris sloughed off the walls and ceiling without pause. Like being on a rollercoaster, there was no stopping until the ride was over.

The music intensified as she neared the door—which was growing to resemble the shape of a tombstone more than a door frame. With each step, the room beyond took shape. Added definition, a puzzle almost complete. Objects began to solidify into quantifiable things.

It was a mirror to the rooms she had passed, except for one very profound difference—the second bed had not been recently vacated. It was still occupied.

A woman lay prone along the top of the soiled mattress. Countless tubes, clogged with yellow and brown gunk, snaked from her body, turning her into something Lovecraftian. A deep, oppressive odor billowed out past Olivia, a stink made of equal parts feces and blood. The woman was not alone in the room either. Three people, clad in doctor's garb, hovered around the woman like alien observers. Their scrubs, which had grown moldy, hung off them in tatters.

Horror, deep and vast, filled her.

She had no memory of covering the distance from the door to the bed, but she must have. In a moment, she was amongst the figures standing there, looking down on the woman. Bandages, discolored from infection, entombed the woman's face. Her eyes, staring blankly, the rich brown in them gone to a dull matte.

She wanted to cry, to scream, but her mouth stubbornly did not respond to such commands. All Olivia could do was look down on the tortured woman. One of the doctors—his face hidden behind a grotesque mask—placed his hand on her shoulder and whispered in her ear. His breath smelled like soaked cigarettes and stale coffee.

"It's time, Olivia."

Like bullets, his words penetrated her head, pushing everything which made her human out the other side.

"No!" she yelled, her mouth finally free. "I can't! She's my mom!" She felt this should be enough, but it was not.

The husks in medical garb continued to stare.

In front of her, the thing in the bed shifted. Delicate strings of something wet, slimy, stretched between the writhing form and the mattress top. The woman—her mother—opened her mouth to an impossible degree. The few teeth remaining clung to blackened gums. She let out a long, tormented cry.

The soles of Olivia's sneakers squeaked as she shuffled backward, away from the room. She wanted it all to go away. As she retreated, she collided with the far wall of the hallway behind her. Oddly, though, it didn't feel like a wall at all. It was hard and cold, but it only abutted her legs and rear. Olivia reached a probing hand back, and her fingers traced along the obstacle she was resting against. It was wet, and it vibrated, like the purr of a great sleeping beast.

She wanted to turn around but for some reason found she couldn't pull her gaze away from shrieking woman before her.

"It's time, Olivia." This time the voice was disembodied. It came from all directions and none at the same time.

Behind her, the beast began to roar. Only, it didn't sound right. It was too mechanical to be a living thing.

"It's time!" the voice boomed.

It shook everything around her. Dust and debris rained from the ceiling. Olivia released her own scream, pressing her hands to her ears.

Having seen enough, she willed herself to look away, to turn from the doctors, from the room...from her mother...and run. As soon as she did, she saw what she had been resting against. It was the front of a car. The vehicle stuck out like the wall itself had partially birthed it. She could not see through the windshield but knew who was inside. Small, delicate flakes of snow drifted down around the car.

How it could be snowing in the hallway never once entered Olivia's mind. It just was. She was about to speak, maybe even scream again, when she felt a hand fall on her shoulder. The skin was pale, almost translucent. Blue-black veins peeked through the flesh. The fingernails had fallen to ruin, ancient filth blackening them.

"Olivia, it's time."

The windshield of the car exploded outwards. Thousands of cubes of glass hit her like buckshot. A woman, her face torn near off, followed the glass like a human cannonball, smashing into Olivia.

Only, it wasn't a woman, not any longer. Now it was a man. It was Liam. And instead of glass, it was thousands, millions, of tiny white bits.

Pills.

CHAPTER 17

Olivia sat up. Sweat caused the unfamiliar dress to stick to her back. A series of tremors overtook her body, and deep breaths came in racking waves, each threatening to become lodged in her throat before bursting past her lips.

A terrifying moment of confusion settled in her mind as she took in her surroundings, not recognizing them. The sparsely decorated apartment was utterly alien, a mock-up meant to deliver the illusion of a real place, but one lacking the touch personal history imparts. Nothing more than window dressing, a store-front display meant to mimic real life.

Like an ocean tide, her memories came back in, and she began to recognize Alex's apartment. The candles on the dinner table still frolicked—not as violently as before though, since the balcony door had been closed. A brief, blessedly distant flash of lightning lit across the bare walls, tape-covered vent, and small dinner table—complete with ornate portrait hidden behind it.

The nightmare continued to shock her, even as it faded from her conscious mind. She hadn't dreamed so vividly, so horribly, about her mother in months. She knew the nightmares were her penance, a jail sentence she would never find parole from. Her curse for refusing to take her mother off life support, for allowing the woman she loved to wither and wilt for a whole year. It always played out the same way—only this time, it hadn't. At the very end, she had seen Liam in place of her mother. And there had been something else.

"Fuck," she muttered, rubbing her eyes.

White. Small, white circles. But nothing else. The nightmare was already fading away.

Olivia sat up further and raked her fingers through her sweaty hair. She hadn't even remembered falling asleep. After telling Alex about her mom, the two of them had retreated to the couch. She recalled the feeling of heaviness which had assaulted her arms and legs once she sunk into the cushions.

"Alex?" Her voice had taken on the quality of broken glass.

Other than the low rumble of the thunder—just now catching up to its visual counterpart—the place was silent.

Olivia rose slowly to her feet and felt her stomach begin to freeze with dread.

Where's Alex? How long have I been asleep? The answer to the latter question was somewhat obvious. It was both still dark out and the storm was still banging, so she hadn't been out long. As to where Alex had gone, the rational side of her brain insisted he was in the bathroom, but for some reason, she wasn't buying that.

She grabbed one of the candles from the table and made her way down the small hallway to the master bedroom. It, along with the bathroom attached, were empty. Olivia was going to try the guest room when she heard a sound coming from the living room.

A deep scratching along the surface of the apartment door, followed by a tremendous thud.

She quickened her pace, returning to the living room just in time to see the doorknob twist furiously. Another bang. The door shuddered. A spike of fear impaled her to the floor.

When Alex had pulled her into his home, he had locked the door, both the deadbolt and the chain. He had also slid a small shelf across the back. But now, she watched impotently as something attempted to batter its way in. Both the chain and the barricade had been removed. Only the deadbolt remained.

Crack.

Olivia flinched. She could see the splintering wood in the candlelight. The single lock would not be enough.

I have to hide!

The closest thing to her was the couch. She had to physically shake the paralysis from her limbs for them to respond. With a start, she jerked forward and dropped to a huddle behind the piece of furniture.

One last bang sent the door flying open. A chunk of splintered wood sailed over Olivia's head and clattered against the wall somewhere behind her. A shaft of red reached into Alex's living room like a rapidly expanding monolith of light. It shot past Olivia's hiding spot, stretching all the way to the dinner table. She looked down at the candle still lit in her hands and quickly blew it out. A column of thin, scented smoke wafted into her face.

Her heart bounced and vibrated in her chest, like a teacup sitting atop a running washing machine. Despite the grip of terror which held her, she had to see what had just entered the apartment, had to see what was coming for her. She peeked around the corner of the couch.

Two Infested stood motionless in the entranceway, both of them men. One clad in nothing but a skin-tight pair of blue underwear—which looked almost black under the glare of the red lights—the other wearing flannel pajamas. Glistening insects squirmed from their open mouths, tasting the air around them.

She wanted to look away, to pull her head back—along with her sanity—from the edge of the couch, to unsee the things before her, but she was locked in place. Frozen. And could only continue to stare as the twin bugs sank back into the cavernous ruins of the mouths they exited through.

As soon as the parasites were out of sight, the Infested began to move. Blue-underwear spasmed a few times before skittering forward and to the right, cutting in front of the darkened television, on a collision course with the kitchen. Meanwhile, PJs, with a surer foot, marched straight ahead, his path leading directly toward the couch.

Olivia pulled herself away from the edge and pressed as hard into the back of the couch as possible. Her fear was so great she was sure her body would shut down under the strain. Lines of whimpering gibberish began to seep from her mouth, and she jammed her knuckles up into her teeth to quell it because no amount of issuance from her brain would stop the sound. She tried to remember where she had left the fillet knife, but that information was utterly blown from her mind, lost in the hurricane of terror overwhelming her thoughts.

When the Infested passed her, he did so close enough his pajama bottoms momentarily caused her hair to reach out in a static grasp. He reeked of alcohol, and she realized she wasn't the only person in the New Leaf hitting the bottle that night.

Eyes wide, Olivia struggled to remain still. She bit down on her knuckles hard enough to break the skin, the sour taste of blood registering on her tongue.

The Infested had continued on into the dining room, his movement a random dance between quick, shuffling steps and slow, languid swaying. Movement that was utterly inhuman. He came to a stop at the dinner table, the remaining candles creating an orange halo around him.

Olivia felt completely exposed, as helpless as an infant forgotten outside with a stray dog beginning to circle. She screamed at herself to run, but the command was distant, like the neural pathways of her brain had become elongated, stretched corridors with no endings. Just as she was starting to get it through to her feet that now was the time to function, a great crash bounced from the kitchen.

PJs spun around, his slack-jawed faced pushed forward like some disturbing hybrid of a human and an Irish Pointer. Olivia went rigid, her back sinking deep into the worn fabric of the couch, willing the furniture to swallow her completely. The Infested's mouth warbled back and forth several times before the insect inside emerged. The thing's antenna only tasted the air for a moment before it was sucked back in and PJs rushed for the kitchen. He hadn't seen her.

Olivia crawled back to the edge of the couch and peeked around the corner. The front door was wide open. She could make it. She could run right through the door, and the Infested would never know she was there. All she had to do was move.

She hesitated though, thinking of Alex. Was he in the apartment? She should warn him. But the barricade had been removed, the chain unlatched. If he had left, the only lock he would have been able to engage would have been the deadbolt. Was it possible that, twice in one night, she could awaken to find the person she was with gone?

A second crash from the kitchen, the shatter of glass, and the uncompromising jingle of silverware on a tile floor forced all other thought from her head and caused her to flinch.

"Run, goddamn you," she whispered to herself.

It didn't matter. Her body had betrayed her. Olivia was stuck fast to her hiding spot, her fear having grown roots. She told herself she would stay where she was, and maybe the Infested would miss her. Maybe they would leave.

Just as she was convincing herself this was possible, something began to tickle the top of her head. She craned her neck and looked up the back of the couch. The Infested in the blue underwear had climbed onto the cushions of the couch and now leaned over the back, the parasite ejected partially from the host's mouth, swayed like a snake, its antenna flitting across her upturned face.

A wild arc of electric adrenaline lit her body up like a Christmas tree. An animal scream blasted from her mouth. The bug disappeared into the Infested's face seconds before he launched himself over the back of the couch at her. She pushed away from the furniture and watched horrified as the Infested crumpled to the spot she had just been occupying.

From the corner of her eye, Olivia could see PJs emerging from the darkness of the kitchen. He threw himself across the top of the island, sweeping a pair of empty water bottles off in his wake, and came to a crash on the other side. As soon as he hit the ground, he was already rising back up in pursuit of her, filing the space between her and the exit.

The movement of three bodies through the apartment sent the candle flames to flicker, causing the world around Olivia to shake. She was rapidly running out of floor to maneuver through. With no other direction available to her, she fled deeper into Alex's place. Her only options were the balcony or the second bathroom, but neither would keep her safe for long. She thought briefly about the possibility of climbing to a neighboring balcony, then dismissed it as insane. She could never perform such a feat. There was no escape. She needed something to fight the Infested with.

Cutting across the dining room, she bumped into the dinner table hard enough to rock the jarred candles, the flames juking violently from the impact. Her fingers scrambled across the surface in search of something, anything, which could possibly prolong her existence. There was nothing. No salvation to be found. Her mind screamed to keep moving but was cut off as she was hit from behind.

The blow threw her forward onto the table, the candles spinning off like tops, most of the flames blinking out. She tried to yell, but a powerful hand gripped her by the neck and yanked her back. The Infested who had her began to attack. He scraped his fingers along both sides of her face, causing a series of burning hot trenches to blare from her cheeks. He moved like an animal, ferocious speed and power. Brief glimpses of flannel pajamas peeking from in-between flashing limbs. Finally, his hands came to a tight grip around her neck. The pressure was extraordinary. The already darkened apartment dimmed dramatically. Olivia fought for breath that was just not there.

A flash of movement drew her away from her attacker. The second Infested. The deranged man smashed into both Olivia and the pajama-wearing monster choking the life out of her. The impact sent all three of them to the floor. She sucked in a lungful of precious air as soon as the iron-tight grip strangling her neck released. Olivia crawled toward the table and noticed one of the jarred candles had rolled underneath it. The dense glass was warm in her hands. Somehow, the flames had defied the odds. Two were still burning.

When PJs scampered after her, she spun around and brought the thick jar across his face. A demented spray of lavender wax peppered his cheek and forehead. The impact rocked his already dislocated jaw, shifting it off to the side. As damaging as it appeared to be to the structure of his face, the Infested did not stop coming for her.

"Get away from me!"

Olivia thrust the candle forward. A thin, almost clear blanket of flame spread out from the mouth of the jar across his pajamas. Again, she caught the scent of booze. Given the way the fire devoured the Infested's clothing, she thought some must have spilled on him earlier in the night.

For the first time, she truly saw an Infested react to something. The man-puppet began an insane dance of uncoordinated movement through the apartment. The flames spread across the flannel, singeing the fabric black in its wake. Thick, choking smoke billowed off the Infested.

Olivia, eyes as big as saucers, watched as the moving inferno fell into the other Infested. The insects began pulling themselves from the destroyed mouths. Overhead, the sprinkler system spun to life, bringing the storm in from outside, a manic beeping accompanying it.

Eyeing the computer bag still sitting on one of the dinner table chairs, Olivia picked it up and swatted at the nearest bug. It pulled back inside the man's mouth just before she could make contact.

Seeing her chance, she stumbled past them. The oily smoke billowing off their blackened skin made her light-headed, and she emerged once again into the red light of the hallway.

CHAPTER 18

The smoke alarm continued to shout as she ran. The stairwell door, a metal rectangle painted beige, bobbed before her. In a moment of madness, Olivia was sure she was getting no closer to the exit, like the door hung on invisible string and was being pulled along, just out of her reach. Taunting her with its closeness.

Her own apartment door stood open on the left of the hallway. She slowed as she approached it, sure Rian was still inside, waiting to fly out at her like some demon from the deepest hell.

The pull of her apartment only held her in its gravity for a moment before she was able to break free and leave the open door behind. She briefly wondered if she would ever grace the space between those walls again. It was a horrible thought, but one, in the moment, which seemed all too real.

Her forward movement stuttered. Her and Liam had not lived long enough in the apartment for it to become home, but it did hold her prized possession—a thin, red-leather bound photo album. Even given its slight size, the black, plastic-covered pages within were only half filled. Still, each photograph residing in the album Olivia knew as well as she did any other thing in the world. Nineteen pictures of her mother, taken from ages four to thirty. The last, which had been snapped with a disposable camera at her mother's thirtieth birthday party, showcased a smiling woman who looked startlingly like Olivia, a fact brought up every time Olivia ran into an old aunt or uncle. She loved that photo the most because it was the closest match to her own memories of her mom. A smile which could melt hearts, and eyes as fierce as all hell. Olivia often wished she was half the woman her mother had been.

But the desire to charge into her apartment, to liberate that single piece of her life, was not enough to risk facing Rian again. Even the thought of the child caused her legs to reinvigorate, pushing her away from Apartment 2506.

The stairwell door finally loomed before her. As she reached for the handle, she was jolted backward by the door blowing open. In front of her, a massive man in jogging shorts and T-shirt came stumbling in. Even under the fabric of his top, Olivia could see his rotund belly sway back and forth with his movement.

"Help me!" he bellowed, a deep sound like a foghorn.

Under the unforgiving red light of the hall, his eyes looked like sunken jewels in the bowels of his chubby face. They twinkled with fear.

Olivia stepped back, and he struggled forward. He shook and twisted, his doughy arms reaching for something on his back, but his impressive girth greatly limited his reach. Massive oceans of sweat patched his shirt under his arms, neck, and saggy boobs. It glistened like oily dew on his bald head.

"It's on me!"

He threw himself against the wall, the impact creating a deep thud. The vibration running up Olivia's leg revealed the weight behind the crash. Dragging himself off the wallpaper, he quickly shuffled back to collide with the opposite side. As he did so, he yanked the shirt over his head and flung it aside. His gargantuan gut, round and stretch-marked, bounced and swayed.

It was obvious the man was not an Infested, but he was in some sort of hysterical panic, and as he plowed forward, she kept taking a step back. Looking over her shoulder revealed her own apartment—growing closer as she back-peddled—and beyond that, the open door of Alex's place, thin tendrils of smoke snaking past the frame.

"Stop! Please!" Olivia begged, but the man continued to act the part of a human wrecking ball and smashed himself against the nearby walls.

Just as she was sure that he would run her over, he seemed to misstep, his feet crossing each other, and he tumbled forward. His large body bounced upon hitting the floor.

As soon as he was down, Olivia saw what was assailing him. Gripped to his fleshy back like a demented backpack was one of the insects. Unlike the others she had seen though, this one was not partially wedged in an open mouth. The bug was long and narrow and stretched most of the way down his length. A nightmarish collection of stick-like legs held fast to the man's flab. A thin, tubular abdomen wiggled about while half a dozen whip-like cords jutting from its sides thrashed the air. The thing started to move quickly once the fat man hit the floor, scurrying up his neck and over his head.

He began to writhe and scream, panic turning his sausage arms into ineffectual clubs. Olivia watched as the bug slid across his face, its legs raking his cheeks and eyes, before forcing itself—headfirst—into the man's mouth.

He tried to fight it. He tried like all hell, but his doughy fingers could not stop the terrible creature's momentum, and even as he bucked and gagged, it was able to push itself farther in.

The sound of the man's jaw breaking was akin to that of a piece of driftwood being crunched under a tire.

Whether it was from the snapping bones or the blocked windpipe, the fat man started to slow his manic jittering. With a final visible push, the insect disappeared through the now slackened mouth. Saliva and broken teeth decorated the man's lips. Fresh rivers of blood rolled down the round mounds of his jowl like a macabre waterfall. A deep gurgling, the sound of a garbage disposal working through the contents of a scraped plate, emanated from the man's mouth. Little bubbles of fluid popped along the sides.

It happened so fast Olivia could scarcely believe it. Even after witnessing the impossible several times since waking on her bedroom floor, she wouldn't have thought one of the insects could get inside a host that quickly.

He continued to twitch, but they were small tremors, nothing like before. His bulging stomach, looking like a giant ball resting atop his waist, rose and fell in small, fitful bursts. The man was still breathing somehow, but it was not natural.

A large crash, which came from one of the nearby apartments—hers or Alex's, she couldn't tell—caused her to start moving again, only then aware she still held Alex's laptop bag. She thought of dropping it but then realized, as sad as it was, the leather satchel was her only weapon. She clutched it and continued forward.

The large man before her had fallen in a way he was blocking most of the hallway. His size was such she would have great difficulty stepping over him. She would have to hug the wall.

Walking gingerly, she approached the mound of flesh, staring at the stretched hole of his mouth as she did so. Olivia had no intention of passing by his head, so she pressed herself against the right wall and began stepping over his legs.

Please don't move! Please don't fucking move! She was sure she could see his body tensing, his muscles rippling under the flab, his arms about to come alive, to reach for her. *I can't take anymore.*

Olivia pushed past the man, the laptop bag held tight to her chest, and started for the stairwell door. She looked back only once to make sure the bug, now firmly nestled somewhere inside that doughy body, had not emerged to pursue her, before she exited the 25th floor.

CHAPTER 19

The first thought to cross through Olivia's mind upon entering the east stairwell was she had wandered into a vast vertical tomb.

Echoes from the door closing behind her bounced off the walls, coming back in a taunting chorus of whispers. The air was dry, which was odd given the humidity of the rest of the building. A sharp tang of dust and metal, the scents of a construction site, invaded her nostrils, and familiar scarlet lighting illuminated the landing before her. She could see what appeared to be smoke or dust swirling in the crimson haze. Beyond the cone of red, there was only darkness. Olivia had assumed the stairs would have something more substantial than the red bulbs for emergency situations, but if anything, the lighting was actually worse.

She rushed forward to the railing, leaned over the side, and looked down. The stairwells in the building were wide, almost luxurious in the amount of space they occupied. The three-quarter turn design left an empty, square shaft dropping straight down the middle to the ground floor. Under normal circumstances, she could see all the way to the bottom. The bright, no-nonsense fluorescent domes attached to the underside of each flight's stairs, gave a sharp, sterile definition to every step. Now, however, all those bright lights had been snuffed out. The only thing remaining was the two-bulb unit stationed above each floor's door, spilling its puddle of bloody light, leaving the stairs themselves lost in the dark. It gave the impression of looking down on a series of red-tinged islands, lined-up in a row, floating in the vastness of space.

Olivia steeled herself for the coming descent. She reasoned that, even moving at a slower pace due to the darkness, she could probably make it to the lobby in a few minutes. A hundred and eighty seconds. She could do that. But then, her thoughts started to shift—a ship being blown off course by the winds of doubt. What if she were to fall? The stairs in the darkened sections were nearly impossible to see. She could picture herself missing a step and tumbling forward, screaming in pain as she lay on the unforgiving stairs, a sharp splinter of bone stabbing through the skin of her shin. Helpless, as the Infested—called by her torment—fell upon her. She wouldn't even have to fall. She could simply run full into one of the creatures. The darkness between landings was practically absolute. There could be an Infested lurking in the black, waiting for her to come to it.

Determined not to let her fear of what might happen keep her stuck in the New Leaf for one second longer, she took a couple deep breaths and tensed herself for a sprint.

Olivia, focused on the task at hand, almost ignored the soft whine from the door behind her. Only when alarm bells began to peal in her brain did she react.

Her body jerked forward toward the nearest set of stairs, the blanketing darkness concealing the steps calling her. In that precise moment, she did not care the closest stairs were the ones going up, just that they were the nearest option.

The door yawned open, and a huge form shuffled out, coming to a stop in the middle of the landing. Standing, like some mythical creature—a demigod from the depths searching for its sacrifice—was the fat man. His eyes, which had rolled back into his head, snatched the red light from the air, turning the two wet orbs into bloody marbles. His mouth hung twisted and broken.

Olivia held her breath, afraid to make a sound. She was sure she hadn't retreated up the stairs far enough, that the edges of the emergency light could still reach her, would point her out to the monster before her, but she was too afraid to move, to exhale.

The behemoth stalked forward, his flabby belly bouncing along the way. Angry lines broke the skin along his loose back, signs of the insect's ascent up the mountainous terrain of his body. He stalked ahead to the railing. Once there, the Infested froze.

The bug poked its head free from the man's mouth, its antenna tasting the air. The thin, string-like sticks continued to dance for several seconds before the creature disappeared once again into the cavity it resided in. The massive Infested slowly began to turn in her direction.

It knows I'm here. It can see me or sense me. It knows I'm fucking here! her mind screamed. It took every ounce of willpower not to flee in blind panic. The only thing keeping her in place was the realization that if the bug had truly seen her, the Infested would not be walking, but rather rushing her.

Olivia gripped the railing, keeping her eyes on the big man in front of her, and started backing up the stairs one step at a time. Her bare feet were wet and clammy with sweat, and her soles slid along the hard surface of the stairs. The Infested continued ambling forward, his own feet naked, until he reached the bottom step. There he seemed to sway for a moment before he stretched out one of his oversized mitts, grabbed the railing, sending a vibration up the shaft into Olivia's own palm, and began to climb. It only took four steps before he was gobbled up in the darkness surrounding them.

Too afraid to turn her back on the thing, even though she could no longer see him, she continued backward up the stairs, her pace as quick as could be under the circumstances. She knew the landing for the 26th floor was nearing. If she could keep quiet, and keep moving quicker than the behemoth before her, she could make a break for it once she reached the light above.

Risking a look over her shoulder, she saw the lit landing bobbing like a scarlet ghost, each step causing it to grow closer.

Go now! she demanded.

Spinning around suddenly, with the full intention to run up the remaining stairs to the 26th floor, she instead lost her balance, thanks to the swinging weight of the computer bag she had slung over her shoulder. She tried to adjust, but the gloom only accentuated her dizziness, and she fell backward, the edge of the steps scraping painfully up her spine.

A quick yelp burst from her mouth. Olivia smacked her hand over her lips and stared, eyes wide, into the darkness. Maybe the Infested wasn't as close as she feared, or hadn't heard her. A second stretched into ten, with only silence to fill the time in between, and then a great shuffling of feet from six or seven steps below erupted. Heavy pounding—the sound of hams being dropped on cement—issued forth as the huge man began to charge.

All pretense of stealth evaporated from Olivia's mind. She regained her footing, hand swinging through the air until her fingers found the hard edge of the railing, and began scrambling up the steps.

The red circle of light above called her. Olivia tried to think, racing up through the blackness, envisioning the 26th floor, a carbon copy of her own. She could sprint down the long hall, looking for some sort of refuge along the way, but if no safe port presented itself, she could continue to the west stairwell. Once there, she could keep going all the way to the bottom. Olivia knew it was not as simple as it sounded. Her encounters with five different Infested just on her own level of the New Leaf Building attested to that. Still, there was no better option available, so she just had to hope it would work.

Olivia broke free of the black shroud veiling the steps and felt her heart stutter in her chest. The door allowing entrance to the 26th floor was covered over with something.

Shiny, dark spots the size of cats or small dogs obscured the doorway. Fear and adrenaline made the world around her shimmer. For a moment, a brief second, she thought maybe the spots were a product of her taxed mental state, but then they started to move. Spindly legs jutting from the sides, they skittered about the surface of the door.

It was covered with the damned insects.

Her momentum kept her moving, but the sight caused her to shift her weight to her left as she entered the landing, sending her off at an angle, smashing against the railing. The things on the door appeared to be agitated by her presence. They hissed at her and jockeyed for position. Behind her came the ever-advancing thud of the pursuing Infested.

She had to keep moving.

Skirting the door as much as possible, sure at any moment the horrid bugs would come at her like a swarm of over-sized locusts, she once again entered the darkness of the stairs and continued her ascent.

There were only two floors above the 26th—the fitness level and the penthouse—and with that realization came a new, frightening one. Both doors had electronic locks. A key card was required to enter the fitness level, a simple plastic square with a magnetic strip on the back and a stylized green leaf on the front. Every resident of the building received one—she could even picture her own, sitting in a bowl with some spare change and a couple of paper clips next to the microwave.

Would the door automatically unlock with a power outage? She scoured her brain for any recollection, any half-remembered moment regarding the locks, but came back with nothing.

Olivia glanced over her shoulder, catching a quick glimpse of the Infested emerging from the darkness into the red light of the 26th floor landing. He looked even bigger, like some great primordial beast stepping from the mouth of its lair in the dead of night. He didn't hesitate or slow as he passed the insects collected on the nearby door. Instead, he just plowed forward, until the shadows of the stairwell ate him up again.

Her lungs burned, and she rounded the last bend leading to the fitness level. She could barely bring in a mouthful of air before her body forced it back out. Olivia wasn't sure what it felt like to suffocate but thought the sensation tearing her chest apart must be pretty close.

Please be unlocked please be unlocked please be unlocked, blasted through her mind repeatedly like an insane mantra.

As it turned out, her concerns regarding the lock were a moot point. Wedged halfway through the threshold separating the landing from the fitness level was a woman. She wore a pink bathing suit, but it looked purple under the bloodshot eye of the emergency light. Her face was puffed-up and heavily beaten.

Olivia squatted next to the woman and reached out for her, thinking for a moment she was still alive. Her fingers pulled back suddenly when she saw the lump jutting from the side of the woman's neck. She had never seen a broken neck before, but she knew the protrusion was not the sort of thing you found on a living person.

Behind her, the obese Infested continued shuffling up the steps. No heavy breathing, or yelling, or grunting came from him, just the continuous slap of his fat feet on the stairs. Any thoughts of respecting the dead vanished as Olivia pulled the door open and stepped over—and partially on—the dead woman.

The body kept the door from closing. Screaming, she grabbed the corpse by the hair and bathing suit and pulled. The woman was surprisingly heavy and, at first, didn't move very much at all.

The immense Infested appeared from the darkness so quickly it almost looked like a magic trick, his chubby hands groping the air before him.

"Move, goddamn you!" Olivia tensed her tired muscles, leaning back with all her weight, and dragged the body free.

The door swung closed at a maddeningly slow pace.

As soon as it did, the metal door began to thunder and shake, the lock stopping it from opening banged like a steel drum.

Letting out a laughing moan, she crumbled to the floor, her back to the door.

"Thank you, thank you." She sighed, her hand resting on the shoulder of the dead woman. Struggling to breathe—she couldn't seem to bring in enough oxygen—Olivia started to cry, deep, coughing sobs, each one shaking her body.

All the while, the door behind her bounced under the rage of the Infested.

CHAPTER 20

FITNESS/POOL LEVEL

The assault on the door continued unabated for several seconds before abruptly stopping. Still safe behind the metal barrier, Olivia leaned over and pressed her ear to the door's surface. Muted thuds of a heavy gait could be heard faintly from the other side. It seemed the Infested had tired of the pursuit and was retreating down the stairs.

Olivia rose on legs which felt more like hot putty than flesh and bone. She let her heart rate slow and her breathing return to something approaching manageable before pushing away from the exit.

The air was thick with humidity, much more so than her own floor had been. Olivia found it hard to breath the moist-heavy atmosphere after coming in from the oddly dry and dusty environment of the stairwell. The deep, bitter scent of chlorine filled her nostrils. Even though the pool was separate from the rest of the floor—accessible only through a pair of change rooms—its cloying stink gave away its presence.

Olivia had delighted at the sight of the fitness level upon first moving into the New Leaf. Separated into four distinct areas, the penultimate floor in the building was an exercise junkie's heaven. The biggest piece of real estate belonged to the pool, an Olympic-sized monster bookended by a pair of jacuzzis on one side and a sauna on the other. Next came the cardio room. Not really a room, per se, seeing as the entire floor was open concept—except for the pool—but it was the easiest way to differentiate the unique sections. An army of ellipticals, stationary bikes, and treadmills stood in military-perfect rows. Banks of televisions looked down on the equipment like prying eyes.

Off the cardio room came the weight room. Olivia had imagined throngs of meatheads pumping iron filling the space, but with the slight population of the New Leaf, the weight machines were left mostly neglected. Last, and the closest thing to a real, enclosed area, was the yoga room. Three mirror-fronted walls faced a square patch of floor lined with mats. Yoga balls of various colors, along with small pyramids of hand weights, littered the sides of the space.

From her position at the east stairwell exit, Olivia could see into the cardio room, and she let out a sorrowful moan at the sight greeting her.

The red lights, which had plagued her since stepping from her apartment, were absent. The fitness level was free of the horrible things, and all at once, Olivia prayed for their return. The only light, which sifted in from the tumultuous, night-time sky through windows along the front wall, did little to illuminate things.

She wished she knew the time. It was still so dark out, but was the dawn approaching, or was she buried in the middle of the night? Morning would bring some semblance of sanity, she was sure of it.

The idea of wading into the darkness of the fitness level was enough to keep her stuck to her spot by the exit. She wanted to remain where she stood, a fixed element of the room, just another inanimate object free from scrutiny. But she knew that was not practical. Until she found a place to hide, she would be in danger.

In the dark, the cardio room felt even bigger than it was. The whisper of light coming through the windows was just enough to reveal the orderly lines of equipment. That whisper became a scream when an explosion of lightning bathed everything stark white. For a moment, just a blink really, a horde of strange, unfamiliar silhouettes greeted her. Metal and plastic machines with jutting limbs became voids in the backlight of the electric flash.

There was something else as well.

Something which might have been a trick of the sudden light, a phantom image sliding across her corneas as a result of the unexpected illumination. Just before the flicker of nature's fury died completely, Olivia thought she saw a shadow detach from the rest and move across the floor.

Feeling utterly exposed in the open space, she spun in a circle, looking for somewhere to go, to hide. Near the stairwell exit was a nondescript wooden door. Her brain deduced, given the room's position near the stairs, a storage room lay beyond. She couldn't remember if she knew this for a fact, or it was the product of wishful thinking. Either way, it had to lead somewhere safer than where she currently found herself. Olivia hurried toward it, grabbed the handle, and yanked.

She half expected the door to be locked, but with an audible click, it swung freely under her pull. Although dark, she could see enough to realize the room was quite small. The smell of cleaning products and cheap paper towels wafted out, revealing her guess of storage room to be correct. Another slash of lightning, followed by a terrible boom of thunder, shook her, causing her to scurry in and pull the door closed behind her.

Mercifully, the closet was tiny. Only a few tentative steps forward, and she bumped into the extent of its depth, her fingers dancing along a series of shelves.

Olivia sank down to the floor and clutched the bag close to her chest. The leather of the computer case was cooler than her fevered flesh, producing a small shudder through her frame at its touch.

Her breathing continued its slow return to normalcy. If only she could get her heart to stop its mad tempo, but that was probably too much to ask for. She doubted her heart would ever beat normal again—a never-ending storm of blood thundering through her veins.

Olivia stared at the door in front of her, which had been blown away into nothingness, thanks to the dark, and started to see strange shapes. These figures born from the absence of light danced and twisted, will-o-wisps marching in a bizarre parade. Her mind wandered.

She thought of Mrs. Elliot. Could the elderly woman ever have foreseen what terrifying sights fate had in store for her? Beaten to death in the hallway of her home. Olivia thought of Rian. Such a sweet boy. Innocence personified. Transformed into something horrible. She thought of Alex. The young man had been lying to her, of that she was sure. But why? He had saved her life, only to then abandon her. Where had he gone? She thought about her mom. What would she have done in this situation? Would she have been brave, or would she have run screaming? And lastly, but most profoundly, she thought of her husband. Somewhere, lost in the middle of this hellish nightmare, was the man she loved. Was he alive? Was he dead? Or worse somehow still, was he an Infested?

Thinking of Liam brought back the nightmare and its strange message. What did it mean? Her thoughts wandered throughout the hallways of her memory. Liam had prepared their drinks. She thought, at the time, it was too dark in their apartment. When she asked Liam to turn on some lights, he ignored her. Was he creating the mood, or was there some other reason for the darkness? Like a buoy revealing itself in the lights of a ship on a foggy night, the orange pill bottle came into focus in her mind. And just like that, the picture began to coalesce. It was almost too obvious, now that the idea was present in her head. She hadn't drunk too much.

She had been drugged.

"But why?"

Had he been trying to get me high? To what end?

The helplessness of it all made her feel nauseous. One thing was for sure in her mind. Liam held the answers she was looking for.

"Oh Liam, where did you go?"

CHAPTER 21

EARLIER

Liam broke from the elevator doors as soon as they opened enough to allow him escape. He had been turning over the conversation in his mind during the short ride up from the 25th floor. What he had heard whispering through his cell phone had unnerved him more than he would have thought capable. The voice had been horse, scratchy, a rasp made all the more pronounced when converted to digital and blasted through radio waves into his device. And there had been the meaning behind the words. Each syllable as serious as a fired bullet.

The smell of the nearby pool acted like a balm on his nerves. Some of his best memories came while swimming. He could still recall being held in his mother's arms while she waded through the community pool when he was a toddler. Of course, nobody believed it when he said it, but it was true. When he reached college, he happily joined the swim team, a move which would ultimately introduce him to the first love of his life.

He was practicing one night, swimming laps, when a pretty young woman came in for a late-night dip. She ignored him at first, instead keeping herself at the far end of the pool, but as time went on, they drifted closer together. A brief bit of small talk turned into a full-blown conversation. She said her name was Olivia, and she was a freshman. As they climbed from the water, Liam asked if she wanted to grab a drink somewhere, had expected her to turn him down, but she accepted.

He had been happy, for a time. The path seemed pretty clear—finish school, move in together, marriage, a career, and then a baby. Except somewhere along the way, while in the career phase of his plan, Liam started to have regrets. Olivia was an attractive enough woman, but he was no slouch either. On more than one occasion, he would catch women sending flirting glances his way. He couldn't help but wonder what it would be like to kiss those women, to fuck them. Once the idea planted in his mind, he couldn't stop thinking about it.

And then there was the daily existence with his wife. He had to admit, her general needy attitude had been a turn-on at first. She was desperate to keep him happy, like a good wife should be, but as the years piled on, it became annoying. His own pride kept him with the woman. Liam wasn't going to be the kind of guy who ended up divorced, especially since he was the bread winner of the two. He'd be paying alimony for years.

When the offer to live in the New Leaf Building was given to him, Liam had almost turned it down. But then, the reality of such a move set in, and he eagerly accepted. The hours away from his wife were like breaths of fresh air. He devoured those moments. It required a bit of acting at home—he didn't want Olivia to think he enjoyed being apart—but Liam was up for the task. Besides, he didn't put much stock into his wife's intelligence.

A second, and even greater, benefit of living in the high-rise was it was there Liam met the second love of his life. It happened quite organically. Shortly after moving into the New Leaf, Liam, enjoying the added perk of the pool his new home offered, had met Audrey. As soon as she exited the changing room, towel in hand, he was smitten. Besides clearly being younger than he was and quite attractive, she also had an air about her, like she needed no one, and that was just fine. This attitude, which he would later discover was fairly accurate, greatly intrigued him.

She gave him that look, the one he had seen from other women before, the one he failed to act on. Not this time. Discretely stuffing his ring into the small, mesh-lined pocket in his swim trunks, Liam had waded over to the woman. He wasn't sure what he was going to say but was saved from having to figure it out. Audrey took to him almost immediately.

The first time they fucked, it was in the sauna. He was sure somebody would find them but somehow didn't care. Audrey's body was a new land for him to discover, to conquer.

Liam found an excuse to not be home certain nights of the week, only he was still in the building. It was a dangerous game, but one he was certain Olivia wouldn't be able to figure out.

He could recall the exact moment he knew he needed to be rid of his wife. Liam had just come from Audrey's apartment and was sliding the key into his door when he was hit with such a feeling of despair. That sensation only widened, like a yawning chasm, when Olivia smiled and asked how his day was. Such a small moment, yet one which revealed to him he could never be happy again with his wife. It was over.

Once again, he considered divorce, but it made him ill to think about it. What would people say? The blame would be put on him, especially with Audrey on his arm so soon after.

Putting thoughts of the past from his mind, Liam hurried through the lobby—the elevator door sighing closed behind him—and entered the fitness level proper.

The New Leaf had several night hawks. Folks came and went at all hours. It struck Liam as odd, given the building's distant location to anything of relevance, that so much of the population appeared to work at odd times. Because of this, he had been worried he would run into a handful of people working out but saw, much to his relief, only one machine was in use.

A woman in charcoal grey tights, a pink heart on the ass, and a purple sports bra ran hard on a treadmill. Under different circumstances, he would have been thrilled to take in the view Audrey's posterior offered while in motion. The heart bounced in the most pleasing of ways, but he was nervous and jittery, his mind being pulled in too many directions to settle on any one thing.

She must have caught sight of his reflection in the windows facing her. Before he could reach out or say anything, she slapped her palm on the big, red stop button and turned to look at him. If the slant of her eyebrows was to be believed, she was not impressed by his presence.

"What are you doing here? You shouldn't have called me, and you damn sure shouldn't be talking to me now." Even though Liam was the only other person around, Audrey delivered her question and statement in a conspiratorial whisper.

What am I doing here? Liam had to admit, it wasn't the wisest course of action. The last thing he should be doing—on that night of all nights—was going anywhere near Audrey. His plan, the original design he had slaved over for weeks, called for him to be cruising to the city. He had purposefully left something at work—nothing all that vital, just important enough that made his returning for it seem plausible. From there, he would stop for a drink, but not before using Olivia's phone to send himself a text message. A short and cryptic bit of digital text which would paint the picture needed.

Of course, all this was turned upside-down by the unexpected phone call.

"I know, I'm sorry. But I didn't know what else to do. Something came up. Something...unexpected." He tried to sound strong, in control, but failed.

"But you did it, right? I mean"—she glanced around the room, her voice lowering—"she is gone, right?"

Liam shushed her. "That part is done. I mean something *else* has come up."

He recounted the odd phone call to his mistress. Audrey seemed to consider this turn of events before pursing her lips.

"Whew, you had me worried for a second. Whoever called you can't possibly know what's going on."

When he opened his mouth to interject, to insist the caller had said things, things nobody could possibly know, Audrey held up her index finger to keep him silent.

"And even if they have an idea, they clearly aren't going to call the police. They would have done it by now. So, go see what they want, and then get the hell out of here. Nothing has changed, right?"

Even though he knew he shouldn't, Liam grabbed her ass and pulled her into him. She was hot, sweating despite the air conditioner, and it aroused him immensely. Olivia was lying somewhere below, and he was pressed against Audrey. He could have fucked her right there if he knew nobody would interfere.

"Okay. I'll try and call you tomorrow, but I'll probably be at the hospital or something for most of the day, so it might be later." He planted a kiss on her.

"I love you, baby." Audrey turned back to the machine and set the tread rolling again.

Liam wanted to say more, but the sudden pounding of her feet felt as sure an end to their conversation as anything could.

Standing in front of elevator doors, Liam steeled his nerves as much as he could and jabbed the call button.

"Alright, let's get this done."

He pulled his phone from his pocket and checked the time. Depending on the next handful of minutes, he might still be able to get the night back on track. A better day was awaiting him. Liam only had to grab it. He deserved it.

The door slid open before him. "Oh-seven-two-five," he muttered as he entered.

The rows of buttons beckoned, and once he had used them, the door began to close. Just before it sealed shut and the elevator whirred into motion, he glimpsed a crumbled piece of paper sitting on the thin carpet outside.

"Shit!"

He jammed his hand into his pocket, the same pocket he had pulled his phone from. The torn, rejected note he had yanked from the pad, the one he had stuffed in his pocket for later disposal, had fallen out. Liam frantically tried to halt the elevator's progress, but now that it was moving, nothing seemed to stop the lift. He would have to retrieve it when he came back down.

Hopefully, it would still be there.

CHAPTER 22

Lost in her own thoughts, Olivia realized she had been caressing the computer bag. Alex said the computer died on him, but what if it had a spark of juice left? The screen would easily light the small confines of the room. Even if it was only for a handful of seconds, she would be thankful.

She sat down and fumbled with the clasps before freeing the device, pulling the computer out, and placing it on her lap. Olivia thought she would need to feel along the keys—like braille—in search of the power button, but as soon as the lid was lifted, the screen jumped to life, blasting light into her face.

Under the unexpected assault, Olivia looked away until her eyes could adjust before returning her attention to the screen. Her gaze skated along the surface until coming to a rest on the battery icon in the bottom right corner.

It was still a quarter full.

She stared at the small icon before looking at the image immediately next to it. The wireless symbol had an angry yellow exclamation mark superimposed over it, signifying a lost connection.

At least he was telling the truth about that. But why lie about it being dead? If there was no way to use the device for help, what did it matter if it had any juice left or not? There had to be another reason why he did not want her looking at it, one she was eager to discover.

The desktop on Alex's computer was a cluttered mess. A schizophrenic collection of files and icons dotted the screen like so much debris after a windstorm. She scanned over the various news apps and library short-cuts making up the bulk of the digital detritus. The file folders, all titled with nothing more than a six-digit number—*dates?* she wondered—gave no clue as to what was contained within. Olivia decided to pick one at random but halted before opening it, noticing a file already open, a small blue tab at the bottom of the display revealing it was just minimized.

It was labeled *Eosphoros.*

Scrunching her nose, she stared at the strange name, a small buzz beginning to vibrate through her head.

Where have I heard that before?

It was immediately familiar, and yet she certainly had no idea what it meant. Then it hit her. Back on the 25th floor, after her encounter with Rian, she had stumbled into the hall and watched as the boy's mom, Chloe, pulled herself forward. With her dying breath, Chloe had practically spat the word.

Olivia restored the file to the screen.

Eight sub-folders appeared. She scanned them, looking for something helpful, an electronic life-preserver which would begin pulling her free from the smothering mystery of the night, and quickly found it.

A file named The New Leaf Project.

A feeling of dread settled over her. She was so thirsty for knowledge, for some shred of understanding, yet she was also afraid of what she might find. She had learned at a young age things could always be worse. What if her own ignorance of the events surrounding her was the only thing keeping her sane?

Shaking away the doubt, she opened the folder.

Most of the file's contents were news articles about the construction of the building. She briefly skimmed through them but found nothing worthwhile, certainly nothing which would explain the Infested. Next was a blueprint of the New Leaf itself. Somebody, possibly Alex, had highlighted the penthouse and the 9th floor in red. *Labs?* was written next to the latter.

"Labs?" she whispered into the darkness being held back by the computer light.

Lastly, she found a list of names with accompanying photos. Above the names, it said: *Confirmed Eosphoros Employees on site.* The directory was slight. Only about eight or ten names appeared, and of these, only one was immediately familiar—Chloe from across the hall. Olivia leaned forward, scrutinizing the image. Even wrapped in a white lab coat, with safety glasses obscuring part of her face, it was clearly her neighbor.

"What the fuck was going on here?"

The thought of Chloe having some sort of knowledge regarding the Infested seemed absurd, given the woman's tragic end. But yet here she was, apparently having been identified by Alex as working for Eosphoros—whatever that was.

The last names on the list belonged to Vera and Conrad Anderson. There was no image of the woman, but there was of the man. A flare of surprise filled Olivia.

She had seen him before.

It came to her quick enough. The stern, yet proud features were an exact match as those portrayed on canvas in Alex's apartment.

This makes no sense. Alex said the people in the painting were his grandparents.

"Is he their grandson? Why wouldn't he say that?"

Shaking her head—the questions were starting to pile-up on the highway of her mind—she returned her attention back to the picture of the man. Conrad Anderson. Alex had said he and his wife lived on the top floor, the penthouse. Could the elderly couple be up there right now? It seemed unlikely. Even with the power outage and the unexplained loss of cell signals, she felt a billion dollars bought instant communication. They would have been able to reach somebody.

No. She imagined the Andersons sitting on a yacht somewhere, enjoying drinks, oblivious to the fact that, half the world away, people were being tormented, killed, while living in a property they owned.

And then there was Eosphoros.

Chloe had uttered it with her last breath. Alex had a file indicating several people inside the New Leaf were a part of it—whatever *it* was—including the people he identified as his grandparents. The word itself meant nothing to her, but it rang with such an ominous resonance inside her head she felt a need to approach it with caution. If there was some sort of secret organization or company hiding within the skin of the New Leaf, it had to be connected to the Infested.

Her head ached, a throbbing strum which had never truly alleviated since waking. Olivia turned the computer aside, its screen alighting upon a shelf densely packed with toilet paper, and closed her eyes and leaned her head back.

She figured she would spend the rest of the night in the storage closet. It felt safe, even though there was no lock on the door. Olivia reasoned it would only be so long before somebody came to the building. Even with the phones out, people were going to be expected at work. Friends and family members would become concerned when they did not hear from loved ones. It was only a matter of time before help arrived.

The quiet solitude of her surroundings suddenly broke as a sharp sound played through the air. Olivia leaned forward, her head cocked toward the door, and listened, her mind placing the noise almost immediately. It was a cellphone. The familiar jingle—the type that comes pre-set on most phones—playfully chirped, each note ringing a bell of hope inside her.

CHAPTER 23

"Hello? Is somebody there?" Olivia's voice carried through the cavernous area, becoming lost in the blackness around her. She stood in the partially open doorway of the storage room, her face pressed in the crack.

The dimensions of the fitness level made the sound impossible to pinpoint. She knew the phone was close by, thanks to how loud it was, but beyond that, she wasn't sure where to even begin her search. The open concept rooms meant the thing could be almost anywhere. She had hoped she would see a glowing screen, a flashing beacon in the gloom, revealing itself to her. But there was only darkness. She would have to venture forth in search of the device.

She considered bringing the computer, holding it before her like an oversized flashlight, but then nixed the idea. The laptop would slow her down, and she did not intend to stay wandering about for very long.

Olivia left the door open behind her and slid from the tiny room in one fluid motion. She stood still for a moment, building up the nerve to move, to burst forward once again into hell. Rocking on her heels—the floor feeling more like AstroTurf than carpet under her tired feet—she let out a sigh and propelled herself forward. Her thigh muscles protested the sudden activity—they still burned from her desperate ascent up the stairs—but the idea of salvation was enough to liven-up her limbs, to push her into a quick jog. The humid air whispered past her ears, and the forest of exercise equipment stood like a foreboding wood off to her left.

The immensity of the fitness level revealed itself in those tense moments. As Olivia scampered in search of the phone, she felt overwhelmed by the scale of floor, like she had unexpectedly entered a huge warehouse. Vast hangers of blackness yawning dark and empty around her.

Her strategy was to use the single, full wall dividing the pool from the rest of the floor as a guide. Keeping it close to her right as she moved forward not only kept her orientated with the rest of the level, but also eliminated a potential vector of approach for any Infested which might be hiding in the shadows.

Olivia followed the curve of the wall and spotted the elevators. She slowed as she approached the doors, her eyes settling on the twin plastic buttons stationed between them. The call buttons—one with an up arrow, the other down—were dark, two black eyes. Still, she couldn't help herself and jabbed the down button. The plastic clicked inside its metal cradle, but, as she expected, nothing happened.

Unlike the lift doors on the other floors of the New Leaf, the ones stationed on the fitness level were fronted with mirrors. Olivia looked at herself, a wraith lurking in the darkness, a stranger's clothes enwrapping her.

There was something else though in her reflection, some previously hidden element, an unearthed feature she had never noticed before. Under the dirt, blood, and trauma adorning her face like unwanted graffiti, she saw something hard, fierce. It surprised her and yet made her feel alive.

She turned away and continued her search, leaving the dead elevators behind. It wasn't the time for such contemplations, but she couldn't help but notice her legs felt a little bit sturdier, her step a little bit surer.

The phone—complete with flower-covered case—appeared like a precious treasure in the pit of a dark ruin. A flashing glow dancing in time with the ringing pushed back the blackness in rhythmic waves. The thing was lying discarded in front of the changing rooms.

"Thank you! Thank you!" Tears of joy burst from her eyes, and a feeling of such profound elation filled her, lifted her weight, carried her forward.

Olivia dropped to her knees in front of the phone, grabbing for it with fingers gone numb with excitement. A flashing red circle on the bottom of the screen throbbed in time with the ringtone. She slid her thumb along the circle and quickly brought the phone to her ear.

"You have to help us!" she blurted into the cell, her words taking on a near-incoherent quality usually only achieved by the very drunk. "Call the police! We need help at the New Leaf Building."

She forced herself to stop, to breathe. It would only prolong things if she refused to let the person on the other end get a word in edgewise. There was no reply. The only sound she heard was her own desperate heartbeat.

"Hello! Hello!"

She pulled the phone away from her ear and looked at it, really looked at it. The cruelty of the situation settled on her like a toxic cloud.

A simple message emblazoned on the screen. *Alarm ended.*

It wasn't an incoming call. It was a fucking alarm!

"God damn it!" She threw the phone as hard as she could. The device was instantly devoured by the darkness, the sound of a distant crash the only evidence it hadn't simply ceased to exist once leaving her presence.

Wiping away her tears, she rose back to her feet. The defeat had rendered her muscles practically useless. She looked back the way she came, the distance feeling immeasurable.

Olivia took one slow, tired step, when a series of noises halted her.

The sound, a wild clattering of metal, dragged her attention to the weight room. She had heard similar noises before, the unmistakable sound of weights falling to the floor. All at once, the vision of the shadow, that drifting patch of nothing which had seemed to exist in a state separate from the rest, returned.

Something is *in there!*

Olivia peered into the black, sure one of the silhouettes fronting the bank of windows—an elliptical, or maybe a treadmill—swayed slightly. Covering her mouth to keep her breathing from becoming a sob, she continued to look on.

Another clanging of metal made her stiffen. A round, cast iron weight rolled like a wheel along the thin carpet of the exercise floor.

There was no way she could return to the storage closet, not without alerting whatever was skulking in the dark. Turning, she looked at the changing room doors behind her.

Olivia grabbed the handle of the nearest door—the women's—opened it, and ducked inside.

CHAPTER 24

As soon as the door settled behind her, Olivia was lost in a formless space. The changing room was pitch black. She knew the layout, having passed through it several times in the past six months during her frequent trips to the pool, but that knowledge crumbled under the weight of the sheer nothingness assaulting her eyes.

Even though her mind insisted that just feet away on either side of her would be a collection of benches and lockers, these thoughts could not coalesce into a solid reality. For all she knew, the entire room had fallen away into a negative dimension. The darkness was such that it felt impenetrable. The absence of light had been made solid. She wasn't sure she could do it, couldn't move through such an environment.

As a reminder the dark was not the scariest thing occupying the New Leaf, there came a loud, insane series of crashes echoing from somewhere on the fitness level behind her. The sound jabbed at Olivia like a cattle prod, inching her deeper into the changing room. She painted a mental map of the area and determined its entire distance could not be more than ninety feet.

It didn't matter really. She already knew she couldn't retreat the way she had come. If it was an Infested out there, she would be easy prey in her sorry state. And she couldn't hunker down in the darkness of the changing room either. Besides the fact whatever was potentially stalking her could be right on her heels, there was the idea that to remain in such a place would finally hold open the door for insanity to move in. She would just have to get through the black room as fast as possible and pray there would be somewhere safe to hide, some sort of salvation, on the other side.

With her decision made, Olivia was free to acknowledge her other senses. The changing room was ripe with odors. A deep ammonia stench hung in the air, bleach or some other cleaning solution. It was an aroma Olivia was very familiar with and one always catalogued in her brain under *sanitized death*. It was the smell of hospitals.

Visiting her mom in the months following the accident, Olivia had come to loathe that scent. A wash of chemicals designed to cover the stink of piss, shit, and blood. It never did though, not quite. The rot and ruin always lingered at the edges, a reminder a person couldn't escape the horrors of dying, no matter how much they pretended they didn't exist.

You can do this. You've faced worse.

As she moved deeper, the smell of bleach was so strong Olivia almost gagged. It burned her nostrils and made her eyes water.

The floor was wet. Her bare feet slid along the tiles, threatening to shift out from under her completely. Afraid of falling, Olivia found herself sliding forward, the mystery substance on the floor collecting between her toes, like tiny, fleshy plows clearing a path along the tile.

As long as she continued in a straight line, she knew she would come to a wall. There would be a ninety degree turn to the right which led to the toilets, sinks, and showers. Beyond that, the door to the pool.

Her hands groped the stale air before her. It was an odd sensation, not being able to see your own limbs. It made them feel impossibly long. When she did hit the wall, it startled her. Her fingers buckled under the impact. Swearing to herself, Olivia shook the unexpected pain out of her digits before taking a step back, turning right, and continuing forward.

The wetness on the tile began to dissipate. Whatever it was, it had left the soles of her feet tacky. The skin there stuck and peeled from the floor with each step.

The bank of sinks came next. She clipped the edge of one with her hand as she fumbled ahead and then quickly scrambled toward it. Having something solid to hold, something normal like a sink, while lost in the abyss of the change room helped ground her. She wasn't sure how much longer she could tread through the dark without breaking down.

If her mental map was correct, all she had to do was follow the sinks all the way to the exit. Breathing a bit easier, she hurried along.

Beyond the pounding of her own heart—which was an ever-present drum beating through her body—a quick, almost gentle sound disturbed the stillness of the room. Olivia halted, her fingers tightening on the edge of a sink, and stared around blindly.

The sound repeated, a soft crinkling noise.

Like a plastic sheet...*Or a shower curtain.*

The shower stalls—a duo of cubbies opposite the sinks and next to the bathroom stalls—were tiled floor to ceiling and had thin, plastic curtains for privacy. She recalled a large sign next to the door informing residents they were required to shower before and after using the pool. Olivia always questioned the reason for this. She certainly never abided the rule herself. But she had seen the odd woman using the stalls from time to time, so she guessed the showers served a purpose.

Now though, all she could imagine was an Infested, standing in the confines of the shower, like a demon in the mouth of hell. It didn't matter the curtains were so thin and her movement had most likely been enough to cause one of them to shift slightly. All reason had been blasted from her mind many hours ago, replaced with a permanent sensation of dread.

Her fear tore at her insides like a ferocious animal, and without giving it another thought, she burst forward in a sprint toward the door, her feet slapping the tile in staccato fits.

The shower curtains came alive, the sound of plastic bags caught in a sudden wind, making her run harder. She expected hands, gore-stained appendages, to reach out, grasp her, pull her into one of the shower stalls, turning the tiled walls into her tomb. But nothing grabbed her, and no Infested lunged through the darkness.

She slammed face-first into the door, and something crunched in her nose. A firework display of pain lit through her head. Olivia barely noticed though, instead focusing entirely on escaping the room. As soon as she felt the hinges of the door respond to her weight, releasing a shaft of light along the right side, she pushed herself fully into the endeavor and tumbled out of the room.

Olivia's feet slipped on the wet tiles just beyond, sending her careening backward, spilling her to the floor. Her head bounced once off the unforgiving ground before everything went fuzzy around the edges.

CHAPTER 25

Olivia found herself staring up at the sky. A creeping ivy-vine of lightning snaked through the clouds. Confusion settled like mold along the edges of her migraine, causing her head to buzz.

Am I outside?

It was hard to remember. But no, that didn't seem right.

The ghost of unyielding darkness hovered at the back of her consciousness, reminding her she had just escaped the changing room. Blinking away the tears which sat in her eyes like pearls, she heaved herself up to a sitting position and looked around. She was poolside. Shady pockets smudged the corners of the rectangular space. The illusion of being outside came as a result of the massive glass ceiling above her.

She winced and reached back, probing her scalp along the back of her head. Her fingers returned with small dabs of blood on the tips. Another injury to go along with the rest.

Torrential rainfall smacked the various glass surfaces encapsulating the room, creating a constant chaotic chatter sounding more like amped-up radio-static than bad weather.

The pervading thought in Olivia's mind was to lay back down, but even if she had imagined a terror in the changing room with her, she certainly had not invented the commotion she had heard in the weight room. Something was definitely out there, something which could be moments behind her.

Olivia took a deep breath and peered up once again at the tumultuous sky. The clouds appeared close enough to nearly hit the building. Just as she was going to look away, she noticed something odd about the penthouse looming above the fitness level like a gravestone.

Topping off the New Leaf was a two-story ode to opulence. Each of the two levels was roughly a third the size of a regular floor—at least, that's what she had deduced when looking at the building map shortly after moving in. She had never set foot up there but had found herself staring at it from time to time while swimming with Liam.

Olivia had assumed the penthouse was empty, awaiting some person of incredible wealth to rent the unit. As it turned out, the place had been home to Conrad and Vera Anderson all along. The thing which caught her attention this time was the bank of lights shining from the many windows.

The penthouse has power!

To make things even stranger, she was almost positive she could see a dark silhouette standing in one of the windows. Thanks to the rain and the distance, the person looked more like the suggestion of a human being than a real, living entity, but squinting her eyes, Olivia had no doubt somebody was up there. And as much as she thought it was her own paranoia, she couldn't shake the sensation whoever loomed above was looking directly at her.

Was it Conrad Anderson? Was he aware of what was happening under his feet? But then she thought, what if he wasn't? What if the penthouse had its own power supply? What if, right now, the old man was simply taking-in the storm, completely oblivious to what hell was enfolding below him? Or maybe it was his wife, Vera. Up late to use the bathroom, wondering why the lights in the pool were off. Regardless of the answers, one thing was suddenly very clear to Olivia, the penthouse appeared to be safe from Infested.

She rolled over and climbed to her feet. The room tilted drunkenly, but after a moment, it settled, and Olivia was able to move again.

The first thing she noticed was the body in the pool. A woman floating face-down. The water was so still the corpse looked like it was stuck in glass. This visual deception was ruined though by the shifting cloud of blood staining the darkened water. It moved and undulated as if being manipulated by unseen forces.

A manic bang bounced from the men's changing room. The sound revved the engine of Olivia's heart, causing a low moan to emanate from her mouth.

She looked around for a place to hide, realizing the mistake she had made. The pool was a dead end. The only way out was the way she had come. And hiding spots were in short supply. She could slide into the pool, stay pressed to the edge, let the murkiness of the water keep her hidden. Olivia imagined an Infested finding her like that and knew it was the wrong choice. It wouldn't even have to come in after her. It could just wait. She would never be able to get out fast enough to evade them.

A smattering of lounging chairs gathered in the corner like a herd of animals made of plastic and rubber. Most of them were folded, and even the ones that were opened would not offer much cover. Both hot tubs presented the same issue as the pool—albeit on a smaller scale. That only left one viable option.

The sauna.

In the gloom, the steam room looked more like a cave sticking out of the far wall than a sauna. An ominous and foreboding structure, like a wood-lined crypt.

At least there would be a door between her and the Infested. And, if she remembered correctly, the room was lockable by a crude wooden latch from the inside.

With the decision made, Olivia quickly covered the distance to her intended destination, all the while peeking over her shoulder at the changing room doors, expecting one of them to blow open, an Infested bursting free.

As she approached, she noticed the bulky, wooden door was slightly ajar. Beyond was utterly black. Coming to a stop, she peered into the sea of ink filling the squat structure but could see nothing of its interior.

Over the course of the night, the darkness inside the New Leaf had become a living thing, a beast prowling the rooms and corridors. It made Olivia feel small, insignificant. She promised herself that if by some miracle she survived the evening, she would never go anywhere without a flashlight for the rest of her days. She bit her bottom lip and slid through the open door. As she turned to secure the latch on the door behind her, she was stopped by a sudden shuffle of feet erupting around her.

A tiny form burst from the abyss and collided with her. Olivia yelped, a sound which quickly soured into a moaning scream, and she thrust at the thing. Her fingers impacted something soft, fleshy. Thoughts, like cannonballs, tore through her mind. Rian had found her. And now, even in the absence of light, she was convinced she could see the boy—dried, caked blood staining his smooth chest. His eyes, cold, accusing, dead.

She tried to backpedal, while at the same time kicking a leg at the wraith swarming her.

"Ouch!" a small voice, already thick with tears, cried.

Ouch?

Olivia stumbled backward from the sauna. As she did so, a faint curtain of light from the windows sneaked past and fell along the shape of a child.

CHAPTER 26

"Shh, shh, it's okay," Olivia blurted, not sure what else to say.

The child, exposed by the pale light of the pool room, was revealed to be a little girl. She attempted to rocket past Olivia. "Don't hurt me!"

Just before the girl could escape, Olivia snatched her arm and pulled her close. Thoughts of Rian still resonated, but they were evaporating quickly.

"Look! Look, I'm not like them! I'm not going to hurt you!"

The kid jerked and bounced in her grip, a human-shaped ball of chaos. Even though she was small, the fight in the girl was impressive. It took everything Olivia had to keep hold of her.

"Please, you have to calm down. I can help you, but you need to stop fighting me."

It did not escape Olivia she was practically re-enacting her first encounter with Alex. It was somewhat shameful when she realized the little girl in her arms was putting up more of a struggle than she had.

"Please!" she all but begged the child. "I'm not going to hurt you!"

The little girl looked at her, eyeballs crazed like a wild horse's, before slowly, almost regretfully, settling down in Olivia's grip.

"I don't want to die," she said, her voice high, like tinkling glass.

Olivia positioned herself fully in front of the kid. "Shh, no, you're not going to die. I promise."

It was ludicrous to give such an assurance. The entire building was a death trap, a monstrous shooting gallery. But still, in the moment, to win the small child's trust, Olivia would have promised the moon.

With the oath made, the girl gave up the fight altogether and sunk into Olivia, her small arms wrapping around her, sobs racking her slender frame.

Whispering into the top of the girl's head—the child's hair thick with the scent of strawberry shampoo—Olivia asked, "What's your name, honey?"

Judging by her appearance, Olivia pegged the kid at being somewhere in the neighborhood of eight or nine years old. She was very pale, and a smattering of freckles stood-out on her skin. Her hair was long and fine, as if made of gold thread. She wore a pajama set with a large, cartoon unicorn on the front.

"My...my name's Emma."

"Hi, Emma, I'm Olivia. What happened? Why aren't you in your apartment? Where're your parents?"

Emma seemed to react to Olivia's name, her small hand going briefly to the pocket of her pajama bottoms, but it was only for a moment, and then her gaze seemed to shift past Olivia and fell onto the pool. A series of dimples formed along her delicate chin as her crying intensified.

Olivia turned and followed Emma's line of sight. She saw the black form floating softly in the water, and all at once, she knew the partial answer to at least one of her questions.

"Was that...Was that your mom?"

Wiping away a patch of snot forming in the space between her upper lip and nose with the palm of her hand, Emma looked Olivia in the eye and slowly nodded.

"Mommy works nights," she said between sniffles. "She comes swimming with her friend before work. She sets her alarm clock so that she isn't late. I had a bad dream, and when I couldn't find my daddy, I came looking for her. I saw my mommy's friend in the door. She was hurt really bad. And then I found Mommy in the pool. And then..."

"Then what, honey?"

"Then..." Emma returned her gaze to the water, her eyes unfocused, like a war was being fought across her vision, one side demanding to see the truth in the pool, the other doing everything it could to relieve the child of the burden. "I saw Daddy."

"What about your daddy, Emma?" She hated pressing the child, but if the girl's father was an Infested, she needed to know.

"He was—"

Overhead, the rain began to pick up once again. This time, it was accompanied with something else, a sound akin to thousands of rocks being scattered across a tin roof. Both Olivia and Emma turned to stare up at the glass ceiling. Countless small, white pellets jumped like albino fleas along the panes. Hail. The racket was tremendous, a constant machinegun assault of clinks.

Olivia could feel the girl tense, her narrow limbs going stiff like petrified branches. "It's okay. It's only hail."

"No," Emma said, her voice no more than a whisper. "Not that. Him."

Stabbing fear slid between her intestines, and Olivia followed the little girl's gaze once again. An Infested—wearing a blood-caked T-shirt and shorts—stepped out of the men's changing room and into the hazy light wafting in from above.

Afraid to take her eyes off the man, to even breathe, Olivia was only vaguely aware Emma was still talking.

"It's my daddy."

CHAPTER 27

The Infested emerging from the men's changing room did so with a jittering shuffle. Olivia had noticed something similar in the movements of the Infested which had invaded Alex's apartment, but even those had not been this severe. It was as if the bug buried in the man's esophagus had reached such a level of control, the man now moved more like an insect than a human.

Olivia slapped her hand over Emma's mouth, catching the scream she knew must be bubbling up the kid's throat, and pulled her deeper into the shadows.

The thing that used to be Emma's father moved all the way to the edge of the pool and then collapsed to his hands and knees. With the man's mouth agape, the bug inside him slid out until half of its mass hung like a grotesque fruit from a human tree. Its antennae waved around, even skimming the calm water of the pool, before it pulled itself back into the safety of its host.

The Infested returned to an upright stance and began skittering around the edge of the pool in the opposite direction from the sauna. Olivia felt sure the thing was looking for them. It had followed her to the change rooms, and now it was searching for her. The blitzkrieg of hail razing the windows above turned out to be a small miracle, as it effectively smothered any noise she or the child were making. For the time being, the Infested did not know where they were.

As much a relief as it was to watch the thing move away, Olivia knew it would only be seconds before the man-puppet navigated the circumference of the pool and ended up finding them standing in front of the sauna door. Her first thought was to drag the girl into the confines of the steam room, snap the chunk of wood to bar the entrance behind them, and hope it would be enough to keep the Infested out. But if it wasn't enough, there would be nowhere to go. They would be easy prey for the creature.

Olivia looked for an alternative and noticed the wall leading back to the changing rooms was awash in shadow. If she could keep the kid quiet, they might be able to sneak along, unmolested, and exit the pool room altogether without the Infested ever knowing. But, other than the blanket of shadow concealing them, they would be exposed for several seconds along the way.

Time took on a sticky quality. Each second—during which Olivia tried to decide the best course of action—felt as if it had been coated in glue, drawing out her thoughts, gumming-up her mental faculties. She could see both outcomes of her intended actions as clear as day, neither projecting a pleasant forecast. But the thought of being confined in the darkness of the sauna as the Infested pounded his way in was enough to snap the cerebral adhesive in her mind.

She had hidden enough for one night. Olivia was no longer content to scurry into the nearest hole like a wounded animal. She was finished waiting for death to find her.

If it wants me, it'll damn well have to catch me!

Emma, whose body had become as rigid as a statue, jumped when Olivia gripped her thin arm and pulled her forward. The girl's mouth was moving, a word tumbling past lips gone white with fear. She was saying, *Daddy,* over and over again.

Olivia watched the creature shamble and twitch its way around the pool. Keeping the Infested locked in her gaze, she yanked Emma off their perch in front of the sauna and ran for the nearest exit.

She hugged the wall, moving quickly, the girl in tow right behind her. The Infested—now passing by the windows—continued to amble along, oblivious of their presence. With the changing room doors growing larger, Olivia realized she had made the right choice.

They were going to make it.

Slowing at the last possible second, just short of colliding with the door, she reached out gingerly and pushed it open.

Preparing herself for the total blackness of the men's changing room—Olivia assumed it would be as devoid of illumination as the women's—she was surprised to see a sheen of white light bouncing off the tiles before them. Her brain, weary and exhausted to the point of near mental shutdown, insisted the light was not actually there, just a figment of her over-taxed imagination. But as the door sighed closed behind them, and the light remained, she tensed, ready for what new horror the night was preparing to throw at her.

A hesitant form emerged from around the bend in the changing room, and a brilliant shaft of light exploded from their hand, a beam of painful illumination zeroing in on Olivia's eyes.

"Olivia!" A voice shouted, the radiance immediately sliding free from her sight, repositioning toward the hard tile of the floor.

The haze of light-butterflies left her vision. It was Alex.

"What?"

It all seemed so inconceivable to her. Was she hallucinating? How could the young man from across the hall, the same guy who had up and disappeared from his apartment, leaving her at the mercy of the Infested, be standing before her?

"Thank God! I thought you were gone." He shuffled forward, his gait awkward.

Olivia shook her head. "How are you here?"

Alex seemed to consider the question and continued closing the distance between them, a look of concern etched across his face, an expression made all the more severe thanks to the harsh wash emanating from the edges of his light. It turned out to be a cell phone wrapped in a flower-covered case—the same phone she had thrown across the weight room in frustration.

"I'm so sorry. I never meant to leave you alone."

She had so many questions, a barrage of inquires waiting to be unleashed. But, she realized, it was not the right time. They needed to keep moving.

Olivia vowed to dig to the bottom of Alex's deception later. Gripping Emma's wrist, she pushed forward, intending to brush past Alex, but stopped when an expression of deep terror demented his face.

She turned to look over her shoulder and caught just a glimpse of the changing room door easing closed.

They hadn't even heard it open.

In the ambient light of the phone, the Infested dashed toward them.

CHAPTER 28

The Infested smashed into Olivia, and she felt her feet leave the ground. Her fingers yanked free of Emma's wrist, and she was forcibly pushed through the air. Both her and her assailant spilled violently to the floor.

In the cavern-like space, a high-pitched scream burst from the little girl. Shrill echoes bouncing off the walls made it sound as if an army of tormented children had suddenly appeared.

Olivia felt her bones grind in protest as she slid across the slick tiles. The air exited her lungs in a whoosh. Before she could think of anything else, the man atop her, the very same man who probably had kissed his little girl goodnight only a few short hours ago, began trying to pummel Olivia to death right in front of his child.

Olivia tried to push the Infested off but was unsuccessful. Unlike some of her previous altercations with the monsters, the man straddling her was not a child, or a sickly senior. He was a healthy man in the prime of his life.

A strange, sweeping light danced across her vision, disappearing behind the form bestriding her. An odd combo of noises—a strained grunt, followed by a meaty thud—filled the air. Her frantic mind finally made sense of the sounds.

Alex, still holding the cell phone, was clubbing the Infested with his fist.

Her neighbor's efforts to dislodge the Infested was effective enough for Olivia to shimmy partially out from under the monster's weight.

She was sure the horrid thing would turn its attention toward Alex, that the Infested would bring his crazed hands to bear on the man's delicate features. But that did not happen. Despite the fact Alex was doing everything he bodily could to hurt, maim, even kill, the Infested, Emma's father paid Alex no mind, instead scrambling to remain on top of Olivia.

"Daddy! Stop!" Emma bellowed.

Olivia twisted her head, her cheek sliding across the floor, to look at the little girl. Emma had retreated to the confines of one of the shower stalls. The tiled walls on both sides appeared like a tightening vice, constricting ever closer to her tiny body in the chaotic beam thrown from the cell phone in Alex's flailing hands.

The Infested arched back, and his shirt, a foreign map with continents of blood decorating the front, stretched as he tensed. He swung his gaze toward the girl, his mouth agape followed a second later.

And just like that, the weight was gone. The Infested pulled himself free of Olivia and began stalking toward Emma.

The child, her form barely visible inside the embrace of the shower stall, cowered like a frightened animal as a nightmare version of her own father descended on her.

Olivia kicked her feet out, the heel of her right foot connecting squarely with the Infested's left knee, causing the stalking man to buckle.

"Run, Emma!" she screamed, knowing her actions wouldn't halt the Infested for long.

The child met Olivia's gaze, her eyes wide. The look, that of some tiny mammal caught in the headlights of a big rig on some godforsaken highway, revealed everything to Olivia. It said Emma was not going to run. She was incapable of such an action. Olivia couldn't blame her. No child—regardless of how tough—was equipped to face down the horror of the Infested.

Apparently, realizing it was going to take drastic measures to stop the Infested, Alex dropped the cell phone and launched himself at the thing. The beam somersaulted through the air, slicing a ribbon across the darkness of the space, before coming to a rest under the sinks, painting a large circle against the far wall.

Emma's dad was quite a bit larger than Alex, and Olivia would have bet all the money in the world the thin man from across the hall would have been no more able to bring the Infested down as he would be able to lift a car, but once again, it was as if the Infested was completely unaware of Alex's presence. So, when the two men collided, it threw the larger completely off his feet.

Despite his momentary success at stopping the harm aimed at the girl, Olivia knew Alex would not be able to halt it for long.

We have to kill it!

She scanned the room and spotted a cart of cleaning supplies partially revealed by the ambient illumination of the downed light. Her heart galloped at speeds she would never have guessed possible, and Olivia rushed over to it, searching for something, anything, that would stop the creature.

Paper towels, a plunger, three rolls of toilet paper, and a bottle of bleach. At the last, her mind sparked, a flare struck from a mental flint, which brought her own earlier thoughts back to her.

Sanitized death.

Olivia pulled the white plastic bottle from the wire basket holstering it and looked back in time to see the Infested shuck Alex free. The move sent Alex colliding with a nearby sink, and the sound of his forehead smacking against the porcelain made her stomach churn. With Alex no longer holding him, the Infested resumed his horrid work and quickly beelined for the child.

Olivia sprinted across the tile floor, her feet smacking angrily with each step. As she ran, she gripped the cap to the bleach and gave it a hard twist. The little white circle danced briefly along the threads holding it in place before spinning free and disappearing like a miniature UFO into the darkness. Warm bleach sloughed from the opening onto the back of her hand, the smell instantly overtaking all other scents.

"Fucking die!" The scream seemed to originate from the deepest part of her, from some previously unknown well.

The Infested turned toward her, his slack mouth giving him a dim-witted expression. In the low light, Olivia could see—or maybe she just imagined she could see—the fine strands making up the insect's antenna peeking from between the split, bloody lips. Apparently deciding the prey coming to it was the better option, the Infested grabbed for Olivia, his weight shifting between feet as he reoriented himself to face her.

Olivia slipped his grasp, and her gaze zeroed-in on the maw in the center of his face. She reached out with a hand of her own. Her fingers hooked over the man's bottom teeth and pulled down. A sick, grinding sensation reverberated through her fingers as the bones of the man's jaw shifted and jutted together.

She tipped the bottle and jammed the open end down into the widened mouth of the Infested.

A geyser of bleach erupted around the edges of his lips, his fingers grasping for the bottle desperately. Olivia refused to let go though. Instead, she slapped her hands on the wide base like a drum, driving the plastic jug even farther down the man's gullet.

The Infested swung his arms violently. One of his spasming fists connected with the side of Olivia's face, and the impact sent stars through her head, turning her knees to jelly. She fell backward, her tailbone crunching as she thumped to the unforgiving floor.

In front of her, the Infested began dancing like a cockroach on a hotplate, his limbs thrashing the air, multiple waterfalls of bleach spilling from the spaces between the bottle and his lips. Finally, he managed to pull the plastic jug free, sending it bouncing to the floor. For a moment, the Infested stopped moving altogether.

Olivia was sure her attack had been fruitless, just a momentary distraction, a desperate bid delaying the nightmare for a few seconds, nothing more. But then, a deep, liquid-fueled belch erupted from the Infested's mouth. He took a shuddering step forward and then bent over, bringing his face within inches of Olivia's own.

A second belch, followed by a noise Olivia could only compare to a rotten melon being tossed to the street, issued from the Infested. She could see something begin to emerge from the man's ruined mouth. In a slurry of blood, saliva, and bleach—which spattered across her face and chest—the insect ejected from its host and fell into a heap of twitching legs onto the tile next to her.

Without the creature controlling him, Emma's father went stiff and toppled to the side.

Olivia watched mesmerized, horrified, as the bug began dragging its bleach-soaked body away from her. It only made it a few feet—emitting a high-pitched buzz, like a nightmarish siren—before coming to a halt. Its spindly legs twitched before the entire thing went still. It was dead.

"Is...Is everyone okay?" Alex's voice penetrated the fog which had begun to obscure Olivia's thoughts.

She rose to her feet and nodded once at the man.

Olivia retrieved the cell phone and held the beam on the withered insect, its gore-slickened carapace reflecting the light in a dizzying pattern of shifting brilliance. After a moment, she directed the light toward what was left of Emma's dad. His eyes stared blankly, a thin line of blood and spit dribbling from his shredded lips. There was no doubt he was dead.

She found Alex slouched near the sinks, rubbing a rising lump along his forehead, but he seemed mostly unfazed. Finally, Olivia turned her attention to the girl.

Emma sat huddled in the corner of the shower, her small body shaking with sobs.

"Shh, it's okay, baby." Olivia laid a gentle hand on the child's shoulder. "You're safe. Take my hand and"—she glanced once again at the dead man nearby—"keep your eyes closed."

CHAPTER 29

Hail assaulted the windows of the weight room. It raked on Olivia's nerves, but for the first time during the entire night, she was not utterly afraid. She had just killed an Infested. Watching the creature die on the floor had transformed it from a thing of unimaginable horror into a bug. Albeit a big bug that could kill her, but still, a bug.

Emma shifted in her arms. Olivia had carried the girl free of the changing room. She feared the child would not be able to break away from her place in the shower stall without help. Only with the darkness—in all its forms—left behind had she felt the kid begin to relax.

Alex walked in front of them, his pace quick and nervous, giving him a bird-like quality. He stopped at one of the padded benches lining the floor and sat down heavily upon it.

"That was fucking crazy." He attempted to push his glasses up the bridge of his nose, but his hand shook so much he missed the mark. "I thought we were dead."

Olivia placed the girl down as gently as her battered body would allow and turned her attention fully to the man. "Where the hell were you! I fell asleep on your couch, and when I woke up, you were gone. You left me alone!"

He raised his hand, trying to halt her accusations. "I never meant to do that. I thought you would be safe. I thought the deadbolt would be enough. Besides"—he glanced back to the changing room—"you seem to be capable enough."

His words stopped her. All evening, she had been searching for Liam, sure she couldn't survive on her own, and yet she had managed. Ever since the accident which robbed her of her mother, Olivia had hidden from life, afraid to make any sort of decision in case it was the wrong one. When she met Liam, there was a tremendous sense of relief. He always knew what he wanted and was more than happy to make the decisions for the both of them. But even then, during the long nights when he was working late, she couldn't help but to wonder if that hadn't been a form of running as well.

Olivia pushed away the uncomfortable line of thinking, returning her attention to Alex and his list of lies. "And then there's all the weird shit that seems to hover around you. A letter from the owner of this building, from Conrad Anderson himself, addressed to somebody named Meredith."

"Olivia, please," Alex begged, but she couldn't stop now.

The dam was broken. The flood was coming, and there would be no halting it.

"That's not all," she continued. "You also have a family portrait featuring said *billionaire* tucked behind your dinner table! You have a full wardrobe of women's clothes in your bedroom. And your computer!"

Alex jerked. "My computer?"

"Yes, your computer. The one you said was dead! The one with a bunch of Eosphoros crap on it!"

It appeared a switch had been flipped in him. He reached out and grabbed Olivia by the arms, his grip tight. "You have my computer? Thank God! When I went back to my place and saw it was gone, I was afraid everything was lost. Where is it?"

She hadn't expected him to react in such a profound manner at the mention of his laptop. Olivia stared at him, and he released his embrace, taking a step back. The sour stink of his sweat filled her nostrils, his breath buffeting across her face in hot waves. She slowly raised her arm and pointed across the cavern of exercise equipment, toward the storage closet. Alex blew out a relief-filled sigh and started making his way across the room.

"Okay, yes, you're right. There is a lot that I didn't tell you, and for that, I am really sorry," he said over his shoulder, moving away from her. "But you have to believe me that I had nothing to do with any of this. In fact, I was trying my best to stop it, permanently.

"Let me get my computer, and I'll tell you everything I know, everything about Eosphoros."

Alex placed the laptop on the bench and snapped it open. The screen immediately returned to life. The digital ghost-light from the display bathed across his face, turning his already pale complexion into a cadaver's.

Emma huddled next to Olivia. It was clear the kid was in shock, but she was quiet, and under the circumstances, Olivia figured that was about the best that could be hoped for.

"How much did you see?" Alex nodded to the screen of his computer.

"Not much. Just that there is something called Eosphoros, and it has a connection to the New Leaf and the Andersons."

"Right, well, we'll start with Eosphoros and then get into the Andersons later."

Alex gazed into the computer screen, his finger finding the brim of his glasses—giving them a small nudge—before speaking. "Eosphoros has existed for a long time. I'm talking, like, hundreds and hundreds of years, predating the Renaissance. Its exact origin is mostly lost to history, but from what I've been able to piece together, it began as something of a European medieval think tank. A small collection of society's brightest coming together, rebelling against the religious dogma of the age, in the pursuit of scientific enlightenment. One thing that is known though is that it was founded by a single woman, Helena, the first Matriarch of Eosphoros."

He slid his index finger across the touch pad, highlighting a folder as he spoke. Inside was a series of image files, each a painting depicting a circle of people performing various feats.

"Eosphoros was instantly ostracized and persecuted by the church, of course, but was mostly tolerated because of the admiration that it received from the citizens. The group was seen as a bright spot amidst a world gone dark."

Olivia looked at each image closely. "So, what happened next?"

"Eosphoros grew. Soon, the small collection of advanced thinkers was a fledgling society. And in a snap, Eosphoros went from a nuisance to the church to a threat, and they became a target of holy retribution. A raid, backed by Pope John the twenty-second himself, found Helena killed and the rest of Eosphoros scattered. The remaining members, including Helena's daughter, went underground. They left Europe altogether and found refuge in central Asia."

Alex exited out of the current crop of images and leaned back, looking at Olivia.

"Who knows what would have happened had the church not gotten involved. Eosphoros was working—thinking—so far ahead of their time."

"But—" Olivia began.

"*But* the church *did* get involved," he finished. "And, in a lot of ways, that involvement led to what came next."

A series of goosebumps rose across the skin of her arms and neck. It was a bizarre sensation, given the rampant heat stifling the entirety of the high-rise. The ominous nature of his remark, "what came next," made her want to ask—beg—him to stop talking. But she was afraid to interrupt the narration, to halt the story.

"Angry, bitter, resentful of the church, Eosphoros turned their attention toward the eradication of that religious institution," Alex said. "Instead of ways to help humanity, they started using their staggering intellect to create weapons."

"Were they successful? Did they launch an attack on the church?"

Alex bit his lower lip and looked from the computer to Olivia. "Yes and no. Yes, they had created something...horrible, devastating, but no, they never loosed it on their enemies—or, at least, not directly. During this time, there was a clash of ideals in Eosphoros. The new Matriarch, Helena's granddaughter, Dominica, wanted to bring more than the church to bow before Eosphoros. She wanted the world, and so, without the approval of the other members, she unleashed their creation to the broader society."

He turned back toward the laptop and launched a new collection of image files. Horrific paintings and illustrations of people dying in the streets. Bodies piled on the back of carts, with more waiting to be picked up at the side of the road. Sinister figures standing amongst the carnage, haunting masks with long beaks obscuring their faces.

"Are these...?" Olivia recognized the images. Her mind reeled at the sheer scope of what Alex appeared to be implying.

He nodded grimly.

"Wait." She felt a sudden need to move but fought the urge, instead shaking her head sharply. "You're telling me that this...Eosphoros was responsible for the plague? The Black Plague which wiped out half of Europe?"

"More like two thirds," he said quietly. "And it wasn't just Europe either. The plague originated in Asia. But yes, that is exactly what I'm saying."

His gaze shifted upward, lingering along the drop tile ceiling before it swung down and settled on her.

"Dominica, the Matriarch of Eosphoros, had taught the world a deep, harsh, lesson—science was as proficient at ending life as it was at bettering it.

"After that, all signs of Eosphoros disappear. The plague was blamed on rats, further reducing the secret society into a ghost, a myth.

"So, what's the connection? What does Eosphoros, medieval, enlightened thinkers turned mass murders, have to do with the New Leaf?"

"Well, like I said, Eosphoros went underground. The only evidence that they were still operating is conjecture at best. But if you know how to connect the dots, you can trace their influence across the years. Empires and religions have both benefited from Eosphoros's unique talents. Although the church had greatly diminished the organizations numbers, it failed to wipe it out. And, most importantly, the Matriarchal line endured as well."

"Matriarchal line?" Olivia interrupted him.

"Oh, right, sorry. I mentioned that Matriarch. Basically, Eosphoros is always fronted by a woman and heir of the first Matriarch, Helena."

"You mean," Olivia said, starting to understand, "all the Matriarchs since the beginning, since Helena, are descendants?"

"Yes. It is the Matriarchal line. Each reigning Matriarch passes the mantle on to their daughter, sister, niece, or other female relative."

Despite the horror of what Eosphoros had wrought, the idea of something of its sort existing for so long made Olivia feel numb. A female-led initiative founded during humanity's darkest days had been responsible for changing the world.

"So"—Alex cleared his throat—"like I was saying, the Matriarchal line survived, and in the early twentieth century, under the hand of Matriarch Mary Rosen, Eosphoros re-emerged."

Olivia pulled the collar of her dress to free the heat building between the fabric and her skin. "It's hard to imagine something like that being able to exist in the information age."

Alex smiled and nodded. "You're absolutely right. It can't. When Eosphoros resurfaced, it was a very different entity than when it vanished. Gone were the clandestine outings and secret rituals. In their place were board meetings and corporate mergers."

"They became a company," Olivia said, starting to put the pieces together which had been buzzing like flies in her brain.

"Specializing in weapon development." Alex exited back out to the desktop of his computer. "Over the last hundred years, the core company, Eosphoros, has buried itself in a multilayered shell of countless other companies and corporations, each utterly disposable and in service to their main objective."

"And the New Leaf? Us?" She looked between Alex and Emma. "Are we a part of the research?"

He nodded slowly. "I believe so, yes. The entire New Leaf project is nothing more than a field test set in a first-world nation. Eosphoros has done similar experiments in the past, but always somewhere poor, backwater. Third-world countries.

"Each resident of the New Leaf was very specifically chosen to represent as large a slice of Western life as possible. Most culled from smaller companies owned by Eosphoros. In many cases, the people have no idea they actually work for the larger entity."

Olivia tried her best to follow along, but it was a lot to digest. The realization Liam was employed, in some roundabout way, by these people—and what's worse, that he, and her by default, were actually chosen—boggled the mind.

"So, if what you're saying is true, then why now? The New Leaf project is years away from completion. Why let loose the Infested tonight?"

Alex looked sickly, his pallid skin shiny with sweat. "That brings us to the Andersons. Vera Anderson is the current reigning Matriarch of Eosphoros. Under her watch, the company has grown to new heights. But a few months ago, she fell ill, and her husband, Conrad, has been acting head until Vera recovers, or until she dies and a new Matriarch can be found.

"The problem is, Conrad has always been a bit unhinged, and it has gotten steadily worse since Vera's illness."

"Why would he be allowed to run Eosphoros?" Olivia asked.

"We're talking about a secret organization with some very deep and dark roots. Who knows why they do *anything*? Plus, in all the years since its birth, Eosphoros has never been without a Matriarch. This is uncharted territory."

A stuttering flash of lightning invaded the weight room, sending wild, thin shadows reaching across the floor. The rain continued unabated, but the hail had died down.

Olivia looked at Alex for a long moment. The young man seemed to be aware she wanted to ask him something, and he stiffened in anticipation.

"How do you know all this? You said the people in the painting were your grandparents. Is that true? Are you Conrad and Vera's grandson? If so, why are you here instead of up there?" She tilted her head up to gaze at the ceiling, through it, toward the penthouse. "Why are you trying to bring them down?"

Alex stood up, his hand falling over his mouth. "Yes, Conrad and Vera Anderson are my grandparents. And as to the *why* I'm not up there...well, it's a long story." Hard resolve fell across his face like a shroud. "And family or not, if I can put an end to the madness that is Eosphoros, then, well, I have to."

CHAPTER 30

Olivia's head swam with questions. She wanted to know more about Eosphoros, more about the Andersons and the New Leaf, and most importantly, more about Alex. Under the dire circumstances they found themselves in, she felt the man had no reason to lie about anything he had told her, but still, his revelations—large as they might be—felt like only the tip of the iceberg.

"Have you spoken to them?" Olivia asked.

"My grandparents? No, not entirely. Like I said, my grandma is very sick. From what I've been told, she suffers from severe dementia. Her body is fine, but her mind is gone. And grandpa is...well, as unstable as ever. I've had zero communication with them for years."

A quiver of revulsion laced with sorrow strummed through Olivia at the mention of Vera's mind being gone. Her mother's withered face, a slack, Halloween mask of its former self, reared in her mind. Olivia had been witness to such a condition, and it was not pleasant, a sight which, until very recently, ranked as the worst thing she had ever seen.

"Which is why, when I received the invite from Conrad, out of the blue, to come live here, I was skeptical, to say the least," Alex continued. "I think he wanted to bring me back—bring me into the fold."

Something about Alex's words did not jive with Olivia's memory. She had seen the invite the young man spoke of, and it had certainly not been addressed to him.

"Who is—" She intended to ask who the Meredith in the letter was referring to, but before she could finish her question, she felt a gentle tugging at the side of her dress.

Emma's wide eyes greeted her.

"What's that noise?" the girl asked.

"What noise, honey?"

The child tilted her head to the right, her ear hitched up. "That noise."

Olivia stilled her own churning thoughts and listened, really listened. It was hard to hear anything beyond the rain, but after a moment, she could indeed hear something. It was distant, a high-pitched hiss—the lunatic squeal of a deflating balloon.

Alex stood up and looked around the room. "Yeah, I hear it too. What the hell is that?"

"It sounds like the monster," Emma said, her voice nearly lost in the short distance between her thin lips and Olivia's ears.

Olivia realized the child was right. They had heard a similar shrill hiss come from the bug in the changing room, just before it died.

"Jesus! Do you think it's still alive?" Alex spoke quickly. He took a stuttering step toward the changing rooms, apparently coming to the same conclusion as to the origin of the sound as Olivia had. "Maybe we didn't kill it."

"No, the bug was dead." Olivia couldn't help but scrunch her eyebrows as a deep memory from her youth pinged through her brain.

When she was five, her mom had agreed to watch a friend's dog for a month while they were abroad. Olivia had been ecstatic, of course. What five-year-old doesn't want a canine pal to chum around with. The dog in question, a sassy Bassett Hound named Bosco, settled in quickly. He would waddle around the perimeter of their backyard for hours after the sun went down, his powerful snout glued to the ground.

Now, as she heard the hiss from the nearby Infested, she couldn't help but think of Bosco and his other nightly ritual. Bosco loved to howl. A deep, bass-filled bellow would erupt from his muzzle, bouncing off the nearby houses, filling the air. Had someone asked Olivia before Bosco came to stay with them how many dogs lived in her neighborhood, she would have been hard pressed to think of even one other. But that first night, when he pointed his nose to the moon and unleashed his mournful howl, within minutes, a half-dozen similar haunting yowls came echoing back in response. When Olivia brought it to her mom's attention, the woman told her howling was Bosco's way of calling his friends.

"They're answering," Olivia said numbly.

"What?" Alex asked.

She glanced around the room, the space suddenly feeling much tighter than its open dimensions should allow. "The bug we killed. I think it was calling for help."

Alex's mouth went slack. "That means..." He began to pace.

Emma moaned. "Are they going to get us?"

Olivia thought about it, her mind retracing her own access to the fitness level. They should be safe enough. The doors were locked, and unlike Alex's apartment, they were made of metal, Olivia herself only having gained access thanks to the body propping open the way. But before she could reassure the girl, she had a sudden, distressing thought.

"Alex, how did you get up here?"

"What? Here? The fitness level?"

"Yes. Did you come up the east stairwell?"

He appeared to think about it for a moment, no doubt trying to identify which stairwell was which. "Yes. No, wait." He pointed toward the far side of the floor. "Is that the east stairwell?"

"No, that's the west."

"Oh, well, that's the way I came."

"How'd you get past the locked door?" She could barely hear her own words over the blood rushing through her ears.

"What do you mean? There was no door! It had been taken down. It looked like it was being repaired or something."

Olivia's mind barely registered everything which had followed *there was no door*. Pushing away from Emma, Alex, and his computer, she ran toward the west stairwell exit. Her heart pounded like a piston in her chest, each thump sending a tremor though her body.

"Olivia?" Alex called after her. "Stop!"

But she couldn't stop. She had to know.

Olivia cleared the corner of the weight room and shuffled past the changing rooms, a tingle of revulsion skittering across her flesh at the memories held within. She directed her attention to the upcoming exit.

Alex was right. The door, off its hinges, was leaning against the wall, a square hole near the knob indicating where the key card lock would go when it was installed.

Olivia froze, staring through the entrance, to the red light beyond—it looked more like a gateway to hell than a simple threshold. She could hear a rampant shuffling coming from the other side. Before her brain could fully send the command to flee, she watched as a vague, amorphous shape began to materialize before her. It appeared, at first, like a tidal wave of shadowy limbs, but quickly coalesced into its real form—a horde of Infested. The lead, a man who was completely nude, a tattoo of a dragon decorating part of his chest, came to a juddering stop. The insect hanging out of his mouth emitted a sound akin to that of a dentist's drill.

"Olivia, what is it?" Alex called from somewhere behind her, his voice sounding like a cheap recording, a deteriorating duplicate of the real thing.

Before Olivia could answer him, she saw the naked Infested tense up, the bug pulling back in. And as if cracked by a whip, the man charged, the rest of the swarm right behind him.

CHAPTER 31

"**R**un!" Olivia shouted.

As she turned her back on the monsters, she noticed something. *They're all men!*

Even as the things fumbled and crawled over each other to get in, to reach Olivia and her two companions, she couldn't help but to realize each and every single one of them was a man and had been all night.

Alex stiffened at the sight but only for a moment before twisting around and breaking into a sloppy sprint. He almost collided with Emma—who had followed behind him. He reached for the girl, but his momentum carried him past.

"I have her!" Olivia yelled, and she broke into a mad dash of her own. "Keep running!" She reached out and snatched the girl's hand, pulling her tiny body along with her.

Olivia watched disbelievingly as Alex diverted from his straight path to the east stairwell exit and instead beelined for his computer.

"Leave it!" Olivia screamed.

"I can't! Everything I have on Eosphoros—on my grandparents—is on there. If I lose it, I lose everything!" he shouted, disappearing into the gloom.

"Don't you have a backup?"

"I do! But it's in my apartment!"

Olivia shook her head. She couldn't worry about Alex and his paranoia, not with Emma in hand. She pushed forward, covering the distance of the weight room in seconds. The entire floor seemed to collapse in on itself, a folding of dimensions. It made gauging the distance to the exit impossible to determine. She was aware of the girl screaming in her grasp, just as she was also conscious of the countless slapping feet pursuing them, but neither thing could break her focus. Her entire being was centered on one action—running.

The corpse of the woman near the east door appeared in the darkness like a familiar landmark. Olivia pulled the child over the body and slammed into the exit, twisting the handle. The door gave under her weight, swinging open. She whispered a small prayer of thanks that the lock had been designed to keep from entering, not exiting. Olivia stumbled into the landing, turning in time to see Alex barely in front of the mob.

"Hurry!" she screamed.

He leapt over the woman—his computer bag bouncing against his side—and joined Olivia and Emma.

The naked Infested, still in the lead, either didn't or couldn't see the corpse and ran right into it, tripping forward into a sprawl. The spill caused a momentary stopgap in the horde behind him. Olivia watched half a dozen forms pile-up over the dead lady.

It seemed the woman had saved her again.

Olivia left the tangle of thrashing limbs behind and directed her companions toward the downward stairs just as the first Infested managed to clear the obstacle and exit after them.

The dry, dusty air of the stairwell buffeted against her face, and she descended. She wanted to be concerned about missing a step, of twisting an ankle in the utter, profound darkness, but there just wasn't any more room for worry in her brain. The little girl—her delicate hand feeling almost doll-like in Olivia's grip—and the stumbling, roiling horde of Infested thundering down the steps behind her occupied all available space.

Olivia wanted to look back, almost needed to, but forced herself to keep her gaze locked ahead. If the Infested were going to catch them, there would be no helping it. No amount of foresight into such an event would save them.

Like a rising fog, the dust in the air thickened the farther down they went. When they passed the door for the twelfth floor, the stuff had taken on a density deep enough to almost obscure the numbers on the door. Miniscule particles, highlighted in the bloody glare, twisted and danced in their wake. Where was it coming from? It made the act of breathing, already difficult from the heat and strenuous activity, a hellish chore.

The downward charge was relentless. As they rushed through the dusty pea-soup atmosphere clogging the landing on level 10, Olivia found a new fountain of energy bubbling up inside of her. One thing she could remember quite clearly of the New Leaf's layout was that there were no residential levels below the 10th floor. Everything from there to the lobby was unoccupied. It meant the threat of danger would be much less for the rest of their descent.

The clatter of Infested still echoed off the walls, but it was clear the horde had not been able to keep the same pace as their prey. Olivia assumed this was thanks to the reckless way the Infested moved. She imagined at least a few of them must have rendered themselves incapacitated, or worse, during the plunge down.

Olivia spun around the last turn before the 9th floor landing and gasped. In the ruby glow from the emergency lights, she noticed something odd about the stairs dropping down beyond.

She gripped the girl tight and came to halting stop. Her lungs burned, and it felt like she was breathing fire.

"Wait!" she yelled to Alex, the man spinning to look at her even as he did as she asked.

Olivia had to take a moment to let what she was seeing fully register. The next set of stairs was gone. Not just lost to the darkness, but actually absent. Leaning over the edge, she could see clear down to the next landing below; a square patch lit in red.

"Where are they?" Emma shrieked. "Where are the stairs!"

Olivia couldn't speak. All she could manage was to shake her head.

"Oh Jesus," Alex said between great, heaping breaths.

Above them, the racket grew. The Infested were getting closer.

Olivia grabbed up the child again and reached out for the 9th floor door, but it didn't open. It had a key card reader like the one found on the fitness level.

"Fuck," she grunted. "We have to go back up a floor."

Alex's mouth hung open to speak, but then he nodded and started to climb.

The ascent was painful, the physical equivalent of moving a mountain. If not for the clamor of Infested crashing down on them with all the inevitability of an avalanche, Olivia imagined she would not be able to coax her muscles to move at all.

Olivia rounded the stairs to the landing for the 9th floor. They were out of time. The pursuing Infested had reached them.

"This way!" Olivia shouted.

Less than a second after they pushed through the stairwell door to reach the 10th floor corridor, it banged open a second time. She had been too afraid to look back while running down the steps, but in the moment, she had to know. How many were still after them?

Three Infested, all men, all in their thirties, all with horrifically mangled mouths, pinballed into the tight space.

"Where are we going?" Alex screamed, rushing down the hall, bringing up the rear behind Olivia and Emma.

Olivia wished she had an answer.

Ahead of them, a door suddenly opened up, and an old woman wearing a nightgown and slippers stepped out into the hallway. Instantly, a portrait of who this woman was painted itself across Olivia's mind. She was a frightened old lady, confused and alone. Hearing the horrible ruckus in the hall, had wandered out.

The elderly woman squared her shoulders so she was facing Olivia, Emma, and Alex—along with the three murderous nightmares behind them—and raised one thin arm. Olivia was sure the woman was pointing at the Infested, like maybe Olivia wasn't aware she was being chased by a trio of monstruous maniacs, but then she saw the gun held in the old lady's hand. The sheen of the weapon collecting the red from the emergency lights turned the pistol—a revolver—into a glowing artifact from another world.

All of Olivia's preconceived notions of who the woman was fell apart.

"Get inside, quick!" the woman shouted.

Olivia, directing Emma, brushed passed the armed lady and entered an apartment bathed in candlelight. Alex was right behind her. As soon as they were out of the line of fire, the pistol roared. Two massive claps, loud enough to give the thunder outside a run for its money.

The gun-toting woman quickly stepped back inside and slammed the door closed.

CHAPTER 32

Olivia was stunned. The night of endless twists had just taken another. With the sound of gunfire still ringing in her ears, she watched the elderly woman scurry to lock the entrance to her apartment. Besides the standard deadbolt and chain each unit came with, three more locks—twin sliding locks and another deadbolt—had been affixed to the inside of the door. Finally, as the secure cherry on top, she hefted a bar from the floor and fit it across a bracket, barring the entire thing. Had Alex had a similar set up, Olivia would still be sitting safe within the walls of his abode.

"Thank goodness I heard you out there," the woman said, moving gingerly toward them.

Before any of the small group could reply, the senior citizen's face contorted into a knot of liver spots and loose skin.

"Damn it! One of them got in!"

The gun jumped back up, stabbing forward—a dog begging to be let off the chain—and pointed directly at Alex.

Realizing what was about to happen, Olivia raced over and stood in front of him. "No, wait, he's not an Infested!"

Switching the gun between hands, like playing some sort of deadly game of hot potato with herself, the old lady took a shuffling step closer to Alex. Olivia could see the woman's knuckles pressing against thin skin. They looked large, deformed, like milky tumors perverting the otherwise passive nature of the frail, old hands.

"Infested? I don't know what you're talking about."

Olivia pointed at the front door and the hallway beyond. "Them! The people with the fucking bugs in their throats!"

Turning her head at a glacial pace until she was looking at the door, the old woman replied, "Them? Those men? They are thugs, criminals, brigands! They only want to hurt us. But don't worry, I won't let them in here." She returned her attention to Olivia and sneered. "And there is no need for such language. Women who swear reveal themselves as being common."

The look in the elderly woman's eyes—the whites turned egg-yolk yellow, thanks to the light from numerous candles—revealed something to Olivia. The lady was not mentally sound. There was a chasm in her gaze, like a large piece of the woman's foundation was missing.

"Please." A ripple slid across Alex's voice as he spoke. "I won't hurt you."

The gun-wielding senior moved closer still, the weapon now firmly affixed to her right hand, the barrel erect—a metal finger pointed at Alex's chest. "Oh no, no, no, you can't fool me. You're just like the rest. A liar."

"That's not true," Olivia blurted. "His name is Alex, and he saved my life several times tonight. And I'm Olivia, and this"—she beckoned the child closer to her—"is Emma. What's your name?" Olivia asked, hoping, praying, she could diffuse the situation.

"Saved your life, you say."

For just a moment, the gun wavered, and the black eye of the weapon staring Alex down shifted. Olivia had a vision of the woman pulling the trigger anyway. After a beat, the pistol lowered completely, eventually sliding home into one of the oversized pockets jutting from the side of the woman's bathrobe.

The old lady groaned and turned away from Alex. "In all my eighty-one years, I've yet to meet a man that I could trust. But with those ruffians in the hallways running amok, I guess I can make an exception." And with that, as if a switch had been thrown, the trigger-happy woman before them transformed into a grandmotherly figure who was all warm smiles. "And my name is Beth. Beth Laponte.

"Now then, can we get you nice folks some iced tea?"

Condensation collected, then dribbled down the can to collect between Olivia's fingers. She imagined her body temperature had risen to an unhealthy degree. First, the sweltering heat in the building, and then the intense physical exertion she had endured throughout the night—coming to a head with a sprint down the entire building. Her internal furnace was burning so hot it threatened to melt the walls of her core.

She brought the can to her forehead and twisted it back and forth. The chilled water hopping off the tin, smearing across her skin, felt like heaven. Beth had told them the secret to keeping things cold during a blackout was to only open the fridge when absolutely necessary.

The iced tea was a cheap, over-sweet brand. Olivia looked at the label on the can and recognized it as belonging to a local grocery store—maybe even one previously owned by Mr. Elliot himself. But the pleasant chill which rolled down her throat couldn't be beat.

Beth's apartment, which was, curiously, slightly smaller than Olivia's own—the ceiling wasn't as high—was decorated to the nines. Dated, patterned furniture, including the sofa she was sitting on, was positioned around the living and dining rooms. Stacks of books sat in neat piles around the place like tiny skyscrapers of literature. Dozens of paintings and photographs hung from the walls. She was amazed a person could so completely fill their living space in only half a year. Groupings of candles stood huddled together on any surface flat enough to house them, illuminating the space to an impressive degree.

"You're lucky we heard you out there," Beth mumbled. She had been pacing in and out of the kitchen since letting them into her home.

Olivia couldn't help but stare at the gun jutting from the pocket of Beth's robe each time she walked by. In the orange light, the handle of the weapon looked like the end of an extremely overripe banana.

"Yes, lucky indeed."

Alex, his iced tea still unopened, watched the woman intently from his seat atop a large, cedar chest positioned against the wall—right where Olivia's television would be in her own home. His eyes shifted in his skull every time Beth wandered between the living room and the kitchen. Olivia couldn't blame him. If she had almost been introduced to the business end of that handgun, she wouldn't let Beth out of her sights either.

"So...Beth," Alex said, easing his way to standing. "The Infest...I mean, the men out there"—he nodded toward the front door—"is that the first time you saw them tonight?"

"What kind of question is that?" Beth's croaked, ancient fingers hovered near her pocket.

Alex raised his hands, concern etching his face with weary lines. "I'm sorry. I didn't mean anything by it. In fact, you helped us out big time. They were after us. If you hadn't come out, we'd be toast."

For a moment, her teeth gnashed together before her features slackened completely and a warm smile stretched her thin lips. "Well, I guess you didn't mean anything by it. You are a man, after all. And to answer your question, yes, we did have an...encounter with them earlier."

Beth moved over to one of the chairs, a wingback upholstered in burgundy, and sat with an audible groan.

"Those men," she said, waving a withered hand dismissively through the air, "will settle down once the power comes back on. Like wild animals, they are. Acting civilized when eyes are upon them, but as soon as nobody is looking, the beast comes out."

Sparing a glance at Alex, Beth leaned forward, her gaze directed toward Olivia.

"Women have to stick together whenever we can," she whispered. Then, turning her attention toward Emma, she continued, "We have to protect each other, keep each other safe from the bad ones."

They sat quietly for a time. The only sound besides the storm was the soft whistle of Emma's purr-like snore. The girl's body had decided it had seen enough excitement for one night, it seemed, and had simply shut-off. The silence would have been almost serene, if not for the occasional bang or, worse yet, scream, which had a knack of arriving just at the quietest moments, just when Olivia felt herself relaxing. It was an unfriendly reminder they were still buried up to their necks in a nightmare. Monsters still lurked the halls of the New Leaf.

"Well, if you'll excuse me for a moment, I need to freshen up. I love a good iced tea, but it goes through this old body quick." Beth pushed herself up from the chair, her arms shaking with the effort.

Now that she mentioned it, Olivia had to use the bathroom as well. "I could really use a pee break myself." She looked toward the spare bathroom. "Do you mind?"

"Sorry, the guest washroom is not working. We've complained to the building manager, but he never seemed to care all that much."

"Okay, then do you mind if I come with you and use the master?"

Beth's eyes widened—a dozen furrows of aged skin bunched along her forehead as a result. "I'd prefer not. I like to keep my washroom private. If you've got to make water, do so on the balcony. The rain'll wash it away."

Under different circumstances, she would have asked if pissing on the balcony also revealed a woman to be "common," but as long as Beth had the gun, Olivia would play by her rules.

"Beth," Alex spoke up from his place in the living room, "you keep saying 'we' and 'our'. Does somebody else live here?"

The old woman laughed, a ridiculous snort which sounded somehow patronizing. "Of course, somebody else lives here. Marianne. My sister." She continued to chuckle to herself as she turned away from the group and started down the short hall to the bedrooms.

"Wait," Olivia said. "If your sister lives her, where is she?"

Beth stopped moving forward, her body rocking slowly. Without looking back, she said, "Marianne is sleeping, and I would like very much for you not to wake her."

Olivia watched Beth shuffle away until the old woman reached the bedroom door. She looked over her shoulder at Olivia, her hand resting on the butt of the gun, before disappearing into the room. A loud click, most likely the result of a lock, could be heard.

CHAPTER 33

Olivia pressed her fingers to the window. Thick, billowy curtains hung from a thin rod running the length of the panes of glass along the top, but the fabric had been bunched off to the far right of the room, held in place by a gold, braided rope. The rain had slowed to a slight pattering against the glass. A distant flash of lighting revealed the storm was on the move, directing its fury somewhere else.

The old woman's apartment was stiflingly hot. Sweat coated Olivia's entire body like a second skin. A tangy cloud of funk hovered around her, a mixture of her own perspiration, bleach, and the rank ichor which had dribbled from the mouth of the changing room Infested. Her limbs ached from dozens of bruises. Small explosions of irresistible itchiness centered around the cuts and scrapes on her face and scalp. Her hand would twitch up wild, her nails dragging across the offending spot, only for her to pull it back and find newly coagulated blood collected underneath her cuticles.

She considered venturing onto the woman's balcony, letting the storm wash away much of the grime the evening had dumped on her, but thought better of it. She doubted Beth had much that would fit her, and the thought of sitting in sopping wet clothing was not an appealing one.

Olivia turned away from the window and moved over to the sofa and the young child lying there. With her dirty clothes and matted hair, Emma looked a fright, a tiny ghoul curled in exhausted slumber.

Beth had never returned from the bathroom. Olivia thought it best, given the tension between the old woman and Alex, that she let Beth simmer down before searching for her.

She looked around, finding it odd that nowhere in the collection of antiques, art, and books was there a clock. Olivia had lost all track of time, like the many shocks to her system she had endured throughout the night had caused her to come unglued from it.

Sitting down, she caused the girl to stir.

"Olivia?"

"It's okay, honey. We're safe. Go back to sleep." Olivia rubbed the girl's head.

The child looked from Olivia toward the windows on the far side of the room and back again. "Is it still storming out?"

"Yes, but I think it's starting to slow down. The worst is behind us."

"Olivia?" Emma pulled herself to sitting.

"Yes?"

"I meant to tell you, earlier, before Daddy..."

A brief wave of pain filled the little girl's face. Olivia hugged her. After the embrace, Emma continued.

"I think I have something of yours."

"What do you mean?"

Emma reached for her pocket. Olivia vaguely recalled the child doing something similar when she first introduced herself. Fishing around inside, the exaggerated way only a kid could, Emma pulled out a folded piece of paper.

"I found this while looking for Mom. It was crumpled. It has your name on it. Is it yours?" Emma held the paper out.

Slowly, Olivia took the folded piece of parchment—crazed lines in the paper reinforcing her claim of its crumbled state. "I don't see how it could be."

Still, she was mystified by the idea her name might be scrawled within, so she unfolded it. Before any writing became visible, Olivia saw the cartoon dog. Her heart skittered at the sight.

My Dearest Liam,
    I am sorry to do this to you, but I can't take it anymore. Every night I put on a false face for you. I deceive you. You think I'm happy, but I'm not. I don't think that I ever could be again. A part of me died with my mother, and it has taken until now for the decay to reach my soul. Please don't blame yourself. There was nothing you could have done.

I will always love you.
Olivia.

"What?" She held the paper in the space between her and the child. "You found this going into the pool?"

Emma nodded.

"I don't understand." She returned to the note. It looked like her handwriting, but not quite. The very end, the last few words, were somebody else's. She couldn't place some of it, but she had received enough cards, letters, and gifts over the years from her husband to recognize the way he wrote her name. He always made the O so grand. The letter had been penned by him but made to look like she had done it.

"Is it a sad note?" Emma's voice carried a tone of melancholy.

Olivia, eyes filling with tears, shook her head.

"No, it's..." She stared at the words, at their meaning, before forcing a smile for Emma. "It's not even for me. It's for a different Olivia."

This seemed to placate the girl, and she nodded.

"Why don't you lay back down, honey? It will be morning before you know it. And we'll all get out of this place."

Olivia waited until the girl had returned to slumber before raising and moving across the room. A mean series of tremors had begun to arc across her body.

"Everything okay?" Alex asked. He had taken up residence near the door. A tactic that would, seemingly, ensure he was the first line of defense against any invading Infested, but would also allow him a quick escape if Beth became unhinged.

"Huh? Oh, yeah." Her answer might have been good enough had she not started to cry.

Alex hurried over. "What's the matter? Besides, you know, the obvious."

Olivia debated telling him what Emma had turned over to her. She couldn't imagine how the note had ended up in a ball on the fitness level, but the message the writing was meant to deliver seemed clear enough.

"I think my husband tried to kill me."

To his credit, Alex took this news in stride. "Um, okay. How?"

She held the torn piece of paper out for him to inspect. As he read it over, she said, "I had a drink with my husband tonight and, soon after, passed out. I've never blacked out like that before. When I woke, I found an empty pill bottle in my kitchen. The label had been torn off, but the medication name remained. Temazepam."

"Sleeping pills," Alex automatically replied.

That makes sense. Olivia delivered a sad nod. "And then, Emma found this upstairs."

Alex regarded the note a second time. "It does look like a—"

"Suicide note," Olivia finished for him.

"Okay?" Alex's eyes shifted through the words applied to the page before coming up to meet her own. "So...why aren't you dead?"

"At some point, I fell out of bed and vomited. I must have puked up the worst of it."

"But, if you don't mind me asking, why? Why would he do this? Are you having trouble?"

"With our marriage? No. Or at least, I didn't think so." Olivia rubbed her forehead. This added revelation felt heavier than any the night had already delivered. "Maybe? I think...I think when my mom died, I never recovered. It was like the car we were in just kept on crashing. A never-ending wreck spanning years. This note"—she flicked the page still held in Alex's hand—"isn't wrong. A part of me did die that night, and it left a hole. That void continued to grow, until the day I met Liam. In him, I found somebody that I could place there, in the hollow, that would stop it from eating away at the rest of me. I think that's what he liked about me, my dependence on him. At least at first.

"God, I'm pathetic. No wonder he secretly hated me."

Alex's mouth turned down, the set of his lips grim. "Bullshit. Besides, that's not a reason to kill someone. People break up all the time. It doesn't usually end in murder."

"You have to know my husband." Even as she was speaking, missing pieces of her life, ones which had been invisible to her, suddenly came into clear focus. "Liam's ego would never allow it. He's so concerned with what others think of him. Leaving me, well..." She laughed quietly, but there was no mirth in the sound. "It would have made him look bad. And even had he tried, I would have fought to keep him. I would have made it tough. I'm too afraid of being alone. Because the truth is, I'm a coward."

Alex shook his head, his sweaty hair dragging across his forehead. "No. You're no coward. I haven't known you long, but you are as tough as nails."

She wished she could believe that, but it felt false. A label meant for somebody else, anybody but her.

Alex folded the paper back up and handed it to her. "Okay, my turn."

CHAPTER 34

"Y ou asked me who Meredith was." Alex took a noticeable breath, his thin frame rising and falling. "Alright, so, you know Eosphoros was founded by my ancestor, Helena, and the Matriarchal line has continued until my grandma, Vera, took over the mantle from her great Aunt.

"It was very difficult for my grandparents to conceive. It led to a lot of strain within the organization. Since my grandma was an only child, if she died, there would be no one to take the mantle of Matriarch. However, all the concern was for naught because, after a time, Meredith, my mom, was born. She would be the couple's only child, but she was a girl, and so it was all they needed.

"I was three when my parents died in a plane crash—did I already tell you that?"

Olivia nodded.

"Right, well, anyway, after that I went to live with my grandparents."

Alex stopped talking. Olivia could see tears begin to roll down his cheeks. She wanted to hold him, encourage him, but she still felt cored by the contents of the note so only nodded for him to take his time.

"Like I said, I was still practically a goddamn baby when they took me in. It's not like I had any say in the matter."

"Say in the matter of what, Alex?"

"Grandma was crazy with grief. Not only had she lost her daughter, her only child, but she had also lost her heir. I guess it was around that time that she must have realized that she had an opportunity to right the ship, so to speak."

He looked at her, his eyes peeking over the top-most rim of his glasses like frightened gophers. It made him appear vulnerable.

"Whatever it is, Alex, I'm here for you." She meant it.

Alex held up his finger for her to wait and hurried over to the counter where he placed his own iced tea. The can jittered a bit in his nervous hand. He popped the tab and tilted it back.

Olivia could see a drop of amber liquid slide down his chin because of it.

Placing the drink down, he returned. "From the ages of three to six-teen, I was raised as a girl."

Olivia was stunned. "You mean, the girl in the painting..."

"Yes, that was me. I was supposed to be the heir to Eosphoros, the next Matriarch. The plan was to raise me as their second daughter, conceived through the miracle of modern science, named in honor of their first, Meredith. Once I was old enough, they would discreetly schedule a surgery which would make it complete."

The enormity, and downright cruelty, of such an act—forcing a child to be something they weren't for personal gain for so long—made Olivia grit her teeth.

"Those years"—Alex wiped a runaway tear from his cheek—"were the worst of my life. Not only was I being forced, brainwashed, into believing that I was this other person, but just the act of living with my grandparents was a crushing weight all its own. Grandma was obsessed with ushering Eosphoros into a new era. Everything she did was in service to that, even in loving me. All of it meant to strengthen Eosphoros. And my grandfather, well, he was so subservient to his wife. Whatever will he possessed had been thoroughly beaten out of him, the cost of which was starting to show by the time I hit my teens. He was clearly losing his mind. In fact, I think after a time, Grandpa believed I actually was his daughter."

Olivia was horrified. She had to clear her throat before speaking, otherwise no words would have been able to emerge. "What happened? Obviously, you left, or got away."

A slow, determined nod preceded a stiffening of his face. "I did—get away, that is. When I was sixteen, my grandparents had to oversee a project."

He adjusted his glasses and turned toward Olivia.

"I had little understanding regarding the nature of their business. I knew they ran a company called Eosphoros, but both my grandparents spoke of it in such broad, general terms, that I could never get my head around just exactly what it was. Overseas projects, contracts, and deliveries. Everything sounded so mundane. I can only assume that the full breadth of Eosphoros would have been revealed to me when I reached adulthood.

"At any rate," he continued, "I made the most of the opportunity and ran away from home. I had enough money saved up to live for a few years, at least."

"Did they look for you?" Olivia asked.

"Of course. Grandma was furious. She threatened me with all sorts of things, from lawsuits to death. But they had betrayed me so deeply for most of my life that I literally didn't care. Besides, I suspected that all their threats were empty. As ruthless as they could be, I think they loved me—at least Grandpa did. And given even my limited knowledge of their activities would be enough to cause them problems if the information got out, they ultimately left me alone."

"That's..." Olivia finally reached out. She took both his hands in her own. "That's horrible. I'm so sorry."

"Yeah, well, I made it through," he said casually, but Olivia could hear the scars the experience had left buried deep inside of him sour his words. "I was content to let it go, let my grandparents go, but I knew I would never really be free of it. Eosphoros is just too big. It would catch up to me one day. Because of that, after hiding for so long, I made the decision to return. To mine their secrets. I devoured anything I could about Eosphoros, about my birthright. As it turns out, my familial connections still carry weight, even in my estranged state, and I was able to dig fairly deep into the roots of my family tree."

"That's one way to get back at them."

Olivia's comment drew a scoff from Alex.

"It's not about revenge, or at least, not anymore. Maybe once, when I was younger, but now...now it's about setting things right."

Alex pulled away from Olivia, her hands falling free from his.

"Anyway, I had hit a dead-end in my research. I was starting to make connections that weren't even there. I thought it was over when, out of the blue, I received a letter. It was from Conrad. It was the opportunity I needed. Considering the letter was addressed to Meredith, I knew that his fragile state had not gotten better. Eager to exploit a potential chink in the armor of Eosphoros, I wrote him back.

"We corresponded for a time. Most of it was nonsense. He clearly believed he was communing with his long dead daughter. But occasionally, he would mention grandma and her illness. A nurse living on site, the twelfth floor, was coming up daily to see to her medical needs."

"Have you talked to him, to Conrad, since you've been here? Like, in person?"

Alex bit his lip. "When I arrived this morning and found that he had taken the liberty of supplying me with a new wardrobe"—he tilted his head toward the dress Olivia wore—"I immediately went to the penthouse to see him."

"What happened?"

"My suspicions were correct. Without Grandma to keep him on his tether, he's completely lost it. For the few minutes we spoke, he rambled near incoherently. He spoke of Eosphoros, of making it bigger than it could have ever been. Of how all it ever needed was a man in charge. When I asked about grandma, asked if I could see her, his eyes would dart around insanely, before saying that she was gone. Gone. Over and over again. I thought I would be ready to face him," Alex said, looking off into the darkness of a nearby corner.

Olivia couldn't imagine how difficult it must have been for him to return. She found new admiration for his courage.

"I couldn't take any more, and so I bailed. I thought about leaving completely, about calling a cab and getting the hell away from the New Leaf and my family forever, but something about the look in my grandfather's eyes…It was like staring into pools with no bottoms. I knew that something was going to happen, something I had to see, to chronicle, and so I stayed."

"Well, I, for one, am happy you did."

Alex laughed. "Listen, I'm thrilled to have met you and all, but had I known this shit was going to go down, my ass would be in a hotel right now."

Olivia snorted, stepped close, and hugged the thin man.

"Have you tried to contact him?" she asked after releasing her embrace. "Since everything went to shit?"

His head bobbed up and down. "That's where I went—when I left you alone in my apartment. I thought if I could get up there, if I could talk to him, I might be able to put an end to this. But if he is up there, he isn't answering."

Olivia recalled the silhouette haunting the window of the penthouse. *Oh, he's up there all right.*

"Why would he end it though? If this is an Eosphoros experiment, wouldn't this, all this"—she waved her arms around her—"be planned to the nth degree?"

"But that's what I was saying earlier. This isn't right. The New Leaf project isn't supposed to be initiated until all three buildings are constructed. This—tonight—is impromptu. According to everything I can find about Eosphoros and its practices, what's happening here is different. It's unprecedented."

She waited for more, but like a spent balloon, it appeared as though Alex had nothing left to vent. All the new information swirled through her mind in a dizzying cyclone.

"You think it's Conrad, don't you? He's gone off the deep end."

His reply came in the form of a small nod.

CHAPTER 35

They stood together near the balcony door, watching the weather play its hand across the landscape. Olivia realized they had both just emptied their souls to each other, and she, for one, was exhausted for it.

Olivia laid her palm against the glass. "Okay, I guess the question we need to ask is, how do we get out of here?"

"Well, the stairwell is obviously out. In retrospect, it makes sense that they would collapse them. I should have saw it coming. The New Leaf was designed as a testing ground, a massive petri dish made of metal and concrete. Eosphoros wouldn't make it so that the rats could simply walk out the front door. I think it also explains why the cell phones aren't working either. Everything is under their control." He pursed his lips. "At least we know what caused the huge bang while you were passed out."

Olivia turned from the glass. "Shit. But there must be a way, right? Your grandfather wouldn't trap himself here."

Alex appeared to consider this. "The blueprints for the building show a helipad on the roof. But even that would only be accessible through the penthouse. And, unless you have some demolition gear, we can't get in there."

Something Alex had said earlier came back to Olivia. A thought triggered by talk of the Anderson's residence above them. "Wait, you said—"

"What are you talking about?" Beth's voice pulled both Olivia and Alex away from their conversation.

"The storm," Olivia quickly replied before Alex could say anything. "It looks like it might be slowing down." She didn't trust the old woman.

Beth moved gingerly, like her bones ached to the point of near incapacity, and stopped near the slumbering form of Emma. "Is she your daughter?"

When Olivia had first married Liam, she had imagined a day when they would have children, happy little souls filling their home with laughter and joy. It always seemed like a foregone conclusion sitting on the horizon of their lives. She thought now how silly that way of thinking had been. The death of her mom should have taught her nothing was assured. And with the reality of what had transpired within the walls of her home earlier in the night, the idea of children with Liam had completely evaporated.

"No. We found her upstairs. Her dad, he was...trying to hurt her."

Beth shook her head and blew out a whistling sigh. "I know too well the horrors a father can inflict upon his child."

The old woman leaned over, her back creaking like the hull of some ancient ship, and caressed Emma's hair.

"She reminds me of Marianne. I swear, when we were kids, that girl could sleep through the end of the world. I would shake her and shake her, and just when I would start getting scared maybe something was wrong with her, she'd spring to life, scaring me half to death."

"I always wanted a sibling." Olivia smiled. "Marianne sounds like fun...I'd like to meet her."

A pregnant pause filled the entirety of Beth's apartment. The old woman's face was slack, her eyes momentarily unfocused. "Well, you can't. She's resting."

Alex looked over at Olivia, his eyes going wide for a moment.

"I just think," Olivia said, "that maybe we could all sit together, until this thing blows over."

"I said no! My sister, God love her, is too trusting. Until I know you lot mean us no harm, I'll let her sleep." She looked between Olivia and Alex, her gaze ultimately settling on him.

Feeling the tension thicken, Olivia tried to change the subject. "Have you always lived in this area, Beth?"

"What? No." Beth left the spot next to the sofa and sat heavily in a rocking chair off to the left. "I grew up out west, on the coast."

"Oh, I've always wanted to see the West Coast," Alex said, his tone light. "Is it as beautiful as I've heard?"

She glared at him, her lips a collection of whitening creases. "No, it's not. I grew up in a house that had only one bedroom. We—me and Marianne—shared it with our father."

"That sounds rough." Alex chuckled nervously. His hands fidgeted in his lap, betraying any attempt he made at trying to look relaxed.

"Rough?" Beth snarled, rising to her feet—a move made almost comical thanks to the rocking chair. "'Rough', he says. Typical man."

Olivia could see Emma begin to stir as a result of Beth's elevated volume. She wanted to shush the woman but was keenly aware Beth's knobby hand had returned to its place near the handle of the pistol, the weight of which caused her pocket to sag.

"Sorry, I was trying to be glib," Alex said, his palms held out in a calming gesture.

"Let me tell you something," the old woman growled. "My childhood was a thing of misery. Sharing a room, a bed, with an alcoholic father... Well, there were some really awful nights."

"Listen, Beth, I really didn't mean anything—" Alex began.

"You never *mean* anything, do you?" she snapped back.

"I'm sorry? I don't know—"

"You men. You take take take, but hey, you don't really *mean* it. You take whatever you want, whenever you want it!" Beth vibrated with rage. Flecks of spittle snuck past her thin lips with each word. "We were little kids!"

A dawning understanding of the old lady's situation filled Olivia. Beth had been abused by the very person who was supposed to love and protect her.

What an awful weight to carry, Olivia thought. She imagined traumatic fissures formed by Beth's father had existed in the woman for years following the abuse, only to be forced wide at the hands of the Infested.

"And then tonight, after so long," Beth continued to ramble, "he found us. I told her, I told Marianne not to open the door, but she's younger than me. She forgot what they, what he, was like. She forgot the way they invade your life. There is no safety. Not even in your own bedroom. They still come in. They have their way. I tried to tell her, but I wasn't forceful enough, and she opened the door!" Tears slid down the craggy surface of her cheeks.

Olivia knew she should be trying to calm the woman, but still, she asked, "Who came? One of those men from the hallway?"

Fully crying, Beth nodded.

"And your sister opened the door, didn't she?"

"I warned her. I warned her that something wasn't right. I went to get our gun, but it was too late. She opened the door, and he was there. It was our father."

All at once, Beth was no longer a crazy person with a gun, but rather a very frightened old woman, lost in the house of mirrors she called her memories.

"Where is your sister, Beth?" Alex asked, his voice barely above a whisper.

When she didn't reply, he took a step toward the hallway to the bedrooms.

A rusty, metal ball formed in Olivia's stomach. She was about to tell Alex he had misread the situation, had falsely interpreted the old woman's frail state as a sign of surrender, but never got the chance.

"Don't you dare!" Beth roared.

Emma burst awake, a small, frightened yelp bursting from her, confusion and terror widening her eyes to a near impossible degree.

"Beth, wait." Olivia stood, her attention being split between the adults in front of her and the frightened child next to her.

"I know what you want! You and your sick, disgusting desires. Hard, calloused hands on young, innocent skin!" Beth stumbled forward, her fingers darting down to the weapon secured in the baggy pocket of her robe. "You can't have it! You can never have it again!"

"Beth, please!" Alex froze, his hands already in the air.

"I won't let you hurt me again. Never again!"

The gun, two pounds of death, jumped up to fill the space between Beth and Alex.

"Beth, stop! I know..." Olivia was going to say, "I know something horrible happened to you, but it wasn't Alex," but she never got the chance.

A terrible din suddenly filled the space. The horrid boom was followed by a footlong gout of flame blossoming from the end of the pistol.

The sound of a hundred bells filled Olivia's ears, drowning out all other noise. Alex toppled backward, his head smashing the coffee table. The two candles sitting on the surface bounced off, the flames snuffing on the carpet, a puddle of wax already hardening.

Everything fragmented around her, including time. The next few moments came in crazed flashes. Emma ran across the apartment, her mouth stretched wide in a scream Olivia couldn't hear. Beth stepped forward, and her boney arm waved the gun about, a thin trail of smoke escaping from the end. Alex, rolling on the floor, his glasses missing—gone in the tumult—as blood spilled from between his hands which clutched his left side.

She shot him, Olivia's mind screamed. *She fucking shot him!*

Something, some final bond to the life she had, a strand of meat connecting the present to the past, snapped inside Olivia. The resulting shockwave, a blazing hot ring electrifying her to her deepest core, caused the world around her to turn white.

A feeling she had only felt once before, many years ago in a hospital in another city, in another decade.

A doctor, his head bowed, telling her it was over.

Olivia screamed. Because of her ringing ears, the sound was muffled, like she was at the bottom of a pool. Beth turned the gun on her. The sneer reducing her face into a petrified rictus made her look like a wizened troll. Olivia wasn't sure if Beth would fire at her and wasn't about to find out. One hand gripped the old lady's narrow wrist, while the other slapped her hard across the face. The gun fired again, dropping from the woman's grasp.

Beth may have been crazy, but she was also old, and as soon as Olivia's palm connected with her cheek, she crumbled to the floor.

Olivia spun around and searched for the weapon. The room spun with her, like it was attached to her head. Emma, a tiny form huddled in the corner off to her right, acted like an anchor, pulling Olivia free from the haze which had overtaken her. She thanked whoever was listening that the child hadn't been shot in the chaos.

Beth whimpered and moaned, a sound eerily familiar to the one which had come from Mrs. Elliot at the beginning of the nightmare. Her tired, boney frame shuddered in time with her sorrow.

Spotting the pistol—it had managed to fall a considerable distance from the old lady—Olivia scooped it up and pointed it at Beth. Her hand shook horribly, and the gun threatened to tumble from her grasp.

"Why'd you do that!" She was aware she was crying as she shouted at the old woman. Looking back, she saw Alex had stopped moving.

Beth climbed to her feet and stumbled toward the front door.

"Stop!"

Olivia's warning did not appear to reach the woman's ears. Beth grasped for the multiple locks.

Stepping forward, Olivia thrust the weapon out. Everything felt disjointed, unaligned.

"Beth, stop! Please!"

With a loud click, the final lock released. Beth didn't look back as she yanked the door open and wandered into the hallway, her pained moaning trailing behind her.

Olivia stepped forward and slammed the door, snapping all the locks closed. She thought she should go after Beth. The old woman would not last long amongst the Infested. But a glance back at Alex told her she couldn't leave.

She ran over to him and rolled him onto his back. A large black stain had spread across the lower left side of his T-shirt.

"Please be okay, please be okay," she muttered to herself, pulling his top up.

The skin of his belly was pale, almost completely white. The near lack of pigment made the angry red hole the bullet had drilled through his abdomen all the more hellish. A bubbling geyser of blood fountained out.

CHAPTER 36

"How bad...How bad is it?" The words sputtered from Alex's mouth.

With each syllable, a gush of blood pushed out the hole in his stomach. Olivia could imagine the bullet, a small ball of destruction buried in the soft collection of guts filling his belly, a lead-based cancer.

"Stop talking," Olivia stammered.

Somewhere in the room, Emma was crying.

"We have to stop the bleeding."

She pulled his shirt over his head, and a painful moan fell from his mouth. Balling it up, she pressed it against the wound. "Emma! Where are you?"

The little girl, tears and snot dribbling down her face, approached slowly.

"Take this." She nodded to the T-shirt, blood already soaking through the fabric. When Emma shook her head, her eyes wide with horror, Olivia shouted. "He's going to die! Please, Emma, I have to find something to stop the bleeding, which means you're going to have to hold this."

She was sure the kid was going to back away, break from the enormity of the request, but once again, the little girl showed a level of maturity which would make most adults envious and did what she was told.

Free of Alex and his sucking bullet hole, Olivia turned her attention to Beth's apartment. She needed to find something, anything, that could help the man.

A stack of wash clothes nestled in a drawer next to the sink, along with a bottle of cooking sherry in the cupboard above it. The guest bathroom—compete with broken toilet—turned up nothing useful. Olivia rushed for the hallway and deposited her finds on the floor next to Alex before continuing.

The first of the two bedrooms revealed what Olivia considered to be the perfect example of an old lady's room. A single bed, the bedding tucked-in tightly around the edges, sat lonely in the center of the space. Two small dressers, a nightstand, and a makeup table—complete with oval mirror stationed on the back—filled out the rest of the room. She considered rummaging through the drawers but figured it would prove useless. Instead, she moved on to the next room, the bedroom Beth had gone into earlier to be with her sister.

As soon as Olivia cracked the door, she could smell the death lingering on the other side. The room itself was a near mirror image of the previous bedroom, except for the one glaring difference—the dead woman on the bed.

Marianne.

Olivia eased into the space, her gaze fixed on the corpse, disturbed by the sight. The woman had been beaten badly, judging by the damage to her face and neck, but it looked as if someone—*obviously Beth*—had cleaned her up and put her in fresh sleepwear. A thin, peach-colored nightgown stretched the length of the body. When the Infested had attacked Marianne, it must have severed Beth's already tenuous grasp on reality. Olivia found it quite tragic. Marianne would not spring to life this time.

She tried not to look at the poor soul, but the body had the same effect a black hole has on light. Her gaze couldn't break free. Only when a short bellow of torment blasted from the living room—reminding her the person before her was already dead, Alex was not—did she continue her search.

Bypassing the bedroom itself, Olivia hurried into the en suite. She rifled through the medicine cabinet and the standing cupboards on either side of the sink. Her search turned up a roll of gauze, a near-empty plastic container of Tylenol, and a dated bottle of iodine.

It's not much, but it'll have to be enough.

Emma was visibly shaken when Olivia returned, but she had remained next to Alex despite her obvious fear. She had even managed to retrieve his glasses, which sat crookedly on his face.

Olivia squatted next to him and once again surveyed the damage.

The T-shirt was sopping with blood. It dribbled in tiny streams though Emma's small fingers. Olivia grabbed the bunched-up fabric from the girl's grip and lifted it. The hole, which almost resembled an inverted rosebud in the sickly light of the candles, continued to bleed.

"Go, get some water!"

Emma snapped into action at Olivia's request.

"I'm gonna die," Alex said, his voice high, quaking. The words came out in between gasps for air. "I'm gonna die."

"Shut up!" Olivia blurted. "You're not going to die. But you have to sit still. Emma! Water!"

No sooner had she yelled it, then the child appeared.

"Thank you," she said, grabbing the glass of water from the girl's hands.

Olivia spread a few of the washcloths out around Alex's side and dumped the water over the bullet wound. A rusty waterfall slid down the side of his belly, and Alex groaned. Next, without thinking, she spun the cap off the sherry and let some of the amber liquid spill over the lip onto his injury. This time, Alex did more than groan.

Using the remaining washcloths, she dried the spot as well as could be—the blood continued to flow—and then dribbled on the iodine. She expected another reaction, prepared herself for the sight of his tortured body wracking in pain, but he simply let out a wheeze. Finally, she folded the last remaining washcloth, pressed it against the hole, and wrapped the gauze around his body. This last part took some maneuvering, but she managed to get it secured without having to move Alex too much.

As soon as she was finished, Olivia slumped back on to her butt, exhausted. She was sure a crimson flower would blossom through the fabric of the bandage, but other than a couple of small circles, like bloody freckles, the wound seemed to be slowing its release. She had done all she could.

She knew only time would tell if Alex lived.

CHAPTER 37

Once Alex was comfortable—Olivia had positioned one of the pillows from the sofa behind his head—she began a more thorough search of the apartment. It was an all-encompassing hunt. Every nook and cranny was peered into for anything which might help—both with Alex's current predicament and their overall chances of survival.

She had been especially hopeful for more bullets. She figured the pistol, which now sat on the dining room table, must be near spent of ammunition—unless Beth had reloaded the gun after firing at the Infested in the hallway. But her quest for bullets came up empty. In fact, other than personal belongings, there was almost nothing of any use to be found.

"Olivia?" Alex whispered as she returned to the living room.

She crouched next to him and ran her fingers through his wet hair. Even though he was covered in sweat, his skin was cool, clammy to the touch.

"What is it?"

"I have to say something..."

She was afraid he wouldn't be able to finish his thought, but after a visible swallow—his Adam's apple sliding up and down inside his sunken neck—he continued. "I have to apologize."

"Shh, Alex, there's nothing to apologize for."

"No. This was my fault. I waited too long. I should have tried to stop Eosphoros sooner."

"Please," Olivia begged. "Please, stop. You did everything you could."

Fresh tears rolled from Alex's eyes, lost amongst the sheen of sweat already coating his face. "I'm just sorry that you and Emma"—his eyes slid to the side, as if he were actually searching for the child—"are going to die here, with me. You deserve better."

Olivia leaned in and kissed his cheek. Her lips came back salty. "I'm not going to die in here. And guess what? Neither are you."

Alex looked pained, but his eyes remained focused. "But there's no way out. The penthouse is unreachable."

She shook her head. "That's not true. Before Beth returned from her bedroom, before she...I was going to ask you of the nurse. You said your grandfather employed a nurse living within the building to take care of Vera, right?"

Confusion clouded Alex's face, but he managed a small nod.

"You mentioned that she lives on the twelfth floor. Do you know the apartment number?"

He groaned as a violent tremor momentarily crept across his body, causing his breath to come in short, ragged waves. Olivia continued to caress his head, his clammy skin feeling like wet rubber under her touch.

When the moment passed, Alex licked his lips and brought his gaze to her. "Why?"

"The nurse, her job would have been to see to Vera's needs every single day. I highly doubt Conrad was always around, which means she would have needed her own access to the penthouse."

Despite the torment he was obviously suffering through, Olivia couldn't help but notice the twinkle of hope revealing itself in his eyes.

"Yeah, yeah, you're right." He tried to sit up, but his body betrayed him, and he slouched back to the floor.

"Stop trying to move. You're making it worse," Olivia whispered. "Stay still."

"Right, right, sorry." He practically bit the words off as he spoke them. "So? Do you know?"

He licked his lips again and feebly reached for his glasses, still sitting awkwardly across his face. "She lives in apartment twelve-fifteen. I know because this morning—God, it seems like so long ago—my grandpa, during his insane rant, mentioned her. Wanting to know exactly what was wrong with grandma, I asked if I could speak—" A fit of coughing interrupted him. After a series of worsening retches, he wiped his mouth with the side of his index finger and continued. "Speak to the nurse. I asked where she lived. He told me, but then seemed to reconsider and said instead to stay away from her because she had been very bad."

"What does that mean?" Olivia asked.

Alex shrugged, which in turn produced another eruption of coughs, albeit a smaller fit.

"Okay, okay." Olivia rubbed his head one more time before standing back up. Moving over to the table, she grabbed the gun. "I'm going to find her, and then I'm going to pay your grandpa a visit. If anybody knows how to get out of the New Leaf, it's him."

CHAPTER 38

T he hallway outside Beth's apartment was quiet. After a check of the peephole, Olivia had unlocked the door and slid from inside. She waited as Emma relocked all the bolts behind her. Each click a weighty knock through the wood, a reminder it might not be so easy to return.

One of the Infested Beth had shot lay in a heap just to the left of the doorway. The bullet had punched a hole through the throat of the man, and, judging by the limp antennae hanging from his mouth, the head of the insect inside of him as well. A mix of brown paste and syrupy blood spattered the skin around the quarter-sized hole. She couldn't help but smile, seeing it. The macabre scene was made all the grislier thanks to the glare from the unforgiving red eye shining down on it.

Olivia turned the pistol to look at the chamber. It appeared to hold six bullets, but at least four of them had already been used. She had hoped Beth would have reloaded the pistol after firing on the Infested, but the black holes in the cylinder revealed she hadn't. Two bullets. Olivia would have to be certain the gun was the only option before using it.

Mentally mapping the quickest route to Apartment 1215, she held the weapon tight and pushed away from Beth's home.

Spatters of blood, a swaying pattern of dark drops, decorated the carpet, proof the other bullet Beth had fired had also found a target. As for Beth herself, Olivia expected to see the old lady hiding somewhere nearby, but there was no sign of her.

The temperature in the building was soaring, but Olivia had become used to the terrible heat. She was amazed at how quickly humans could acclimate. Even more unbelievable was the realization she had been doing just that for her whole life. She had become an emotional chameleon, blending into whatever background life flung at her.

Losing her mom, marrying Liam, even following Alex. All those moments, those shifting colors in her personal kaleidoscope, had been a reflection of her own unwillingness to face reality, to be her own person. It was why, she knew, she had to see the night through to the end. It didn't matter if there were a million Infested prowling the halls. To stay in Beth's apartment waiting for death to come, to snuff her out, would have been unbearable.

The stairwell door opened smoothly, almost as if in defiance of the horror which had taken up residence in the building. She had planned to charge up the two floors she needed to ascend, but the deathly quiet filling the space made her stop. Instead, she slowly made her way down to the 9th floor, to the edge of the landing before the drop off. Without the thundering panic the horde of descending Infested had inspired earlier, she was better able to look at the strange void where the downward steps should be.

There was no doubt about it. Alex had been right. The stairs were clearly designed to collapse. Leaning forward, careful not to lose her balance, she could just make out the mechanisms which had been used to hold the steps in place.

When she tilted further out, something caught her eye. Through the cloud of dust collecting like a dense fog at the bottom, the red emergency lights below cast enough illumination to make out the crumbled heaps of the fallen steps. A jagged mountain range of manmade material poked and jutted from the bottom of the stairwell. Just as Olivia was about to pull back, she saw something in that rubble, a tiny, broken form barely visible in the light.

It was Beth.

Olivia put her hand to her mouth. "You didn't know. When you ran, you came this way and didn't see that they were gone."

Looking down on the twisted remains, a sight somehow made worse by the distance and poor visibility, Olivia felt tears wet her eyes. Even having shot Alex, Olivia knew the woman didn't deserve such a fate. Beth was a victim, just like the rest of them, just like the whole building. Every life contained within, every experience, every decision, every first kiss, first heartbreak, every lonely night and moment of joy, all of it, thrown away for numbers and money.

A lone, deep shuffling from above pulled her away from her ruminations. Moving back from the drop-off, she inspected the 9th floor door. It was locked tight, but the glow from the card reader revealed there was power coursing through the unit. It highlighted the importance of the level. On Alex's computer, the 9th floor had been marked with the word *Labs* next to it.

Can there actually be a laboratory in there? It would have been an outlandish thought a short time before, but as Olivia stared at the solid light of the functioning card reader, she felt the idea wasn't so far-fetched.

The shuffling from above grew louder. With no idea how to get through the door, Olivia turned away and started back up the steps.

She moved quickly though the darkness blanketing the stairwell, but that deep, primal fear which had assaulted her earlier while doing so was gone. After facing such horrors, there was something almost calming about the black filling the space between landings. As if, well in its embrace, she could convince herself the nightmare was gone, over.

Whatever was producing the noise above failed to make itself known by the time she reached her destination. She eyed the door, a large black 12 stenciled along its surface.

CHAPTER 39

12TH FLOOR

Olivia entered the 12th floor cautiously. The emergency light just inside the door was on the fritz. It sputtered, sending bloody bubbles reaching down the hall in front of her.

The corridor itself appeared clear, but the doors were mostly opened. Splinters and other bits of debris peppered the carpet before each threshold. She couldn't tell if the damage was the result of Infested breaking in or out. Either way, it illustrated the fact that hunkering down anywhere in the New Leaf did not automatically equal safety—something she could testify to firsthand.

As she passed one of the open doors, she turned her attention within and nearly screamed. Sitting just inside the entrance, backlit by a battery-powered lantern, was a slumped figure. It was a man, the first male corpse she had seen all night besides Emma's father and the Infested Beth had gunned down. The body was not what she found horrifying though. It was the trio of insects fighting over which would be able to take over the dead man's body.

They rolled and hissed, a tangle of stick legs and thrashing antennae. It appeared the bugs had started to outnumber their potential hosts. It also appeared the body did not need to be living for the things to take control.

Olivia raised the pistol toward the scene, her finger tight on the trigger. She wanted to kill them, wanted to see their horrible, nightmarish bodies blown to bits. But after a moment, she relaxed her grip on the weapon. Leaving the creatures fighting, she returned her attention to the hall before her and continued moving forward.

Apartment 1215, which, like all the apartments in the building, was announced by a brass set of numbers stuck to the front of the door, stood before her. A series of scuffs marked the front, along with a couple of cracks in the wood, but otherwise, the door appeared sound. Olivia pictured the Infested smashing against it before moving on to easier pickings.

She reached out and tried the knob. It twisted a fraction of an inch before stopping dead. It was locked.

That was a good thing, Olivia reasoned. It meant the nurse might still be alive.

A crash, followed by a distant scream caused Olivia to raise the gun and point it down the hallway. She thought she saw movement, something quick, a dark blur passing through a splash of scarlet light farther down. Even with the pistol, she felt completely exposed. Deep fear began to slide across her intestines, and her stomach began to cramp.

After trying the handle again, she quickly knocked on the door. "Hello? Is somebody in there?" She stood directly in front of the peephole.

When there was no answer, she knocked again, louder.

"Please! I don't have one of those bugs in me. If you let me in, I might have a way to get out of here."

No reply.

She shifted her gaze up and down the hallway. While turning to her right, she saw the movement again. This time, it was impossible to ignore. Something was darting in and out of the open doors a half dozen apartments down. Bringing the gun up, her mind screamed that what she was seeing was not an Infested. It was too low to the ground and moved in sporadic bursts.

"C'mon."

She kicked the door—out of frustration more than any sort of belief it would open the way for her. She hadn't really considered the idea she might not be able to enter the nurse's apartment at all, which in hindsight seemed like a big mistake.

The clattering of glasses, followed by what sounded like a large piece of furniture toppling over, crept from somewhere nearby.

She leaned back and saw the apartment next to 1215 was accessible. With no clear way of accessing the unit in front of her, Olivia scurried over to the open door and ducked inside.

A dead woman greeted her.

Olivia tried not to look at the body but couldn't help it. The woman, clad in silk pajamas, was propped up against a couch, her face caved in. It reminded Olivia of a jack-o-lantern she had once come across while walking home from school many years ago. Halloween had passed, and the carved pumpkin had been left to rot on somebody's front steps. The angular features had all started to sink in on themselves. A cloud of fruit flies, like hundreds of moving freckles, dotted the orange skin.

She turned away from the corpse, but it was too late. Her stomach flopped, and a string of bile raced up her throat, forcing Olivia to swallow it back.

One thing was immediately certain—the woman had not gone down without a fight. The windows on the far side of the room were all smashed. Wind and rain turned the curtains into tortured ghosts slapping inward. Water covered the floors and dinner table—which was pushed much closer to the windows than Olivia's own.

Moving slowly, she passed through the living room. The humid wind blowing through the shattered windows splashed against her. There was an ironing board standing forlornly off to the side, and a small collection of clothing lay scattered around the floor. A sheet of water had settled along the hardwood in the dining area, turning it into a slip-and-slide. Olivia shuffled carefully, navigating across the space, angling toward the small storage closet stationed between the kitchen and guest bathroom.

Sitting on top of the dinner table was a sandwich—or at least it looked like it may have been a sandwich at some point. The rain came in far enough to reach the table and its contents, turning the bread of the sandwich into a sort of gelatinous mush.

She scrounged through the closet and found a small yellow toolbox. Slapping the container down on the kitchen island—placing the pistol next to it—she snapped the clasps and looked inside. An electric screwdriver, complete with various tips rattling around in its base, a hammer, and a few nails were inside.

Hefting the hammer free, she bounced it momentarily in her hand, gauging the weight. She wasn't sure how effective it would be, but figured with enough determination, she could break her way into the neighboring apartment with the tool.

Having made up her mind, she started to turn when a noise halted her.

Footsteps slapped the wet floor behind her.

CHAPTER 40

Olivia snatched up the weapon and spun around, the gun and hammer acting like counterweights in each hand. Bringing the pistol to bear before her, she steeled herself to see an Infested rushing for her.

But that wasn't what she saw.

Backlit by the red light of the hallway was a small, slumped form. It darted off to the left, disappearing behind the couch, then into the kitchen. Olivia shook her head. Whatever it had been was no taller than waist height.

She remembered her encounter with Rian earlier, but this was different. This wasn't a child. It had weight, density.

Olivia stepped backward toward the shattered windows, keeping the gun leveled before her. A piece of glass bit into the heel of her foot, but she was too focused on what stalked her to feel it.

A squelch echoed from the kitchen tile. Whatever was in there, it was moving quickly.

She stared into the darkness, the horror of knowing something was inside the null space, peering out at her, was almost too much for her mind to handle. Olivia wanted to run, make a break for the hallway, return to the safety of Beth's apartment. But to do so would be to give up. If she went back, she would never find the courage to leave again. Instead, she took another couple of retreating steps.

The rain slashed in through the ruined windows behind her, patting against the back of her legs. She kept the pistol aimed at the kitchen.

When she was just starting to wonder if the thing was going to make a move for her or not, it separated from the black.

The gun roared to life, but it was out of pure panic Olivia had fired, and she knew right away she had aimed too high. The thing barreling toward her was an Infested after all, its mouth a slack oval. But, unlike all the others she had seen, this one had no legs.

The Infested shimmied across the floor at a frightening speed using only his hands. Two smooth stumps, ending just above where his knees should be, thudded and skidded on the wet hardwood. Olivia screamed and tried to run, but the water beneath her feet caused them to slide out from underneath her. She fell sideways into the table, tipping the whole thing over. The water, which had pooled on the surface, came washing down atop her.

During the tumble, the gun had broken free from her grasp. She saw it spin across the wet hardwood, coming to a stop against the fireplace.

The Infested grabbed the hem of her dress and began to pull himself up her body. Olivia screamed as she tried to kick the thing away. It was no use. The Infested had already hauled his bulk up past her knees and was reaching for her hair.

Dirty, wet fingers raked across her belly. The thrashing of their two bodies slapped at the soaked floor. The insect peeked out of the man's ruined mouth, like some sort of hellish mole. It began to shriek.

She knew what it was doing. It was calling its friends.

Terror at the prospect of a swarm of Infested filling the destroyed apartment was almost too much to bear. Olivia snapped her head around and saw the hammer nearby. She hadn't even realized she had dropped it. Grabbing the handle, she swung the tool through the air, connecting squarely with the side of the Infested's head. A wet crack, like a snapped chicken bone, filled the air.

The bug, possibly realizing how exposed it was, quickly pulled back into its hole.

She swung the hammer again, grazing the Infested's forehead. A deep, angry gash opened where the hammer had touched. The blood, which immediately started pouring out, was diluted and washed away from the rain reaching them as they struggled.

The Infested brought his fist down across the side of her face. The blow momentarily paralyzed Olivia's body. For an agonizing moment, she had no control over her limbs. With nothing else to do, she arched up and slammed her head into the thing's mouth. The sudden flare of pain which came with the attack shocked her body back into life. The few remaining teeth inside the Infested's maw broke free and clattered to the wet floor.

Scrunching her legs, her knees reaching up to her chest, she thrust out, launching her attacker free from her. The man skidded awkwardly along the soaked hardwood.

Olivia scrambled to her feet and immediately began searching the chaos surrounding her for the gun. It was so dark, and there was debris everywhere.

She looked over her shoulder and saw the Infested right himself. He charged like a demonic chimp.

Lightning etched across the sky, and white brilliance flashed through the broken windows, turning a trillion-watt spotlight in their direction. In that moment, Olivia could see the revolver. The weapon sat amongst the scattering of clothes that would never make it to the ironing board.

She started for gun, but the legless Infested hooked her foot, sending her spiraling to the floor, a small tide of water rushing away from her.

"No!" she screamed as she kicked.

Like before, the Infested clawed his way up her body. All the while, Olivia continued to drag the both of them closer to the handgun.

As soon as her fingers brushed the handle of the weapon, she snatched it up and rolled over. The Infested scurried to remain on top of her, while at the same time scratching for her face. An ear-piercing wail burst from the man's mouth.

Olivia jammed the barrel of the gun into the Infested's open mouth. Nearly half the weapon slid past his shredded lips, and she pulled the trigger.

The pistol bucked like a wild stallion. A section of the Infested's back, just below his neck, blew open like the petals of a bloody flower. A fountain of gore, including what appeared to be part of the insect's head, showered out like nightmare confetti. The man reeled back and slumped off to the side.

Olivia sat on the wet floor, panting, staring. What pulled her from her trance was a clicking sound. It took her several seconds to realize the noise was coming from the gun.

She looked at her hand dumbly. Her finger was still pulling the trigger.

Like a snake with its head cut off, the digit continued to contract. Each time, the cylinder would make one-sixth of a rotation, the hammer falling on spent shells.

CHAPTER 41

It took several minutes for Olivia to regain her composure—a feat of Herculean proportions. Her whole body quaked, and her breath rushed from her mouth in maddening waves. She couldn't slow it, no matter how hard she tried.

The gun felt like a thousand-pound weight in her fist. It was suddenly so heavy she imagined it would stretch the tendons running through her arm until they snapped like frayed rubber bands, would yank her shoulder clean from the joint. She let her fingers relax along the warm grip, and the weapon dropped to the floor. The single thud it made—a simple knock on the hardwood—belied the sheer size of the thing to Olivia's mind. Looking down at the gun, she desperately wanted to join it, to just let her muscles go limp, to collapse to the ground.

She took a few stumbling steps away from the head-blown carcass crumpled before her, away from the shattered windows and the howling wind beyond, away from the bedlam littering the apartment's dining room. Turning her back to the chaos, she could imagine, even for a moment, she was inside a normal place, a safe place. Somewhere sanity still reigned. A living room organized around the television, remote on the coffee table.

Soft, oversized cushions perfect for leaning into while watching a movie. Approaching the couch, and those large cushions, Olivia half sat, half collapsed into it. Even still, her body refused to give up the shakes.

The TV, a black rectangle mounted on the wall, looked more like a perfect absence of a television. As if somebody had snuck in while the woman—lying stiffly on the floor next to the couch—had been ironing her clothes for another day of the grind and had silently cut a hole in the wall where the TV used to be.

Staring at the dark screen, Olivia pictured a well-groomed weatherman, with his startlingly white teeth, promising the viewers the morning sun would bring a much nicer day. Clear skies and, blessedly, much more comfortable temperatures. Of course, he wouldn't be saying this because he was most likely at home, sleeping soundly next to his trophy wife, dreaming of cold fronts and El Nino. Blissfully unaware that somewhere nearby, certainly within one day's drive, there was a building crawling with Infested. A place so terrible, so nightmarish, if he were to see it, he would never waste another second of his life reporting on the weather again.

Olivia shook her head, turning away from the television, and looked back toward the scene behind her.

"Okay, think," she mumbled to herself. Sitting on the comfy couch while Alex was dying, even for a few minutes, seemed selfish to her.

She had planned on smashing her way into the apartment next door, but that was before her tango with the legless Infested, before she fired the last two bullets in the gun. Olivia realized she would have to come up with another way to gain access to the nurse's apartment, and quick. She didn't want any more company of the variety she just suffered through.

With a slap of her palm against her forehead, she rose from the couch. "Think, think, think."

It was hard to focus. The last gunshot had been too close to her ears, filling her head with a warbling ringing sound.

Another fork of lightning marched across the sky. She could scarcely remember a storm raging for as long as this one seemed to be. It was fitting, she guessed. It would almost be an insult to face such horrors like the Infested on a beautiful night.

While looking outside, she noticed that, ironically, the only glass which had not been split, cracked, or outright broken was the balcony door. Something in her mind, some growing idea, made her squint her eyes.

"The fucking balcony!"

CHAPTER 42

Careful not to slip along the wet floor, Olivia hurried over to the glass door and slid it open. The wind outside blew in howling waves. It shifted and moved with unpredictable fury, like a cornered beast biting anything getting near enough. The rain, a slave to the wind, assailed her from all sides as soon as she stepped onto the balcony.

So much for the storm beginning to dissipate, she thought.

The trees surrounding the building rocked violently back and forth. From her distance, standing at the railing, it made the woods wrapping around the building look more like an unruly crowd of giants than a copse of trees. She tried to see any sign of the city on the horizon, but the storm was too fierce, the distance too far. Below, lined in neat rows in the guest parking lot, stood a collection of black vehicles.

"That's weird."

The residents of the New Leaf Building were afforded underground parking. The lot below was for visitors. In six months of living in the high-rise, she hadn't seen more than a few vehicles parked in the spaces provided. Olivia knew the cars could not be coincidence. Certainly not on the night the Infested were unleashed.

Turning around, away from the cars below, she tilted her head back and looked straight up. She wondered which balcony belonged to her, tried to count, but decided there was no reason for it. Olivia knew that she would never live there again. Besides, all she was doing was stalling.

The apartment layouts in the New Leaf alternated from unit to unit. If one had its bedrooms located down a short hall on the right, the neighboring apartment would have its rooms down a short hall on the left. This layout resulted in every second pair of units having back-to-back balconies. She knew by the location of the balcony she stood on—along the left of the apartment—the nurse's balcony would be separated by nothing more than a small patch of wall.

Olivia took a deep breath, leaned out over the railing with her head tilted to the left, and took in the distance between the two balconies.

She guessed the space between was about five feet. The wall separating them was a nearly featureless slab of white concrete.

"How am I going to do this?" She took a step back and looked in at the dark apartment. She would need something to help her get across, a way to bridge the gap.

Sidestepping the dead Infested, Olivia returned to the living room and began searching for anything useful she could use to navigate across the space between balconies. The best thing would probably be a ladder, but she doubted she would find one. She considered stacking the chairs, but that wouldn't work either. As she scanned past the comfy couch, she once again saw the ironing board.

The board was old. It reminded her of one her grandmother had owned when Olivia was a child. The surface, covered in a red floral print, had no fewer than a half-dozen triangular burns in the fabric. She gave it a heft, trying to judge its durability. It felt sturdy enough, but that didn't mean it would be able to hold her weight. Placing her hands on the top, she pushed up, lifting her feet off the ground. An ancient groan issued from the joints of the metal legs, but the board held.

If I'm quick, she thought, *I won't be on it for more than a couple of seconds.*

Her plan was to close the legs and place the board between the two sides, effectively creating a raised walkway. But as soon as she dragged her impromptu bridge out to the balcony, she realized it wasn't going to be that easy. Hefting the ironing board up, she pivoted so it cleared the top of the railing and positioned it toward the nurse's apartment.

No matter how much she tried, she couldn't find a way to keep the board steady.

"Fuck." She yanked it back, staring at the object.

Olivia tipped the ironing board over, reopened the legs, and once again extended it over the railing. This time, with the legs down, she was able to use them like hooks and catch the railing on the other side. Once secured, the make-shift bridge extended across the distance—albeit at a tilted angle.

She gave it a wiggle, searching for any give, but there wasn't any.

"This is so stupid."

What she was about to attempt was insane, maybe the most ill-conceived thing she had ever done. But Olivia knew there was no other course of action open to her, not really. If she wanted to help Alex and Emma, if she wanted out of the nightmare, she would have to make the trek between balconies.

After retrieving one of the felled chairs by the coffee table to use as a stool, Olivia climbed up and placed a tentative step out onto the edge of the board. It shifted under her weight. She was sure it would simply pull free of the shoddy set-up and plunge to the ground below, but after that initial re-settling, the ironing board remained firm.

The rain splashed against her face, making it hard to see. The nurse's balcony suddenly appeared to be separated by an unimaginable span of concrete. Reaching out with her right hand, her stomach to the building, she was able to slide it across the wet surface of the outer wall. She had hoped she would be able to reach all the way across, but in practice, she realized that was a ridiculous dream. The reality was, she was going to have to fully commit and shimmy across the ironing board with nothing to hold on to.

I can't do it!

Careful not to lose her balance, she stepped back down from the railing.

"This is crazy. I can find another way in."

Even as she tried to convince herself, Olivia knew she was wrong. Time was rapidly running out. She needed to get next door. It was her only chance of finding a way into the penthouse.

"Damn it!" She spun around and looked at the crooked ironing board clinging to the railing.

Without giving it another thought, she hurried back out to the balcony, climbed the chair, and maneuvered across the ironing board. As soon as she did, her balance shifted, and the makeshift bridge listed to the side. Olivia could feel her feet losing traction on the tilting board, just before one of the metal legs broke off, jarring the entire thing loose.

In a surreal moment, it appeared as if it were the building itself that was moving, leaning away from her, a lilting colossus falling backward. One second, she was staring at wet concrete an inch from her face, and the next she was looking at turbulent sky. She was about to fall twelve stories to the parking lot below. She briefly, insanely, wondered if she would land on one of the black, luxury cars.

Instinct more than any sort of coherent thought saved her. As soon as the ironing board began to give beneath her weight, she pushed off with her feet, propelling herself toward the next balcony.

For a moment, a single moment in her mind, everything around her came to a sudden stop. The ironing board, already tumbling free of its mount, hovered mid-collapse. The rain sat in the very air around her like a swarm of frozen locusts. Thorny vines of lightning stabbing down from the dense cloud cover illuminated the world around her like a massive, tangled coil of rope light. Olivia, hanging over a hundred feet above the earth, her hand, snarled into a claw, gasped at a wet railing.

And then it all started again.

Her fingers wrapped around the metal. As she thudded against the railing, an angry boom of thunder filled the world. The sound dwarfed every other noise, like hearing the voice God.

Olivia let out a bellow and forced her other arm up, her hand securing a space on the railing. As soon as she had both handholds tight, she frantically hoisted herself up and over, falling awkwardly onto the unforgiving concrete of the balcony. A shock of pain announced itself along her back and shoulder from the impact, but it wasn't debilitating and certainly couldn't pull the smile from her lips.

The rain pelted down on her, pooling in her closed eyes as she breathed heavily. It wasn't just that she was still alive that had turned her mouth into a grin. It was that she had done something so truly stupid, yet so utterly brave, a thing she would never have imagined herself doing, even for one second, before this wretched night, a feat she had outright labeled as impossible earlier in the evening, which made her smile.

Rising to her feet, rolling her right arm in an attempt to lessen the angry kink which had just been born in her shoulder, she leaned over the railing. The ironing board, a small white teardrop amongst the black asphalt of the parking lot below, made her outright laugh.

CHAPTER 43

Olivia cupped her hands on either side of her face and peered through the glass of the balcony door. She couldn't see much. The blinds on the other side had been drawn. Normally, that would mean no way to see in, but there must have been a window open somewhere inside the apartment because the blinds, which ran vertically, swayed gently. Every few seconds, a slash of light from within would find its way past them, only to be snuffed out when they shifted back.

An empty coffee can full of cigarette butts sat on the balcony. The yellowed filters floated in the collected rainwater like miniature boats lost at sea.

She wondered again if the nurse was inside the apartment. Surely, she imagined, the woman would have heard Olivia knocking on the door. She wondered at the nurse's mental state. A frightening thought presented itself to her. What if she was about to walk in on another Beth? Another fractured mind broken from the strain of the Infested, just waiting to unleash itself on Olivia.

"Well," Olivia leaned back to look across the gap toward the balcony she had just left behind. "It's not like I can go back." Grabbing the handle of the balcony door—it was warm and wet from the rain—she prayed the small lock on the inside was not in place.

If it was, she would be forced to smash the glass to get in and would probably cut herself in the process. Luckily, the lock was not engaged, and the door slid open easily.

She reached out and pushed her hand through the blinds cascading down on the other side. Two of the slats parted for her probing fingers, and instantly, a stab of light fell through the opening. It glared directly into her eyes, causing her to squint. In the electric glow, she thought she could see a dark form, impossibly tall, standing in the dining room.

Heart bouncing, she let out a small yelp and retracted her hand. The slats quickly fell back into the place, blocking her view of the apartment and the giant inside.

What the fuck was that? her mind screamed.

She had been so quick to launch herself irreversibly toward the nurse's home, she never stopped to think what new horrors could be awaiting inside.

Olivia backed-up until the railing abutted the small of her back. The rain hit her head and shoulders. She barely felt the water though. Her entire focus was turned toward the open patio door and the wall of blinds before her. In her mind, she saw some tall, thin Infested, a true monstrosity reaching as high as the ceiling. Arms as long and narrow as a tree branch, reaching out, covering the length of the dining room in one ghoulish swipe.

When the seconds began to pile-up and still nothing emerged, she steeled herself for another look.

Inching ahead, her hand shaking despite her best efforts to keep it steady, she parted the curtains a second time. When the light blared out at her, she kept her eyes open and peered into the apartment, ready for whatever she had witnessed earlier.

What she saw was horrific but couldn't hurt her.

A high-powered flashlight, the sort advertised on late night info-mercials, sat on the middle shelf of a curio cabinet. The intense beam was angled such that it lit across the dining room, coming to a rest on the blinds by the patio door. The thing she had glimpsed—the tall, black form—was actually situated halfway between the curio cabinet and the spot where Olivia stood.

It was a woman, the nurse, still in her scrubs.

She hung from the dining room light fixture, a leather belt cinched tight around her neck. The woman's raised position created the illusion she was impossibly tall. The chair she had used to secure her makeshift noose lay tipped. A small pool of urine had collected beneath the nurse's dangling feet.

Olivia kept the woman in her sights—the utter stillness of the body was almost surreal. It looked more like a prop, a gag found hanging in any number of fun houses and haunts which popped-up around Halloween. Except it was in the middle of summer, and this prop had pissed itself when the belt tightened.

She freed the flashlight from its home in the cabinet and swept it through the space, purposefully avoiding lighting the corpse before her. The apartment was neat, organized. The only sign something was wrong, besides the obvious suicide, was a large shelf tipped backward so it leaned against the front door.

It was a good thing she hadn't tried to break in, eyeing the shelf—*the thing must weigh a ton*. She would never have been able to move it. It was a miracle the nurse had been able to do so herself.

What if she didn't? Olivia thought. *Maybe somebody else is in the apartment?*

She swung the light around like a club, illuminating the corners of the living room and dining room, the cupboards and fridge beyond the island in the kitchen, and down the short hall leading to the bedrooms. Even as she did so, Olivia felt like there was no need for her search.

A person doesn't hang themselves unless they are alone. It was one of those things Olivia couldn't possibly know yet felt like there was no other answer, and so she accepted it as the truth.

Having seen enough, she finally turned the light on the woman suspended from the ceiling. The nurse's face was a swollen, purple mess. Her eyes bulged from their sockets, red with burst blood vessels. Her tongue, which stuck out of her mouth like a half-eaten eel, was thick and dark. Snot and mucus, which had dried into a pattern of cracked tiles along her chin, revealed the woman had done the deed hours ago.

Olivia stepped in closer and found she recognized the face. A vague familiarity filled her. "I've seen you before." She was almost sure she had shared an elevator ride with the woman on more than one occasion.

Letting the light slide down, away from the deceased's face, Olivia saw something sticking out of the left pocket of the nurse's scrubs. A bit of paper. It was positioned such as to be impossible to miss.

Olivia snatched the paper as fast as she could, afraid in some way the nurse would burst to life, muscles creaking and snapping against the effects of rigor mortis in an attempt to stop Olivia from invading her privacy. The action caused the body to sway gently, but the nurse remained stiff, forever frozen in that terrible moment when the lack of air finally caused her life to stop.

Olivia quickly retreated into the living room, leaving the sofa as a barrier between her and the dead, before looking at her find.

She directed the flashlight toward the folded sheet, turning the paper brilliant white under the powerful eye of the light. Olivia opened it. Rows of tight, neat handwriting scrawled from one side of the page to the other. The penmanship was on a level Olivia could only dream of. She realized, with a surreal sense of déjà vu, she was looking at a suicide note. Only this time, she thought it was the genuine article.

This is all my fault! It began. *My name is Abigale Campbell, and I never meant for this to happen.*

CHAPTER 44

Olivia peered back at the body hanging in the dining room. Abigale. Knowing the nurse's name somehow lessened the horror of it all. It said the woman had lived a life. She was a real person, not just another tragic number, a statistic for Eosphoros to analyze.

Returning her attention to the letter, she continued to read.

I've made a terrible mistake. I only wanted to help. You have to believe me. All I had to do was give the old woman her shot.

Olivia knew which old woman the nurse was speaking of—Vera Anderson.

I still don't know what was actually wrong with her. She is physically sound. I would even say overly healthy for her age, but her mind is just...gone. Mr. Anderson hasn't given me much information regarding that part of her condition. Normally, I would want to know such things, but the money is good, and so I do as I am told. Every day, I was to go up to the penthouse and give Mrs. Anderson her medication—something to do with her blood-sugar, although it is clearly not insulin—feed her, do her exercises, and well, just sionally, she'll wander a bit, as if her body is remembering a routine that her mind has long forgot. Her husband, my employer, usually supervised my time there.

Mr. Anderson frightened me. He would storm through the penthouse, talking—sometimes screaming—to himself. His favorite subjects were his wife, somebody named Meredith (a mistress?), and Eosphoros (whatever the hell that is). If Meredith is a mistress, then the man has a cold heart as he makes no effort to hide the name from his poor wife. I once asked if everything was okay, if he needed me to contact somebody who could possibly help him. His own mental state is not that much healthier than Mrs. Anderson's. In reply, he nearly bit my head off! I honestly though he was going to attack me.

Still, like I said, the money was good. Really good! I would never make the same amount of cash in the public sector.

"Jesus," Olivia whispered to herself.

From what Alex had told her, his grandfather was an unhealthy man. She couldn't imagine what it must have been like to be in his presence nearly every single day. Then again, he was a legitimate billionaire. People would take a lot of abuse if it meant more zeroes in their paycheck. Giving her head a shake, she returned her attention to the letter.

Everything changed last week. Mr. Anderson was gone—some business out of country (or so I was told). Truly alone for the first time in the penthouse—I don't count Mrs. Anderson as I don't feel she knows I am there, even when I am present —I couldn't help but let my curiosity take over. I snooped. Had I known what I would find, I never would have looked where I wasn't supposed to. Hell, had I known before what I know now, I would have laughed at Conrad Anderson's offer to come work for him in the first place. But, sadly, I didn't.

The elderly couple have amassed an amazing collection of items over the years, the biggest display of which is in Conrad's library (a room I was told never to enter). It was while marveling over these things that I noticed something odd. The red elephant. It opened a hidden door. I was actually pretty excited. I had found a secret room! What I saw in there was...I can't even describe it! But my God, it was the most awful thing I'd ever witnessed.

The delicate swirls and loops of the writing began to degrade, as if the fear the woman had felt that day had traveled from her memory, down the pen, and onto the page.

I was so scared I stopped going up to the penthouse. There was no way I could return. I wanted to call Mr. Anderson, tell him that he needed to send somebody else to take care of his wife, but he left no way to contact him. So, instead, I simply left her. Jesus! The woman can't even tie a shoe, and yet I left her alone. I have no idea if she is eating—she's certainly not taking her medicine. I almost went back for her, I really did, but then I thought of the library and couldn't find the courage.

All week, the guilt of what I had done drilled holes in my stomach. Finally, this morning, I couldn't take it anymore and went back up. I thought I would find the old woman injured, or maybe even dead. A sad, lonely corpse alone in that massive apartment. But when I went to her room, the bed was empty. She was nowhere to be found. I wondered if she could have left, wandered free from the penthouse?

To make matters worse, Mr. Anderson had returned home sometime before. The man charged through his home in a mad rage. He demanded to know what had happened to his wife, but I had no answers. I tried to speak to him. I tried to tell him that I was sorry, but he was deranged. He dragged me in to the library and showed me what I had seen earlier, only, in that moment, I realized that I hadn't seen anything. Standing there, as he practically frothed at the lips, I witnessed the full extent of what is hidden in the walls of Conrad Anderson's library.

I can't un-see it. All this time, that thing, that fucking horrible thing, has been right here. It's been here, in the New Leaf, all along!

He took my keys and told me to go to my apartment and wait. He said he'd call me back up later to discuss my future status in his employ. I was so scared. Conrad Anderson is a powerful man. He can destroy me. So, I waited. I realize now I should have run. Run as far away as I could. But hindsight is 20/20.

Now, the power is out, the phones aren't working, and I have no car. Just like Vera Anderson, I am a prisoner in the New Leaf building.

Olivia pulled the page closer, holding it right before her face. The writing had become frenzied to the point of being nearly illegible.

I can hear them! Skittering in the vents. Screams in the hallway. I have to get out of here! But all I can see is that...thing in the penthouse, and I'm too afraid to leave.

The rest of the letter was unintelligible. A scrawled mess—the complete devolution of Abigale's tight handwriting. A few words jumped out at Olivia though, like small literary islands floating in whirlpools of black ink.

...Something below.

...key card. I don't know what it's for.

The last paragraph, a return to neatness, clearly written after the above, revealed the nurse's sorry fate.

I can't take it anymore. The sounds are awful. The things are everywhere. I've barricaded my door, but I doubt it will hold for long.

Please, if you find this, Conrad Anderson is a monster! He is responsible for everything!

And then:

I'm sorry, Mom and Dad. I'll always love you. I never meant for any of this. I just wish I could see you one more time.

The woman's name was printed so close to the bottom of the page, some of the words looked like they might fall off.

Olivia let the letter flitter free of her hands, and it see-sawed down to the dark floor. A paper snowflake falling amidst a summer storm.

Had I not purged the Temazepam from my stomach, would someone have found me the same way I had found Abigale?

CHAPTER 45

Olivia stood alone in the dead woman's apartment, her mind spinning. The letter had presented more questions than answers, but one thing which had stabbed her brain like a hot poker was the line about Conrad Anderson taking Abigale's keys. Getting to the penthouse was the only way out, and like a slammed door, that option was now closed to her.

"There's nothing left." She had clawed, fought, bit, and shot her way to a dead end. The New Leaf would be her grave after all.

She listened to the rain, which splattered against the windows in fits, her thoughts drifting two floors below to settle on Alex and Emma. Their own hope of escape, of life beyond the miserable night, had been denied as well.

Olivia directed the flashlight toward Abigale one last time, she noticed something sticking out of her pocket. When she had pulled the letter free, she must have also partially revealed what else resided there. Olivia made her way toward the unfortunate woman and retrieved the item—any fear of the corpse bursting to life long gone.

It was a plastic key card, the back of which was solid white with a single black magnetic strip along the top. The front was a flat grey with a red E in the right corner.

Eosphoros.

"Wait." Olivia hurried back to the letter and picked it up. The page felt coarse and stiff in her fingers, but the sensation was lost to a sudden rushing of blood filling her head. She scanned through the jumbled section one more time, her eyes finding those random clear words like they'd been struck through with a highlighter.

"Something below?" Olivia flipped the key card in her hands a couple times. "Is this…" She looked up at the body suspended from the ceiling. "Did you manage to get the key to the ninth floor?"

She read the note again, but no further clues presented themselves from the flurry of ink scribbling across the page.

"I guess there's only way to find out." Olivia tucked the card into one of the shallow pockets on her dress.

Grabbing a knife from the kitchen—*it's better than nothing*—Olivia surveyed the bookshelf barring the front door. She put down the knife and flashlight and attempted to pull the unit away from the exit, but it was too heavy. The contents of the shelf would have to be removed if she had any hope of clearing the obstruction.

Stacks of paperbacks and hardcovers tumbled to the floor around her feet. She could practically hear her grade six teacher lecturing her on proper book care techniques. The final couple of novels topped off the pile. Olivia eyed the now empty shelf, hoping it would be enough.

She gripped the edge and heaved forward with everything she had. For a moment, she was sure it was still too heavy, but slowly, she inched it upward until it regained its footing, standing once again.

"Jesus, Abigale," Olivia said between gasping breaths. "You were one strong lady."

Getting the shelf to topple away from the door was quite easy with it vertical again. She rocked it back and forth two or three times before momentum and gravity took over. Olivia jumped back, cringing in anticipation of the resulting tumult. She was not disappointed. The crash was tremendous. It reverberated throughout the nurse's apartment, even causing unseen dishes hiding in darkened kitchen cupboards to rattle and shake.

Not wanting to waste time, especially in case the bang brought unwanted attention, Olivia unlocked and then opened the door. It groaned as it swung ajar, evidence of the damage the weight of the bookshelf had wrought on the hinges.

Olivia started to head out. Just as she cleared the threshold, a deep, all-encompassing beeping filled the air.

"Site-termination-protocol has been initiated," an automated voice bounced down the length of the hallway. *"All remaining Eosphoros employees on site, please evacuate immediately. Thirty minutes until complete cleanse."*

The recording repeated a second time before abruptly cutting off, allowing the silence to rush back in like water into a hole.

For a moment, Olivia couldn't move. The message had effectively stuck her in place. Site-termination-protocol? Complete cleanse? She shook her head. Neither of those things painted a positive picture in her mind.

"It looks like I have thirty minutes."

She gripped the knife tight. The handle was warm and smooth—reassuring— and she made her way to the stairwell.

CHAPTER 46

LABS

Olivia's thoughts swirled like the dust in the air around her as she made her way down the stairs. She found herself thinking about Liam. Despite everything she had gone through, a part of her still needed to know what happened to her husband. Was he alive and in hiding? Or had he become an Infested? Olivia reasoned the answer was more likely to be the latter. With the exception of Alex, she had yet to see a man escape the terrible grasp of the hellish insects.

She bit her lip, her teeth threatening to burst through the swollen skin there. If she saw Liam again, she knew she would confront him, no matter the circumstance. She owed it to both of them to do so.

The pull of the 9th floor was almost enough to sway her from her path. She wanted desperately to report in with Alex, even with the strange notice of a coming "site cleanse." She wanted to let him know it wasn't over yet, that she was still fighting for them. But the possibility of finding him dead, having bled to death, was enough to push her past the exit, to continue her downward plunge for the 9th floor.

Coming to a stop on the floor's landing, she turned the light toward the drop-off where the steps used to be.

Careful of her footing, she directed the beam over the edge. Besides the broken ragdoll which had been Beth, she could also see several male bodies littered amongst the jagged concrete and steel below. She thought of the reckless abandon with which the Infested had pursued her throughout the night.

It seems Eosphoros's trap has also snared a few of their own.

Olivia put the flashlight down and reached into her pocket, pulling the stiff, plastic card free. She slid the card through the device, preparing herself mentally to be denied. But as soon as the key card left the bottom of the thin track, a melodious chirp issued from the box, and the light blinked from red to green. The *clunk* of a lock sliding open filled the landing.

Olivia swallowed painfully—the dust practically choking her—and opened the door. A wave of frigid air rushed out. Chilly currents wafted past her tired frame, sneaking into the stairwell, causing the cloud of dust to dance. She had an immediate physical reaction to the cold. It chilled her damp clothes almost instantly. The heat had sapped her so thoroughly the icy wave was able to take up residence in her bones upon contact. She began to shake.

Olivia stuck her foot in the door so it wouldn't close before reaching down and picking up the flashlight. She felt a great hesitancy to enter. There were answers beyond the door, and she wasn't sure she was up to dealing with them. However, even if she wanted to wait, to collect herself, there just wasn't time. She was literally on the clock. So, with a shuddering sigh, she aimed the beam of her flashlight though the opening and shouldered her way in.

Just beyond the door was a short hallway, which appeared to end in a small room. Olivia's brow furrowed. The arc of light being thrown from the flashlight revealed the room held cupboards, a fridge, and a dolly with several bottles of wine standing stoutly on the top.

What is this?

A light switch sat on the wall to the right. She wouldn't even have considered toggling the small knob, but the drafts enveloping her in a cool blanket screamed air conditioning, and so she flipped the switch.

Fluorescent lights stationed in long rectangles of foggy plastic along the ceiling blinked and popped into life. Staring at the fixtures, Olivia numbly powered-off the flashlight.

The room at the end of the hall revealed itself fully to her as she approached. Besides the things she had already seen, there were also various items resting against the far wall. A whiteboard on wheels, as well as several stands featuring various pie charts and graphs. A podium. Beyond that, a second entranceway.

This new door looked thick, expensive. The high-quality wood—a dark finish with numerous knots in the grain—shone under the all-encompassing wash of the overhead lights.

As soon as she opened the door, she knew something was wrong. A smell, vaguely of burning rubber, crinkled her nose, the kind of odor which could not be natural. But there was something else in the air as well, a sour tinge.

She found herself standing in the mouth of some sort of meeting room. Unlike the small hallway, the lights in the space had already been turned on. A massive, oblong table dominated the center of the space. Thirteen chairs stood around it like toadstools grown from metal and fabric. Slumped in twelve of the thirteen seats were dead men and women.

They wore business suits and pricey looking watches. Leather briefcases and attachés littered the floor around them. Shit and piss collected at their feet, soaking the lush carpet, destroying their designer shoes.

Olivia stared at the strange and unexpected display of death.

The smell of chemicals continued to make her nostrils burn the deeper she walked into the room. Files were scattered around the surface of the table. Twelve of them, to be exact. Each bound in leather with silver clasps keeping them closed, a red E emblazoned on the front.

What happened? Who are you people? She recalled the cars filling the guest lot, and somehow felt certain she was looking at the owners.

The boardroom itself was rectangular. Besides the door she had come through, there was another door—equally as impressive—next to a bank of windows. The room was too small to reach either of the exterior walls of the New Leaf, which meant the windows were interior. What they looked out on was a mystery to Olivia. The view had been obstructed across all the panes by drawn blinds.

For a moment, she thought she saw a bug climbing free from one of the dead people's mouths, but upon closer inspection, she saw it was not an insect at all, just a swollen tongue jutting from dried lips. Still, the thought one of the men of the table could potentially be host to one of the bugs made her approach cautiously.

The body nearest her, a large man with a thick mustache and bald spot, lay slumped forward, his head turned sideways, resting in his arms. Without the proper context, he would look like a man who had decided to sneak a quick nap during a particularly boring presentation. Or at least, he would look like that, if not for the thick snot crusting the hairs of his mustache and the dark veins sectioning the grey skin of his neck and face.

Olivia reached past the man, past his stiff arms, and placed the knife and flashlight on the table. She then picked up the folder in front of him, running her finger over the embossed E before flipping the folder open. Even though she didn't have time to read through the contents, she couldn't stop herself.

Eosphoros – Third Quarter 2019 Meeting agenda

She let out a wild, borderline insane giggle. It had been a board meeting. "How mundane. I would have thought you people would meet in a castle, or ancient tomb."

The next page revealed a table of contents. She scanned through the titles. *Matriarchy. Overview. Projected Sales. Best Environments for Deployment. Government Contracts.* The final listing read: *New Leaf test subjects.*

Olivia slipped past the table of contents and found herself reading a report written by Conrad Anderson himself, regarding the state of his wife.

Attention board members. I know that there has been some concern raised regarding the continued incapacitated state of our current Matriarch and my wife, Vera Anderson. As well as my place as acting head of

Eosphoros. Once again, I will point out that Eosphoros law dictates that until she is recovered or deceased, a Matriarch's spouse will act as head of Eosphoros.

I assure you, I have nothing but the best of intentions moving forward and hope that all of you will continue to bear with me in this time of need. I am confident that Vera will make a full recovery in the near future. In the case that she does not, however, I think it is prudent that we start to look at what comes next. Because no heir exists, it is my belief (as well as Vera's) that I, Conrad Anderson, remain in the Matriarch position for, at the very least, the entire duration of the New Leaf Project.

We can discuss this further at the upcoming meeting, and hopefully, that will be the end of it.

The memo was signed and dated a month previous. Olivia guessed the board was going to make some sort of decision regarding Conrad's continued place atop the Eosphoros mountain.

Moving deeper into the file, she came to the overview section. Most of it was scientific jargon—a fair amount revolving around genetic testing—which meant almost nothing to Olivia. But there was one interesting tidbit which caught her attention.

The Dermagigantes (species D-118) have shown remarkable growth since undergoing the gene-splicing therapy. Aggression levels have increased exponentially. Full parasitic symbiosis achievable in minutes. The continued draw back, one which is proving to be insurmountable for our geneticists, is the continued incompatibility with human females. Hopefully this roadblock will be cleared by the New Leaf Project launch date, but for now, testing will continue using only male subjects.

"The Dermagigantes?" She hadn't really thought of the things as having any other name besides the Infested, or big fucking bugs. As far as names went, she figured it was a fitting one.

It certainly is a mouthful.

Returning her attention to the page, she continued to read.

Despite the best efforts of our geneticists, we have yet to break the hivemind exhibited by the Dermagigantes. This may prove to be impossible, which will mean that the queen will have to remain protected during any sort of deployment.

"There's a fucking queen?" Just the thought of something worse than the Infested made her stomach roil.

Skipping over the bulk of the folder made up of charts, graphs, and sales figures, she stopped at the section titled *New Leaf Test Subjects*.

Since the New Leaf project began two years ago, the goal has been to find a group of test subjects which would represent all walks of first-world life. The research division has carefully checked the histories of all applicants and narrowed the list down to a perfect group which will be called Test Group A (note, Test Group B and C will be discussed once the plans for the New Leaf sister buildings are complete). For more info on Test Group A, please refer to the biographies section at the back of the agenda.

Once all sites are up and operational, the New Leaf Project will commence in its fullest.

Olivia leaned against the table, careful not to disturb the dead man next to her. It was all so formal, so orderly. The fact that a person sitting behind a desk, in a cubicle somewhere in the world, had written this with all the compassion of compiling a grocery list made her queasy.

The remaining pages held various photos and profiles on her neighbors, all given a number based off which apartment they lived in. She saw pages dedicated to the Elliots, Emma's family, even the obese Infested, before coming across her and Liam's entry. Beneath their names, ages, and history, there was a short write-up.

Subjects 2506-A and 2506-B were accepted based on their relationship. Subject A has become disillusioned with his marriage. He has begun an affair with subject 1518 (See: Subject 1518: Scott, Audrey) and has recently started planning the termination of his wife, Subject B.

Measures may need to be taken, if Subject A is successful in terminating Subject B, to keep him on site until testing is ready.

Subject B has been shown to be a submissive. Our analysts predict that (assuming Subject A does not terminate her), Subject B will remain passive when the testing begins, unwilling and unable to fight back. This prediction will especially be true if Subject B is stripped of her husband (Subject A).

Anger funneled up through Olivia. "Fuck you!" she screamed, throwing the leather-bound file at the group of corpses surrounding the table.

The folder frisbeed through the air before colliding with a woman in a pantsuit, her eyes twin balls of white staring blankly into the afterlife.

"You don't know me! You didn't know any of us!" She pushed the man next to her from his chair.

The body fell stiffly, the way a statue might topple over.

Olivia picked up the heavy seat. She could only heft it a few feet from the ground, but it was enough to swing it through the air, letting go at its maximum arc. It spun crazy, like a roller-coaster cart broken free from the rest of the ride, and smashed against the blinds. A sudden, violent crash followed the impact. Several of the vertical blinds snapped free from the track holding them in place and crumbled to the floor, along with a downpour of broken glass.

Any thoughts at continuing her tirade fizzled as she stared through the hole she had just punched through the blinds and window.

Just outside the boardroom was a vast laboratory.

CHAPTER 47

"**I** found your labs, Alex."

On the other side of the glass was a wide, open-concept laboratory. Desks cluttered with monitors, binders, and coffee mugs dotted the floor plan. The closer she crept, the more details revealed themselves, including the dozens of dead bodies littering the floor—clogging the spaces between desks and chairs like weeds poking through the cracks in the sidewalk.

Standing in front of the jagged mouth she had created, Olivia once again was aware of the strange odor which had greeted her in the boardroom.

Poison! She looked back at the collection of corpses slumped in their business attire and quickly slapped a hand over her mouth. *These people died so quickly they couldn't even leave their seats.*

Slowly, she lowered her hand. If the air held something so toxic it could snuff a life in a snap, then it was gone. If not, she would already be dead.

Olivia returned her attention through the broken glass, becoming aware of a faint dinging noise. It was so distant she had to strain to hear it at all.

She stepped away from the window and retrieved her knife from the nearby table before approaching the second door in the room, which she now knew exited into the laboratory.

When she pushed the door open, it only swung free halfway before meeting with resistance. She leaned through the gap and saw a small cart lying on its side against the door. Slumped near it was a person, complete with lab coat and yellowed goggles.

Putting her shoulder into it, she heaved the door open and exited the boardroom.

The lights in the lab were brilliant and cold, like arctic sunlight. She was sure no shadow could exist under such a powerful glare.

The room seemed to be a work area. All the desks and chairs had been arranged in such a way that any one person would be able to observe any other's work without having to move far from their own.

The laboratory's occupants appeared to have been going about their jobs when they were poisoned. Unlike those in the boardroom, some of the people in the lab had made an attempt to escape their fate. A few bodies lay sprawled in moments of panic.

Oliva moved through the room—the tomb—and came to a set of sliding doors. At her approach, they whooshed open gracefully. Beyond was a square space filled with canisters, beakers, and a plethora of high-tech equipment. Like the previous room, dead lab technicians and scientists lay crumpled in sad heaps.

She wanted to call out, to see if somebody, anybody, was alive, but was too afraid. The laboratory was a graveyard, and she was terrified to see what was hiding amongst the dead. In her mind, she could picture things skulking between the desks and cubicles, waiting for something to draw its attention.

Olivia sidled up to one of the nearby computer screens—a flat monitor stationed next to a metal canister with a glass front. A young woman lay slumped over in a chair before the computer. Her face was mercifully turned away from Olivia, hiding the ugliness of her death. Olivia peered through the glass and let out a frightened yelp. Floating in a greenish liquid within was a Dermagigantes. The fluid, which appeared thick, like emerald-tinged oil, seemed to diminish the bug's proportions.

The screen, which had reverted to a screensaver of a swirling kaleidoscope of colors, returned to life when Olivia gave the mouse a shake, revealing whatever the young woman had been working on before death had found her.

An image surrounded by various notes dominated the display. It seemed the main focus of the research at that station had been on the insect's appendages, specifically the whip-like protrusions coming from the end of its abdomen.

Olivia once again gazed into the tube, this time ready for the creature within, and found herself eyeing the stringy strands floating from the end of the bug.

It seemed the Dermagigantes used the whips to penetrate the back wall of the esophagus. From there, they bored through the tissue until contact with first the spine, then the brain, at which point, full control of the host body was achieved. Beneath the information, a secondary note had been added, proposing host bodies retained full awareness, even though they had no control. Further tests had been scheduled to determine the validity of the proposal.

Olivia brought her hand up to her mouth as the words on the screen began to fully register. All night she had viewed the Infested as monsters, murderous creatures driven by rage and death. But the mere thought that buried inside the Infested, like prisoners in jails constructed of their own flesh and blood, were men being forced to watch, helpless, as they committed acts of unspeakable violence toward the women and children they loved, was overwhelmingly horrifying.

She reached out, turning the screen off, and continued moving through the labyrinth that was the Eosphoros labs. Desperate to forget what she had just learned but knowing she never would.

She hurried past another collection of cubicles and entered into a room housing a half dozen massive, sealed tanks, each the size of a small car. Wires, tubes, and ventilation shafts sprouted from the sides like demented growths. Various cameras had been set-up around each unit, ready to catch and document whatever was supposed to happen within. Stenciled on the floor in front of her, in black letters, it read: *Caution, Live Specimens in Use. Clearance Level 7 Only.*

Glancing at the dead bodies scattered about, Olivia guessed the higher clearance had meant very little in the end for the Eosphoros scientists.

Most of the tanks were dark, but two—including the one closest to her—were lit from within with pale, yellow light. Her knees went weak at the sight of the first tank.

Bathed under the sickly glow were numerous Dermagigantes. They skittered and climbed over each other in an undulating wave of legs and antenna. The sight of the tank and its horrible residents reminded Olivia of her childhood. Her mom had loved goldfish, and whenever they were near the pet store, they would go in. As her mom would peruse the various fish types, Olivia would go over the lizard section. She had no interest in the reptiles, but rather their food.

Without fail, there would always be a dirty aquarium—with brown crust clogging the corners—full of hundreds of live crickets. She would press her face against the glass, equal parts repulsed and fascinated at the insects. A couple inches thick, the carpet of crickets at the bottom of the tank was always in motion. Although the Dermagigantes were a long way from the average cricket, standing there in a laboratory full of death, staring into a tank with living nightmares scurrying about, Olivia could picture nothing else.

The second lit tank was empty, although scuff marks on the glass, as well as deep slashes in the floor of the tank, revealed it hadn't always been so.

No sooner had she left the tanks behind, then the automated voice from earlier returned.

"Site-termination-protocol has been initiated. All remaining Eosphoros

employees on site, please evacuate immediately. Twenty minutes until complete cleanse."

"I'm trying," she said bitterly.

After the room with the tanks, Olivia found a winding collection of stalls which she could only classify in her mind as prison cells. Thankfully, they were empty, but her guess as to the nature of the rooms was all but confirmed when she saw the chains bolted to the cement walls, each ending in a manacle which would have fit snuggly around a human wrist or ankle.

Is there no end, she wondered, *to the horror Eosphoros is willing to inflict on others?*

Exiting the cellblock through a reinforced door, she entered into a hallway. After a dozen or so steps, she once again heard the dinging sound from earlier. This time, she recognized it immediately—the elevators.

Breaking into a sprint—her feet howled at the exertion—Olivia blew past the washrooms, as well as a number of unmarked doors which she assumed led back into the labs, until coming toward a wider section of hall complete with twin elevator doors.

A skinny man in a white coat lay sprawled across the threshold to one of the elevators. Every time the door attempted to close, it would collide with his body, ding, and open back up.

She felt like she should be shocked at the sight of the working elevator, but as the door made a repeat attempt to close, she realized it all made perfect sense. The power outage was man-made. While everybody above the lab would be running for their lives from the Infested, the people on the 9th floor would be conducting business as usual.

Olivia stepped over the man, bent over, and pushed him free of the doorway. With the obstruction gone, the door was finally able to slide closed. Heart beating like a drum, she looked at the column of buttons— oddly, all still dark—displayed along the inside wall. She had been blocked at every turn throughout the horrid evening, which is why, in her heart, Olivia knew it wasn't going to be so easy.

Tentatively, she reached out and hit the button for the tenth floor.

The screen above the buttons—a shiny, black display—which usually showcased which floor the elevator was passing when in use, flickered. A digital keypad featuring numbers from 0 to 9 appeared. A smooth, synthetic voice wafted down from hidden speakers.

"Please enter password to unlock elevator."

"Password? What? No!" Olivia pounded the area directly next to the display.

She backed up until her rear hit the far wall, and she slumped to the floor. Olivia wanted to tell Alex she was sorry, to hug Emma and tell her she loved her, to find Liam and...

"No, wait." Olivia rubbed her head as memories began to surface. Something about Liam and unsolved mysteries. "It can't be."

She slowly returned to the digital display and eyed the numbers floating there. Back in her apartment, before the chaos and horror of the night, she had found numbers indented on a notepad. Numbers which had been written by Liam. 0725

Even as doubt demanded the numbers could not be the password to access the elevator, Olivia's finger was already entering the combination.

"Password accepted," the voice intoned. The rows of floor buttons lit up.

Liam had the password. Did he know this was going to happen? She was stunned.

Staring at the options, Olivia realized she had just opened the door to her own freedom. With the elevator functional, she could go anywhere in the building, even the lobby. Instantly, the weight of salvation tugged at her.

I could run. I could get help!

But it wouldn't be fast enough. The New Leaf was so far from anywhere, it would take much longer than the ominous countdown echoing through the building allowed.

But I don't even have the keys to the penthouse! It'll be another dead end. But even this, she knew, was not an absolute. Until she tried, there was no way to say it was impossible.

Besides, she reasoned, *how long would I really be safe for if I run? Conrad wouldn't let me tell the world. I'd have to flee, to hide, forever."* Olivia firmed her lips as the main reason for not backing down from fate filled her head. *I won't leave Alex and Emma!*

The penthouse button clicked softly as she pressed it. The elevator lurched to life, quickly ascending the New Leaf building.

As the floors danced past on the small screen—now returned to its proper function—all Olivia could wonder was why Liam had known the password?

CHAPTER 48

PENTHOUSE

The ride to the top of the building stretched into an eternity. The seconds it took for each new floor number to appear on the screen before blinking away felt like days, years.

16

17

Every now and again the elevator would vibrate, shimmy. It was just enough Olivia had to remain rigid, for fear of falling over. She was tired beyond all her imagining.

21

22

As the lift climbed higher, she was hit with the certainty she would never leave the penthouse. It would be her grave. But she was determined to see the night through, for better or worse.

24

25

Olivia pictured her home for the last six months. She saw the darkened television, the empty pill bottle, the vomit soaked into the carpet of her bedroom, the notepad on the counter—*I almost dog-gone forgot*—and, more than anything else, the photo album full of pictures of her mom. If she did make it back, she would return for it.

26

FL

PH

The elevator slowed to a stop, and the doors dinged open.

Olivia looked down a short, ornately decorated hallway. Various paintings hung from the patterned wallpaper. Gold light fixtures—made to resemble candle-mounted wall sconces of old—glowed with soft, electric light. The corridor looked, to Olivia, like it belonged in some Victorian mansion nestled in the English countryside, not atop a modern high rise.

The hall ended at a large set of double doors. At the sight, Olivia felt her heart begin to race. It appeared her search for the keys to the penthouse had been in vain from the start, as one of the doors was already partially opened.

The doors of the elevator whispered closed behind her, and she hurried down the hall. She held the knife she had pilfered from the nurse's apartment before her, waiting for whatever nightmare might be ahead. When she reached her destination, she took a steadying breath and pushed through the opening.

As she passed the threshold, she was greeted by a grand display. A massive entranceway.

Marble pillars sprouted from the floor like four identical soldiers, reaching up to the ceiling. The walls were adorned with dozens of framed paintings. Sofas of rich, red velvet and antique wooden chairs, hundreds of years old, lined the walls, separated by waist-high vases, marble busts, and suits of armor.

Olivia felt like an invader, a foreign body which had just been introduced into an environment it was never meant to exist in. Each step across the vast display of wealth made her feel small, worthless, as if her mere presence was an insult to those who called the penthouse home.

At the head of the room, opposite the elevators, was a wide archway complete with two massive cherrywood doors—they made the front doors look small in comparison. Twin staircases, rising from either side of the arch, came together above the opening and continued on to a second level—the railing of which peered down at her from above. Patterned runners climbed the steps like flat snakes trying to flee the grandeur of the entranceway.

She approached the doors, noticing for the first time they were decorated in elaborate carvings. Swirling depictions of men and woman wallowing underneath the brilliance of a single figure, a woman with shimmering hair, stars in the strands.

Olivia gripped the handle of one of the doors and gave it a yank. She expected the door to be heavy, to resist her attempts at entering a place she did not belong, but it opened smoothly toward her despite its obvious weight.

The entranceway led to the dining room, a space large enough to practically devour Olivia's entire apartment. A dark wood behemoth of a dinner table dominated the center of the room. Although big enough to host a dozen people comfortably, the table only had one chair, a rather plain looking bit of furniture sitting forlornly at the very end. A crystal chandelier hung suspended over the table, the overall dimensions of which made Olivia think of a spider's egg sack, the diamond-shaped crystals resembling hundreds of newborn arachnids scurrying over the nest.

More artwork—Olivia could only guess at how much money was sitting on the walls of the penthouse—decorated the room. Off to the right, gilded in bronze, was a large, fully stocked bar. Row upon row of bottles lined the shelves behind it. The bar, with its collection of booze, was the first sign something was wrong atop the New Leaf.

A smattering of liquor bottles had tipped over along the bar's surface. Murky rivers of rum and whisky had run together, dribbling over the edge. She could smell the sour-sweet stench permeating the air.

"Hello?" Olivia asked the stillness around her.

Although afraid to bring undue attention upon herself, she couldn't take the silence any longer. Besides, the logical part of her brain insisted the old man had to know she was there, in his home, anyway. Conrad had manipulated the entire evening to the fullest. She couldn't imagine the man missing her arrival into his domain. And then there was Liam.

Is he here...waiting for me as well?

Tapping the point of the knife along the surface of the dinner table— anything to keep the silence from overwhelming her—she asked, "Liam, are you up here?"

She hadn't expected a reply and, as such, was not disappointed when none came.

Off to the left of the dining room was a hallway, to the right a pair of white, swinging doors. Assuming the doors led to the kitchen, she instead turned her attention to the hallway.

A bloody smear on the floral-patterned wallpaper just inside the hall halted her search and caused a bubble of dread to rise from her core. The rust-colored mark, which could have been left by nothing other than a hand, ran along the wall in an arc like a crimson arch. Ignoring everything else, Olivia followed the macabre trail until its end, just outside of a thick, wooden door. The floor in front of the door was spattered in drying red drops. A bloody smear tarnished the shine of the brass handle. Whoever had left the trail had gone through the door.

"Liam?"

No answer.

"Mr. Anderson?"

Nothing.

The blood on the knob was dry, but even still, Olivia used only three fingers to turn it. She quickly wiped the affected digits on her dress right after. As soon as the door clicked, she used her toe to push it open. It was a library. She immediately thought back to the nurse's letter. Abigale had found something in the library, something which had frightened her enough to leave her helpless patient alone for a week.

Olivia entered.

INFESTED

Three of the four walls were faced in bookshelves. The units rose well past the height of the ceiling in the previous rooms. A half-dozen glass displays decorated the middle of the space, each containing an item—statues, artifacts, and ancient tomes. Off to the side of the room was a spiral staircase which curled upward in one corner, reaching to the second floor of the penthouse. The far wall was all windows.

Outside, the rain had been reduced to a mild spitting. Distant lightning, a faded strobe light buried in dark clouds, revealed the storm was finally out of breath.

Olivia stepped fully into the library and noticed a large desk situated on one side of the room. Directly across from it, on the opposite end of the library, was a huge television screen. A fury of static filled the display.

The blood, which continued along the floor, looked like grotesque lily pads on the blue carpet. The trail covered the distance of the library, disappearing around the far side of the desk.

Breathing in shallow bursts, the knife held tight, Olivia followed the trail. Questions pounded her brain.

Where is Conrad Anderson? Where is Liam?

She felt her breath catch in her throat at what greeted her when she rounded the piece of furniture.

Lying on the floor, his face a frozen rictus of pain, a deep slash across his throat, was Conrad Anderson. She recognized him immediately from the image on Alex's computer. The man's hands, twisted and gnarled like petrified vines, reached stiffly for the gash cutting across the loose skin of his neck. Blood, now dried to a black crust, stained the front of his silk shirt.

Olivia jerked back from the dead man. Twisting around, she took in the room, expecting somebody to make themselves known, to come rushing toward her. But the library remained quiet, still. The rain and her own heavy breathing the only things soiling the solitude.

"I don't understand," she mumbled, backing away from the desk and the remains of its former owner.

For most of the night, she had envisioned Conrad Anderson as the puppet master, the man behind the curtain. Seeing him dead on the floor, his life smeared all over the library, did not jive with what she had learned.

Conrad was just another victim!

Turning slowly, fighting to take her eyes off the dead man, she looked outside. The view from the library was that of the pool below. Olivia could see the blue of the water—it shimmered in the darkness like sapphires on black velvet. Even though the body was not visible, she knew Emma's mother bobbed in that water, her flesh swelling. Thinking of that poor woman brought back Olivia's own experience poolside, specifically the revelation the penthouse had power in the first place. But there was something else.

"Wait." She returned her attention to the dead man behind the desk. "I saw someone!"

In fact, she realized she was standing in the exact same window the mysterious silhouette she had seen earlier had been in.

Olivia moved closer to the body. She figured, by his sorry state, the acting Matriarch of Eosphoros had been deceased for more than a couple of hours.

"You look like you've been dead longer than everybody else. But..." Returning her focus to the window, she continued. "Then who did I see?"

CHAPTER 49

EARLIER

Liam exited the elevator into the wide hall which led to the front door of the penthouse. He had almost expected the four-digit code to be bogus. A prank. Staring at the decorated stretch before him, he wished it had been.

He replayed the phone call in his mind for the dozenth time since leaving his apartment. It actually helped to think of the call. It took his mind off what he had done to his wife. Even though he wanted to be free of Olivia, free of her presence, what he'd done to her made him feel numb. If pressed, he would admit this coldness seeping through him was more to do with the terror of being caught for his crime rather than the act itself, but still, he was having severe doubts.

The caller had sounded like a wraith. "You know, the law frowns on uxoricide, Liam," the voice had said. "But fear not, I have no intention of alerting the authorities...That is, I won't do so if you fulfill a simple request of mine.

"You will come to the penthouse, and we will discuss a business trans- action. In exchange for keeping your cowardly act a secret, you will do a it isn't anything that will require much effort on your part.

"I assume you are agreeable to this?"

The speaker only hesitated for a moment before continuing, apparently having no intention of letting Liam answer.

"Good, I knew you would."

"Call the elevator. Once inside, select the button for the penthouse. A prompt will appear, asking for a code. You will enter zero-seven-two-five. It will take you to me."

Liam had scrambled to write the numbers down, and the caller continued to speak.

"I look forward to discussing this further with you in person, Liam. I am sure that we can come to a mutually beneficial conclusion to this matter. And, if you fail to follow my instructions, then I'm afraid I will be left with little choice but to reveal your crime to the police." At that, they had hung up.

Maybe Audrey is right. Maybe this will change nothing. Maybe I can still get away with it. The person on the other end of the phone certainly had presented themselves as being reasonable.

The doors at the end of the hallway were closed. He wasn't sure if he should knock or just go in. As it turned out, neither option was needed.

"I'm happy you decided to come. It would have been such a shame for the authorities to become involved." The tired voice from the phone floated through a small, barely discernible speaker next to the door.

"Well, I'm here. So, now what?" Liam tried to sound tough, firm, but his breath refused to cooperate, leaving him sounding winded.

A static-filled cackle of laughter fell from the speaker. "What a brave boy. Standing before the unknown, fists balled."

Liam looked down at his hands and saw he had indeed clenched them tight. He spun around, his gaze searching the ceiling of the hallway. He saw a small, black eye staring back. A camera. The person on the other end of the speaker was watching him.

"Enough of the games. Who are you?"

"A concerned third party." The amusement from the laughter still floated in the words.

Liam could practically see the smile producing the speech.

"Like I said, I'm here. What do you want me to do?" Liam rocked slightly as he spoke.

"Ah, now see, that wasn't so hard. All things are negotiable. It all depends on what you have to offer. In this case, all I require from you, Liam, is a moment of your time. A mere pittance compared to the years you would no doubt face for having murdered you dear wife."

Liam felt nauseous. "Fine. Just tell me what you want. But after that, it's over. Okay?"

"Agreed. Now, if you would kindly follow me."

Liam was about to ask how he could follow a disembodied voice when the door before him swung open mechanically. From beyond, a light came on.

"We don't have all night, Liam." This time, the voice floated in through the open door.

With nothing left to do, Liam began to follow.

The speakers, each bursting to life in the exact moment he stepped from one room to another, led him on a tour through the sprawling penthouse. First through a magnificent foyer, then the edges of an extravagant dining room, across a sprawling, fully stocked kitchen, through a sitting room with a massive grand piano and art hanging from the walls which would have looked at home in the Louvre.

Each new space presented a level of wealth Liam could only dream of. Wine racks with vintages, no doubt, dating back decades. Pedestals showcasing world-class art and sculptures. Furniture made of delicate fabrics and fine, rich wood. All of it nestled within obvious signs of modernity. Digital screens peeked between antiques. Blue lights of technology blinked past volumes of books which appeared to be weathered by centuries of existence.

Until finally, he was led into a small bedroom. The room was an interior one, which meant no windows. A single bed surrounded by various medical supplies and a lone chair the only pieces of furniture.

"Hello? I don't understand." He began to turn around when something brushed against him. His heart jumped, and a yelp of surprise managed to bubble past his lips before he felt a sharp sting. A hot, searing, pinprick in his neck.

"Shh, Liam. You of all people should how easy it is to drug a person."

He tried to see who had spoken, but it was no use. His arms and legs, indeed his entire body, seemed to collapse in on itself.

"Don't worry. Unlike what you gave Olivia, this will not put you to sleep. What I've given you is just a little drug we manufactured quite some time ago. Over the last few months, I have become quite familiar with it myself. You see, it all but severs the connection between brain and body. Your thoughts will be in there, but you won't be able to voice them, enact them. But fear not, you will still be able to feel. You will be able to *feel* everything."

With his head filling with cotton, he became aware of somebody holding his hand, leading him. And to his horror, he could do nothing to stop it.

His eyes caught fleeting images, but his mind was confused, unwilling or unable to process what he was seeing. Finally, he was seated in a chair. The sound of straps being fastened reached his ears. He demanded his mind to focus, to understand who was doing this to him, but his control was gone. Once he was secured, his capture began to cut away his clothing. He could feel his balls shrivel as the cold air caressed them.

"Well," the voice said, "it looks like we are at the end. But know that you are doing me a great service. And in doing so, your life has now had meaning."

He could hear the shuffle of feet walking away. A door closing—the deep thud of a bank vault.

He tried to talk, to beg, to scream, but he was maddeningly silent,

INFESTED

maddeningly still. Some vital connection from his brain to the rest of his body had been disrupted. A series of yellow lights popped on around him. A harsh sound, the sliding of metal on metal, was followed by what Liam thought was a great release of water. A large, wet thump sounded to his right.

Oh God! Why is this happening to me?

Something began to move on the floor nearby. A slow, clicking noise the result. It grew closer, louder. Whatever made the sound began climbing him. From the very fringe of his sight, he saw a long, slender insect leg tap along his chest.

CHAPTER 50

With the reality of the situation sinking in—Conrad Anderson was not responsible for the horrors terrorizing the New Leaf—Olivia was able to focus her thoughts and begin searching his desk.

There has to be a way to turn off the countdown!

The drawers climbing either side of the back of the desk were locked. She considered, briefly, searching the corpse for a key but couldn't bring herself to touch him. Moving on to the surface of the desk itself, Olivia imagined it matched the mental state of its owner, a mess. Cluttered piles of loose-leaf, books, and folders lay scattered about. At the head of the desk sat a trio of paperweights, three red skulls, each about the size of a grapefruit. She recognized two of the three skulls as belonging to a large cat—like a lion—and a bear. The last, which looked vaguely familiar to her, was quite odd in appearance. It almost looked human but heavily deformed. A bulbous protrusion where the nose should be jutted from the front. In angled downward and partially covered the teeth.

Site-termination-protocol has been initiated. All remaining Eosphoros employees on site, please evacuate immediately. Ten minutes until complete cleanse.

Olivia responded to the countdown with a grunt.

"Fuck! I'll never find it!" The reality was, even if she had an hour, she couldn't thoroughly search the entire penthouse. Olivia swept the top of the desk of some of its contents.

To come so far and still fucking die, up here, alone.

Objects and debris scattered across the floor.

"No, fuck that. I'll find a way."

She stepped over the mess on the floor, and something snagged her attention. Sitting before her was one of the skulls, the odd one she couldn't place. But from this new angle, the origin of species it was designed after clicked in her mind. It was an elephant skull. She recalled having seen one recently on the cover of *National Geographic*. The story had been about ivory poachers. She thought then, as she did now, that without the tusks, trunk, and huge ears, the skull looked nothing like the animal it belonged to.

"A red skull for a red elephant." As soon as the words left her mouth, she was transported back to the nurse's apartment, once again holding the woman's desperate note in her hands. It had mentioned a room, a secret room, found in the library. It had also said something about a red elephant.

She reached down and scooped it up. It was surprisingly heavy. The lacquered crimson surface reflected the overhead lights like burning stars.

Olivia flipped the object quickly, the countdown playing in the back of her thoughts. She inspected every nook and cranny.

"Could this...?"

The button, barely visible just inside the lower jaw, would have remained completely hidden to her had she not actively been searching the paperweight for some clue. How Abigale had noticed it at all, Olivia could only wonder.

Pressing the button caused a soft murmur of machinery to issue from the wall of books to her right. A section of shelving, roughly the size of a door, sighed open.

Olivia stared at the sudden entrance. After her many discoveries of the night, she was no longer capable of being surprised by the New Leaf's secrets.

The hidden door led to a small, dark passage. As soon as she entered, the lights lining the ceiling burst to life.

Motion sensors.

The walls of the short corridor were the antithesis of the rest of the penthouse. Gone were the ornate wallpapers and rich, wood trim, the fine art and the countless displays of wealth. In their place were grey concrete walls and floor.

Olivia shuffled forward, sure she was nearing the end of her journey. A conclusion was fast approaching, a finale that was as much Alex and Emma's as it was her own. Whatever happened, in less than ten minutes, it would be over one way or another. She had ventured into the heart of Eosphoros. All that was left was to look the beast in the eye and let the pieces fall where they may.

She came to what she could only think of as a miniature version of the laboratory found below. A bank of monitors and other devices lined a console to the right. A massive tank, the perfected copy of the ones she had witnessed earlier, stood in front. Something was inside the tank.

Something familiar.

Olivia closed her eyes and covered the remaining distance blind. She didn't want to see.

All night, she had wondered about her husband. Thoughts of their past, present, and future had followed her throughout the New Leaf. And now, as she shuffled forward, those thoughts, those memories, were joined by a thousand more. Every kiss and every snub. Every loving breath and harsh bark. All the sunshine and all the rain. A swirling stream which, as it seemed, was always destined to end with a violent, cataclysmic waterfall. It all played behind the screens of her closed eyelids, like a movie which could not be stopped.

Even as the first tears slid free from the barriers she had shuttered into place, she knew she had to see. There was no more hiding. Olivia opened her eyes, the knife in her hand clattering to the floor.

Somewhere in the recesses of her mind, something let go, some final thread which had bridged her existence before the Infested to her life after.

Staring at what was in front of her, she knew fully, there was no going back.

The tank was a testament, a shrine, to the highest of filths. Blood, grime, and shit spattered the glass walls, turning them into canvases of psychotic abstract art. A thick, viscous fluid coated most of the floor. It caught the illumination from nicotine-yellow light tubes positioned on the ceiling, sending up a urine-colored glare. The source of the liquid was immediately apparent. A canister of metal and glass, a big sister to the one she saw on the table in the laboratory, stood against one corner of the tank. The front had been opened, loosing the contents from inside. The yellow syrup slicking the ground was not the only thing free from the canister. The creature which had been floating inside had been liberated as well.

A tick, some minor quake which started along the left side of Olivia's neck, grew into a full tremor which caused her muscles to shake. She reached up, her fingertips finding the smooth spot behind her ear, as tears continued to fall freely from her eyes.

Liam, completely naked, was strapped into a chair, a seat which would look at home in a doctor's office. But it was no gynecological chair he was secured to and was certainly no doctor which was seeing to him. A bug, like the others but bigger, more terrifying—a collection of spindly legs and an arrow-shaped head—straddled her husband. Its abdomen was wedged down his throat to the point it had not only broken his jaw but appeared to have nearly sheared it from his face completely. The horror didn't end there though.

This was clearly no normal Dermagigantes. This was something else. It was the queen.

Liam's stomach was massive, distended beyond belief, a dozen tears and rips showing how much it had exceeded the elasticity of his skin. His legs, which were spread-eagle and secured in stir-ups, exposed his genitals and anus. Olivia slapped a hand over her mouth at the sight. His ass had been torn asunder—a shotgun blast fired from within his bowels. Blood, feces, bile, and other fluids splashed up to cover his withered penis. The rest slid down his open cheeks, turning into a ghoulish downpour, mixing with the yellow lake already coating the floor.

Olivia's legs gave out at the same time as her stomach. She threw-up on herself as she collapsed to the floor. It was too horrible. Even after everything she had learned about Liam, about his awful, disgusting intentions with her, he was still her husband. She had loved him, and she knew in her heart he had at one time loved her too. She could still see him clearly in the park, down on one knee, ring in hand, as leaves the color of the setting sun wafted down from the autumn trees.

Olivia swiped her hand across her mouth and rose, her legs wobbling for the effort.

"Oh, Liam." She had barely whispered his name, but still, as soon as she did, he began to move.

She jumped back from the glass and watched, the true horror of the situation revealing itself to her like a knife in the guts. Liam began to thrash, his body jumping and bouncing within the restraints. The large insect mounting him held tight, seemingly unfazed by the sudden eruption.

He's still alive!

Pressing her hands to the glass, Olivia yelled, "Liam!"

The man inside did not reply—he couldn't—but his eyes darted in her direction. They were crazed, the whites threatening to overtake the irises completely.

A roiling bubble pushed along the deformed confines of his belly, the skin stretching—a new rip appearing near the bottom of his ribs on the right side. Even through the glass, she could hear the squelching sound which trumpeted from his torn anus. In a small fountain of blood and bits of tissue, a sack tumbled from his ass onto the floor. Only it wasn't a sack at all, but a tangle of four small Dermagigantes.

Newborns.

The creatures pulled themselves apart and fumbled around with all the coordination of baby fawn before angling way from Liam—and their mother—and disappearing into a vent at the far side of the tank, an opening Olivia hadn't even noticed until the things were through it. The vent, no doubt, connected to the main vents and ducts of the building, allowing exposure to the rest of the New Leaf.

Every single one, she realized, brain gone numb. *Every single Infested I've encountered throughout the night was born from Liam.* She hadn't thought of how the creatures were created, but it made sense. They were living things after all and needed to be birthed.

The queen had been using Liam to produce her brood for hours. His body, a ragged piece of meat, an incubator for her progeny. Already, the insect shimmied, repositioned on him, a contraction stiffening its multitude of appendages. Olivia guessed it had just deposited more insects into his guts to grow and mature.

She couldn't take it anymore.

Turning away, her body on some sort of auto pilot, she stumbled over to the console. The room around her began to grow fuzzy at the edge. She leaned on the table and struggled to catch her breath, which raced in and out of her manically. Oliva was sure she would black out, but after a few seconds, her breathing started to return to normal, the room stabilizing.

Not ready to look back at her husband, she instead looked up at the various screens before her. The nearest monitor—a touchscreen, if the lack of keyboard fronting it was to be believed—was lit with numerous lines of information. Things like tank temperature, infection time—which was rounding the five-hour mark—as well as reproduction rate, although this last one said it hadn't been updated in nearly the same amount of time since the initial infection.

In her frazzled state, it took Olivia a moment to realize all this information was referring to Liam and the queen Dermagigantes. Underneath all the multiple readouts and gauges was a red box with two words present within: *Exterminate Experiment.*

She looked at the digital box on the bottom of the screen. Her eyes unfocused, and she stared past the words, the monitor, and the entire New Leaf Building. She saw all the moments she had shared with Liam, millions of snapshots which slowly coalesced into a single second of time. Her index finger brushed the screen so gently she felt the warmth of the monitor on her skin as much as its hard surface. The small box flashed three times before vanishing from the display.

A simple beep of confirmation rung out.

Olivia turned once more toward Liam. The effects of her action were dramatic.

From hidden nozzles along the ceiling of the tank, four gouts of flame burst down upon Liam and the queen. Olivia jumped at the sight. It looked like a rocket ship was about to take off. The fire, blue spears fringed in orange, instantly crisped her husband and the parasite abusing him. The inferno first blackened, then blew free, swaths of his skin. She wondered if the fire would penetrate the walls of the tank, but it had obviously been built for such a thing. She could feel nothing of the hell raging inside, even though she was only a handful of feet away.

After a few seconds, the arcs of flame ceased—a few wheezing coughs of fire puffing from the hidden nozzles before going dark. The chair, the bug, the canister, and her husband crackled and popped, like a bonfire. The floor and walls were scorched black. An audible click issued from somewhere in the ceiling of the tank before a half dozen streams of foam began pouring down, covering the entire scene in marshmallow fluff.

Olivia watched the steam rise from Liam's remains. His form, now fused with the bug which had taken him, was an inhuman tangle of shapes.

CHAPTER 51

"**S**ite-termination-protocol has been initiated. All remaining *Eosphoros employees on site, please evacuate immediately. Five minutes until complete cleanse.*"

The warning pulled Olivia away from the smoldering ashes of her former life. She was reluctant to leave that previous existence, if for no other reason than it still carried weight for her, a burden which would take time for her soul to shed, but time was running out.

Moving toward the second monitor on the console, she saw its screen dominated by a real-time countdown.

4:58

4:57

4:56

"Fuck," she muttered. "There's got to be a way to shut this off."

"You of all people should know there is nothing that can't be achieved, Olivia." A dry voice jumped from the small passage Olivia had wandered through from the library.

Olivia turned and found herself staring at an old woman in a pants suit.

Vera Anderson.

"Judging by the look on your face, you both know who I am and are surprised to see me standing here."

As the Matriarch of Eosphoros spoke, she moved closer to Olivia. With the transition from the corridor to the hidden room, the overhead lights fully revealed her. Her complexion was pale, almost grey—the color of spoiled pork. Her hair thin, wiry strands of white thread.

Seemingly aware of her appearance, the woman brushed her fingers through her hair.

"Excuse my appearance. I haven't been in the best of care lately."

Vera came to a stop.

"It has been a long night, for both of us. But know this, I am truly happy to see you." She spoke with a confidence which belied her poor physical condition. "You are my savior."

Olivia didn't know what to say. She was truly shocked to see the woman. Instead, she glanced back at the screen and its relentless march toward zero.

"Ah, yes. There is no longer need for that, at least not yet." Vera tilted her head to the side, a few slivers of white hair sliding across her forehead. "Cancel site-termination-protocol. Authorization vee-eh-dash-one-eight-one-five."

"Site-termination-protocol cancelled."

The numbers on the monitor vanished, leaving the screen black.

"Now come, my dear." The old woman held out her hand. "Accompany me back to the library. We have much to discuss."

Taking the Matriarch's hand—the woman's fingers were cool, almost waxy—Olivia walked with Vera back through the short hall to the study.

"What happened here?" Olivia asked of the woman next to her. "I need to know."

Vera turned her face toward her and smiled. "'Then you will know the truth, and the truth will set you free.' John, eight thirty-two. The Bible is full of the best quotes, don't you think?" She licked her dry lips. "But worry not, Olivia. I intend to reveal all to you. And then...then I will have a proposition."

A proposition?

Once clear of the hidden doorway, Vera directed Olivia to stand by the windows as she walked over to the chair behind the desk. The old woman let out a long sigh and lowered her frame.

"Time is a cruel bitch, don't you think?"

The question was rhetorical. Vera waited for no reply.

Instead, she locked eyes with Olivia and said, "He liked to watch, you know."

"Who?" Olivia asked.

The old woman tilted her head to the side, her gaze tumbling to the floor and the stiff body residing there. "My dear, loving husband.

"True story. When I first met Conrad all those years ago, I knew one day I would kill him. Past the veil of love and family, of loyalty and commitment, it was there. This undeniable truth hovering at the fringes of our relationship. He was just a tad too unpredictable. So, for that reason, I knew I would end his life." Her voice grew thick with strain. "Do you know how hard that is? Knowing, even as you kiss, caress, make love to the person you have committed your life to, that one day you just *know* you are going to end their existence?"

Vera dabbed at her eyes with the sleeve of her jacket.

"I only wish that I had done it a lot sooner. I could have saved us all some trouble."

Olivia shook her head. "I don't understand. I thought you were sick! You had dementia!"

The Matriarch waved away Olivia's question. "I was never sick. I was drugged, dear."

Abigale's note returned to Olivia. The doomed woman had said her main duty had been to administer Vera's medication daily.

The medicine wasn't helping her. It was keeping her locked away in her own mind!

"Conrad wanted Eosphoros," Vera continued. "But the only way to get it was if I was incapacitated. Not dead, mind you, just in a state where I would not be able to make decisions. Our...*organization* has been around for a long time, which means some of our customs are downright archaic. Nobody else within Eosphoros had the clearance to verify my condition.

As long as Conrad could prove that I was not deceased, he would be acting head." She groaned. "I was always so damn careful, but everybody gets complacent sometimes. I let my guard down, and he took advantage. It happened so fast. One thing I can say, our products are certainly effective. I was drugged daily. My mind screaming, fighting, but the signal being lost between my brain and my body. A bad connection, I guess you could say." At this, she smirked.

It was ironic, Olivia realized. Abigale had died with the guilt of being responsible for Vera's death, but by abandoning the old woman, she had allowed the drugs to leave her system, ultimately setting the Matriarch free.

"When he returned home this morning, I was waiting." Vera sneered. "His panic was something to behold. It was the look a man adopts when he realizes he has fallen into a snake pit.

"He was frantic to find me, but I remained hidden. I watched him with that wretched nurse, as well as with Alex. Poor Conrad was beside himself. I can tell you, when I made my presence known, he was more than a tad surprised. I didn't even have to fight to stick the blade in his neck." She looked again at the man curled on the floor.

"After that, I turned my attention toward Eosphoros—starting with the board. During my time locked away within my own mind, I had come to realize that the organization needs a shake-up. An injection of new blood, if you will. Thankfully, all the New Leaf's controls are accessible from up here, allowing me to gas the entire ninth floor—a safety precaution all our sites enjoy in case of unwanted guests." Vera squinted in Olivia's direction, her eyes turning into sunken pits of liquid mercury. "And then there was the Dermagigantes. With the board needing to be built back up, I knew it would be years until I saw the fruits of my labor. I had invested so much into the Dermagigantes initiative, I couldn't let all that work be shelved for that long."

"You let loose the bugs," Olivia said. "You're responsible for the Infested."

"The Infested?" Vera chuckled. "I like that! It sounds so much better than Dermagigantes or species dee-one-one-eight. But to answer your question, yes, I did. In fact, I considered taking a walk through the New Leaf to watch firsthand but ultimately decided I had been through enough in the past few months and bore witness from up here."

"But..."

The Matriarch laughed. "But the Infested would have beaten me to death? No, dear, they wouldn't have. The Dermagigantes are a very unique creation. In some ways, they are utterly stubborn to our manipulations. Take the fact that, try as we might, we can't get the damn things to bond with women. And then there is the queen." Vera turned to look toward the hidden entrance. "The bugs are marvels, no doubt, but they are fatally chained to the queen. Take out the mother, you destroy the children. But then"—she smiled and raised her chin triumphantly—"on the other hand, we've been able to accomplish incredible feats with the creatures. Feats that warlords and governments would pay *astonishing* amounts of money for. Like the ability to hardwire directly into the Dermagigantes certain limitations. For instance, the fact that we can make them blind to certain DNA strands, like mine, for example. I could walk through the New Leaf with my eyes closed, and the Infested would be no more threatening to me than a group of kittens."

Olivia's head swam with the revelations. First, the knowledge the Infested would not, could not, attack Vera's bloodline effectively answered one of the night's biggest mysteries—how Alex had managed to avoid the bugs at every turn.

If we had only known. He could have marched through the New Leaf with impunity.

It was a depressing thought, considering his current situation. She then focused on what else the woman had said. *The bugs are marvels, no doubt, but they are fatally chained to the queen. Take out the mother, you destroy the children.* Unless the Matriarch was lying, which Olivia felt she wasn't, then by burning the queen, Olivia had ended the Infested plague swarming the building.

Feeling dizzy, Olivia leaned back, her shoulders resting against the window.

"Ah ah," The Matriarch raised a finger. "It may be a lot to take in but stay with me. Like I said earlier, Conrad liked to watch. What I meant by that was that he liked to watch *you*."

"Me?"

A sudden sadness overtook the old woman's face. It made Olivia think of a grieving widow standing beside a coffin.

"Yes, you. Conrad was...not well. He was obsessive.

"I'm sure it will come as no surprise to you at this point, but the New Leaf is fully wired with thousands of cameras. Every hallway, storage room, and apartment are under twenty-four-hour surveillance. Conrad would sit in here and watch the daily lives of all the New Leaf residents." She tilted her head toward the large, snow-static screen across the room. "It became his obsession. And you, my dear, were the star of his own little reality show."

Vera's features grew grim, turning her already pale visage into a grotesque death mask. "He would bring me in here and stand me like a mannequin next to his desk as he watched you. For hours, he would stare at that screen as you wandered around your apartment, bored, alone. Sometimes you would clean. Other times you'd bring out your notebooks to write, only to stare at the blank page before putting it all away. He watched you shower, defecate, sleep. It never grew tiresome for him." Vera paused, no doubt to let the full depth of the invasion that had been enacted toward Olivia sink in. "He especially loved watching you and your husband be intimate. He has that footage saved, in case you are interested in seeing it."

Olivia shook her head, a deep feeling of nausea filling her gut.

"Conrad adored how desperate you were to please Liam. The lengths you would go to keep your husband happy. In fact, my own husband enjoyed those particular displays so much, he would often guide me over to this very desk"—she rapped her knuckles along the wooden surface—"bend me over its top, and have his way with me while it played. Sometimes, when he was really hot and bothered, he would even grunt out your name."

Despite the fact the woman had been the architect of all the misery the evening had wrought, Olivia couldn't help but to bite her lip in disgust. Every word Vera Anderson uttered added another layer of horror to an already horrific situation. More dark, vile truths being brought into the light for all to see.

"He knew, of course, that Liam was going to kill you. I think my husband viewed your life like that of a soap opera. It entertained him." She glared at Olivia. "It sickened me.

"When I regained control of Eosphoros and made the decision to release the Dermagigantes, I needed a host for the queen. Unfortunately, Conrad was already dead, so I had to look elsewhere. As luck would have it, I had already been introduced to an adequate replacement.

"Which brings us to you, Olivia." Vera leaned back. "I certainly never would have imagined, after watching you for so many hours previously, that you would have the steel required to make it here. It wasn't until after I initiated the countdown to cleanse the site that I fully became aware of your movements throughout the New Leaf. It was"—she leveled a smile toward Olivia—"fascinating. So, instead of taking my leave, I decided to remain. The countdown could be deactivated at any point, so there was no worry there. I was curious just how far you would get. Here was this woman, a frightened little mouse, a victim of forces both *in* and *beyond* her control, fighting back against the wheels of fate to forge her own destiny. And in that moment, I had an epiphany."

The Matriarch stood from her chair, stepped over the stiff remains of her spouse, and rounded the desk to face Olivia. "Eosphoros needs new blood. It needs to evolve. The chains of the past, the strict adherence to tradition, had allowed this once great collective to become stagnant. A swamp full of death and decay. Watching you, my dear, I saw the future of Eosphoros. A new direction, a new voice."

Olivia was numb. "What are you saying?"

Vera let out a chittering laugh, like breaking porcelain. "You! I'm saying it's you! We have been through so much but have both come out of the fire the stronger for it. Clumps of metal forged into the sharpest blades. Together, me, the last Matriarch, you, my heiress, the next Matriarch, we can grow Eosphoros to unprecedented heights!"

The old woman reached her hand out.

"Come with me, and I'll take care of you."

CHAPTER 52

Despite never knowing such a life, Olivia could picture what it would be like to live in the world promised by Vera Anderson. Never again would she be afraid of those around her. All the worry—the dread—at what each new day would bring would be gone. And all she would have to do was say yes to the woman before her.

What she's offering is what I've always wanted. I'll never be alone again. In such a position, she would have purpose, direction. The hole in her life would become forgotten in a sea of excess. Yet, even as the images of the future came freely to her exhausted mind, she noticed the pain behind her ear.

Vera Anderson, grinning, moved a step closer, her hand suspended between them. "Come now, dear. There's nothing left here, for either of us."

Olivia stared at her, but instead of taking the offered appendage, she turned to look out the window. Her gaze stretched across the horizon, devouring the landscape, the world. Her fingers caressed the scar she had received the last time her life had been completely altered.

"It's time, Olivia," Vera barked, the mirth from her voice starting to slip away, like a poorly executed accent.

And why shouldn't it? Olivia realized. *It's completely fake.*

Vera Anderson was not happy, not loving. She cared about no one. She was a puppet, a doll dancing at the hands of misery, bouncing and jiving at the fingers of death. The Matriarch was just another kind of Infested.

"What about Alex?" When she spoke, it was so low it barely registered to her own ears.

"What?"

Olivia saw Vera's reflection in the glass shimmy, take an uneasy step closer.

"What did you say?"

Fingering the scar one more time, Olivia thought of her own mother, and a warmth so profound filled her she could barely breathe for a moment. She felt tears well in her eyes before spilling free.

"I said"—she turned to face the Matriarch—"what about Alex? Your grandson. He's still alive. What about him?"

Vera hobbled closer. "That ungrateful brat can burn for all I care. I offered him everything. The keys to the kingdom were his. All he had to do was play a *fucking* part. But he couldn't do it. He wasn't strong enough, certainly not as strong as you. No, Alex decided to flee like a coward in the night. He threatened to expose us, to reveal Eosphoros to the world. So, don't talk to me of Alex. He betrayed me. As far as I'm concerned, he made a choice long ago, and it was a poor one. Now he must see it through to its bitter end."

Fire blossomed inside Olivia's chest, and her anger welled. "Fuck that! Your grandson is a good person, and despite the fucking insanity you and your whack-job husband filled his life with, he managed to pull himself up and face the world." Spit flecked her lips as she continued. "He's shown more courage, real courage, tonight than you probably have during your whole, miserable life."

Vera took a small step back, away from Olivia. Her mouth parted to reveal the edges of her teeth. Her eyes narrowed.

Everything was happening so fast, Olivia felt the earth spiraling away from her, the ground itself disappearing into a void. But then somewhere, deep in the recesses of her mind, she could see her mom. A pillar of good, of every just and moral thing Olivia had ever done, and all at once, the earth was firm beneath her feet.

"You have nothing I need. You are worthless, a soulless thing leeching off of humanity, and I would rather die a thousand times over than accept anything you could possibly offer me."

The Matriarch rocked slightly before Olivia, her face a knot of disgust. Her tongue snuck out past her lips, a thin layer of saliva slickening the surface before being absorbed into the skin.

"Pathetic. People like you never cease to amaze me. Worthless nobodies eager to bite the hand offering to feed you. Oh well." As she spoke, she stuffed her right hand into the pocket of her pantsuit. "The reality is, some of us are made to fuck, and others are made to be fucked. I guess you are the latter." The overhead lights glinted off the object she pulled free.

She has a gun!

Olivia barely registered the danger before Vera Anderson fired.

CHAPTER 53

The weapon roared in Vera's hand, sending the old woman stumbling backward. At the same moment, Olivia felt a red-hot razor's edge slice the side of her arm, spinning her away from the Matriarch completely. She tried to regain her footing, but it was too late. She was already tumbling to the floor.

She looked frantically at her left arm and saw a curtain of blood already running down past her elbow. It was hard to tell, but it appeared the bullet had just grazed her.

"God damn it!" Vera barked from somewhere nearby.

In a daze, Olivia took in her surroundings. The window behind her, the one overlooking the pool, had a small hole punched through it, a dozen crazed cracks reaching from it. The wind from outside whistled past the opening. A frustrated groan pulled her away from the glass and back to the threat facing her.

Across the room, the Matriarch regained her balance. Her white hair hung wildly in front of her face. Clutched in her fist was the weapon. When she noticed Olivia looking at her, she grinned and said, "Isn't this fun."

As soon as the words left her mouth, she brought the gun up, a two-handed grip this time, and aimed at Olivia.

Move!

The gun thundered again.

The sound of splintering wood filled Olivia's ears.

She missed!

Olivia, realizing her luck could only hold for so long, pushed herself off the floor and hurried around the back of Conrad Anderson's desk, landing atop the dead man.

"I just want you to know, Olivia, that after I kill you, I'm going to reactivate the self-destruct sequence. Alex, the child, and whoever else may be hiding in the New Leaf will all come crashing down." The woman erupted into a wheezing laugh. "But not me. No. When the sun rises, a new Eosphoros will rise along with it. And it will be glorious."

A gun shot crashed through the air of the library. Bits of paper and debris exploded off the surface of the desk, raining down on Olivia while she covered, her head with her hands. Another round of laughter filled the silence immediately following.

She's right, Olivia thought. *As long as the Matriarch is alive, people like Alex, like Emma, will always be in danger.*

Her heart fluttered at the realization. She was suddenly pulled through time, in the moments, the seconds, before the car crash, before her mom was forever taken away. Olivia knew she was approaching that patch of black ice, that unforgiving light pole once again. This time, she would face it. She would stare it in the eye, and she wouldn't flinch.

Taking a breath, she caressed the scar behind her ear, for what she reasoned was the final time. She was finished with the past, with the ghosts which had haunted her for years, with the guilt which pulled her into the mire almost daily, with the fear of the future. She was done with it all. And in that moment, she breathed easier than she had in years. A level of freedom which she would have sworn had flown from her life, never to return, came back, filling her.

Slowly, Olivia rose up from behind the desk. "Enough, Vera."

The old woman had made her way across the room, her back pressed against the window with the bullet hole in it. The gun looked heavy in her hand, but the barrel didn't so much as waver.

"Oh, dear, it is far too late. The offer is no longer on the table." She hefted the weapon higher, taking aim at Olivia.

"No, wait," Olivia said, tentatively stepping out from around the desk, her hands held high. "I have to tell you something."

The Matriarch's eyebrows bunched together. "What?"

Olivia took another step closer until she was lined up with the Matriarch. "It involves Eosphoros. Your legacy."

Vere snarled at this, but the gun remained quiet.

Olivia closed her eyes and steadied herself, before opening them again. When she did, she looked past Vera, her gaze focusing on the fractured window. "It all ends tonight."

"Is that so? And just how do you imagine that to—"

Olivia didn't let the Matriarch finish. Instead, she leaned forward and broke into a mad dash toward the woman.

Panic filled Vera's face. The gun, so steady a moment before, bounced through the air in crazy arcs as she pulled the trigger. Flames blossomed from the end of the weapon, but it was too late. Even if one of the bullets hit home, Olivia thought, momentum would carry her forward, like a car sliding on black ice. She covered the distance between them in a second, slamming herself into the Matriarch.

For a single heartbeat, the two women mashed against the windowpane, a painful colliding of bodies, but then, a sharp crack filled the space around them, and the window shattered, causing them to tumble free from the library.

The heat of the night enveloped Olivia as they plummeted. Underneath her, struggling to bring the gun up, which was still clutched in her pale, knobby hands, Vera—grandmother, wife, Matriarch, architect of pain and torment—shrieked.

They landed on the glass roof above the pool. The impact smashed through Olivia's body. It felt as if every bone inside of her shifted. Underneath her, a deep wheeze whooshed out of Vera Anderson. Her bones doing more than shifting by the sound, dry tinder snapping under the wheel of a tire.

They locked eyes for a moment, Olivia's wet with emotion, the Matriarch's hard with rage, before the glass ceiling broke and both of them tumbled down into the pool below.

CHAPTER 54

Olivia floated in the abyss. A deep well of nothingness. The black entombed her, comforting in its emptiness. She wanted to linger there, to hold onto the absence of everything, but something spoke from the back of her mind. A tiny, almost forgotten voice. It babbled words of encouragement.

At first, Olivia was resentful of these affirmations.

What do you know, anyway?

She had been through so much.

Who can blame me for wanting to stay here?

But the voice continued, and the more it did so, the more she recognized it as her own. Except, that wasn't quite right. It was not just her own voice. There was a second just beneath the surface, a twining of her own words spoken through the mouth of her mother. The realization that, in some way, her mom was present with her, in this place of nothing, made the abyss feel uncomfortable. An almost irresistible urge to move, to escape the blackness, filled her.

She gasped for air and broke the surface of the pool. Several currents of pain shot through her body, but she was alive.

Olivia looked up and saw the broken remains of the glass ceiling above her. It looked like a gaping mouth, shards of glass for teeth. The sky beyond, formally a tumultuous nightmare of angry wind and thunder, had mellowed under the opening eye of the morning sun. A few clouds remained, but they had emptied their load and now, tinged in orange and pink, looked almost beautiful.

Struggling to stay afloat, Olivia understood she had almost died, and worse, had been ready to embrace it. And maybe, she realized, she had been dead. Just another corpse in the skyscraper tombstone that was the New Leaf Building, but something made her want to come back. Try as she might, she couldn't recall what it was, but for the first time in a long time, she felt whole. The void was gone.

Bobbing in the water, amongst a collection of debris and the bloated corpse already residing in the pool, was the body of Vera Anderson. A bitter cloud of red staining the water around her. Mercifully, she was face down.

Pushing herself away from the dead woman, Olivia wondered what would happen next. The Matriarch, the mother of Eosphoros, had basically destroyed the company. Olivia had no doubt there were other sites, labs, offices, and employees, but with the entire board exterminated, and both Conrad and Vera gone, Eosphoros was in ruin.

The walk through the changing room had been much easier than before. It was still utterly dark, but Olivia had no more room for fear. She simply stepped one foot in front of the other until she was free of its grasp.

In the area outside the darkened room, she saw an Infested. The man stood half-wilted next to a weight machine. Olivia tensed, ready to defend herself, but the man didn't move. Hanging limply from his destroyed mouth—like discolored dental floss—were twin antenna. Even as she shuffled through the space between herself and the man, he remained completely still. If she needed proof the bugs were useless without their queen, there it was.

The elevator still refused to come when called, so she headed for the stairwell.

A quick stop to the 25th floor, to her apartment, produced Liam's car keys and the photo album of her mother. The latter Olivia clutched close to her chest, like the images inside were crucial to keep her heart beating. And in a way, she thought they were.

It took almost all of the strength she could muster to knock on the door to Beth's apartment. Her left arm had fallen completely numb, and she thought it might even be broken. The rest of her body hummed from the relentless trauma it had endured.

"Emma, it's me, honey."

Cold dread began to freeze the blood in her veins when there was no reply. She thought of an all too plausible scenario. Alex had died, and, being surrounded by the dead, Emma had retreated into herself. A broken doll disconnected from reality. A deep dread began to fill her.

I'm too late!

She quickly brought her hand back up and pounded along the frame. Beth's many locks would be impossible to get past, and there was no way she would be able to repeat her daredevil act of climbing between two balconies again, not in her condition.

"Please! Please!" Her voice began to crack as the sorrow set in.

"Olivia?" Emma's frightened voice barely penetrated the door.

Olivia felt her knees go weak at the sound of that sweet voice.

With sudden, overwhelming tears of relief spilling from her eyes, Olivia leaned closer to the door and said, "It's me, honey! It's me!"

As soon as the child managed to free all the locks and open the door, Olivia had her in an embrace. Emma's small body, warm, alive in her grasp. She had never felt such intense love for another human being before. Not for a long time, at any rate.

"You made it." The voice carried weakly from the other side of the couch.

Letting the girl go, Olivia lifted the photo album from the floor and placed it on a table by the door before moving cautiously over to Alex. He looked awful, even worse now with the light of dawn pouring in through the dining room windows.

"I thought you were dead." His gaze slid across her body, settling on her bloody arm. "And it looks like I might have been right. What happened to you?"

Olivia laughed and crouched next to him, cradling his head. "What can I say? You getting shot looked like so much fun, I thought I would join in. I met your grandmother."

Alex opened his mouth, closed it, then said, "My...grandmother? Vera? Where? How?"

Olivia leaned in and kissed his forehead, salty with sweat. She would tell him. She would tell him everything. But not until later.

Kissing his head again, she said, "We have to get you down to the ninth floor. The elevators are working there. As much fun as this has been, I think it's time to leave."

ACKNOWLEDGEMENTS

This book was many years in the making. During that time, it went through numerous drafts, a hefty restructuring, and a complete and total re-write. Along the way, many kind folks leant their time, thoughts and talents to the cause.

Infested began life as a short paragraph (inspired by the music of Trent Reznor) and a conversation over lunch with my friend Justin Cantelo. Justin's enthusiasm over the idea gave me the go-ahead to explore Olivia's horrible night further.

Easily one of the most important people to the writing of this novel has been fellow author Ben Van Dongen. The hours we spent sitting across from each other in the coffee shop, typing away on our individual projects, is staggering. Nearly every thing that happens in the novel was bounced off of Ben first. It was invaluable to have an instant beta reader constantly available. Cheers to you, Ben!

This book probably would never have been released if not for the day Elly Blake, over coffee (of course) hit me with some hard truths. I didn't want to hear it, but knew she was right, and so made the decision to heavily restructure the entire novel. As it turned out, Elly knew what she was talking about, and here we are.

I would never have typed a single word if it wasn't for the love and encouragement of my family. Almost everything I do is for my wife and daughters—they are the sun to my solar system. My brother, Michael, who basically introduced me to horror stories a million years ago, and still likes talking all things spooky with me. And, of course, my mom. I dedicated this book to her, but the truth is, they are all dedicated to her. I love you mom.

Some other folks that were utterly crucial to Infested seeing the light of day are: Brittni Brinn, Theo Hummer, Michael Drakich, Mick Ridgewell, and all the great people at Write On Windsor for helpful feedback and critiques. In fact, the book had many beta readers, and to all of you, I am eternally thankful. Michelle at Eerie River Publishing for not only loving the book, but swooping in with an acceptance email at exactly the right moment. And Francois Vaillancourt for the insanely awesome cover art (I love that image!).

And a big thanks to you! Yes, you! This is my first novel, and I am ridiculously excited that you read it! In this world of a million distractions, hopefully my little story about people being controlled by bugs was worth your time.

C.M. Forest
April, 2022.

C.M. Forest, also known as Christian Laforet, is the author of the novel Infested, the novella *We All Fall Before the Harvest,* the short story collection *The Space Between Houses*, as well as the co-author of the short-story collection *No Light Tomorrow*. His short fiction has been featured in several anthologies across multiple genres. A self-proclaimed horror movie expert, he spent an embarrassing amount of his youth watching scary movies. When not writing, he lives in Ontario, Canada with his wife, kids, three cats and a pandemic dog named Sully who has an ongoing love affair with a blanket.

Website: ChristianLaforet.com
Facebook: Author C.M. Forest
Instagram: @christianlaforet
Twitter: @C_Laforet
TikTok: @christian_writes_horror

ALSO AVAILABLE FROM
EERIE RIVER PUBLISHING

NOVELS
Infested
Miracle Growth
Storming Area 51: Horror At the Gate
In Solitudes Shadow
Dead Man Walking
Devil Walks in Blood
SENTINEL
A Sword Named Sorrow

ANTHOLOGIES
Of Fire and Stars
Monsters & Mayhem
AFTER: A Post-Apocalyptic Survivor Series
Last Stop: Horror on Route 13
It Calls From The Forest: Volume I
It Calls From The Forest: Volume II
It Calls From The Sky
It Calls From the Sea
It Calls Fromt he Doors
Darkness Reclaimed
With Blood and Ash
With Bone and Iron
Forgotten Ones: Drabbles of Myth and Legend
Dark Magic: Drabbles of Magic and Lore

COMING SOON
It Calls From the Veil
NOTHUS
Shade of Night
Path of War
Void
Elemental Cycle Series

www.EerieRiverPublishing.com

More from Eerie River

Eerie River Publishing, is a small independant publishing house
that is devoted to releasing quality horror, dark fantasy and
dark fiction novelas and anthologies.

To stay up to date with all our new releases and upcoming giveaways, follow
us on Facebook, Twitter, Instagram and YouTube. Sign up for our monthly
newsletter and receive a free ebook Darkness Reclaimed, as our thank you gift.

https://mailchi.mp/71e45b6d5880/welcomebook

Interested in becoming a Patreon member?
Patreon membership gives you exclusive sneak peeks at upcoming books, early
chapter releases, covers art as well as free ebooks and discounts on paperbacks.

https://www.patreon.com/EerieRiverPub.

ALSO BY EERIE RIVER PUBLISHING

It Calls From the Veil - Releasing Summer 2022

SENTINEL by Drew Starling

Made in the USA
Middletown, DE
13 June 2023

32524978R00161